T0278415

THREE THINGS ABOUT Emmy Crawford

ALSO BY ALLISON L. BITZ

The Unstoppable Bridget Bloom

THREE THINGS ABOUT Emmy Crawford

ALLISON L. BITZ

HARPER

An Imprint of HarperCollinsPublishers

To Evie and Jonah—
kids like you give me hope of a better, kinder world

ONE

IT'S 10:02 P.M. AND A fat white van turns a corner, lumbering in our direction. I stop short, palms immediately slick with sweat, and pull Issy behind a row of tall bushes. The paparazzi sharks are right on cue.

Issy and I are the last people on this big dirty earth who should be sneaking out. And channeling cool and calm older sister isn't easy when the dark Georgetown streets are full of potential threats. Yet here we are—Issy, glistening with nerves and excitement, and me, hairs on end as the media van inches closer. I need to get her out of here. "Hey, I forgot my wallet. Can you run back and grab it?"

"Now? We *just* made it out!" Frustration coats her voice, and I can't say I blame her. Both of us getting out the door without waking either parent, our much-younger sister Lucy, *or* our overly enthusiastic dog had been a minor miracle. I don't know if Issy can run that gauntlet a second time. But I know *for sure* Issy can't get in proximity of the paps. Her even noticing them could be catastrophic.

So far, so good—Issy flips her cascading waves over her shoulder, annoyed but oblivious to the white van. "Are you sure you *need* your wallet?"

"Yeah." *No.*

"And you didn't think to throw it in your bag in the *hours* you were nagging me about departure time?"

"C'mon, it'll only take a second," I reply, feigning nonchalance.

"Why don't *you* go back for it?"

I grind my back teeth, willing myself to think fast thoughts. "You're more graceful, and Maple likes you better. Less barking potential."

Issy huffs but marches back toward our house. I position myself carefully, trying to block any chance a camera could capture her. The DC paparazzi are always out for political blood. Blood like mine, and Issy's is even sweeter. Unfortunately my dear sister has zero skills for managing this kind of attention. That's where I come in. I can handle my stuff *and* hers if needed.

And I'd really tried to handle everything for tonight. When you're a senator's kid, covert operations require precision—and if we'd left by my preplanned time of 9:47 p.m., the short walk to a friend's house wouldn't be such a big deal. The shark vans pick up between ten and ten-thirty every night, ever since a bathrobed and slightly mussed picture of Mom, a.k.a. presidential-nominee front-runner Catalina "Cat" Crawford, was snapped in our driveway

2

around that time last spring. (Observation compliments of many late-night study sessions at my street-facing desk.) And though I'm not above sticking my toe into dangerous waters every now and again, that's *not* Issy's jam.

Case in point: just a few weeks ago, I sat for an interview with *Washington Life*, a local magazine covering "DC society." They'd wanted both me and Issy, but Issy declined. In her absence, they titled the piece

Three Things About Emmy Crawford
1. Her current read: *The Jungle*, next on the precollege reading checklist she created for herself
2. Her favorite way to spend a day: "Coffee and CakeCups with my sister Issy."
3. Her biggest dream: "I want to take nationals in debate this season."

(I'd called #3 a goal, not a dream, but I let it slide.)

The article's title was a nod to my debater brain, as I'd shared with the reporter how I perpetually organize the world into lists of three. Overall it was a good, fluffy piece, which expanded on each of those things about me.

But this was a sanctioned interview, whereas the paparazzi happy hour every night outside our house is decidedly not. And Issy, hater of all media, is clueless about the feeding frenzy. Tonight we're late getting out the door because she decided to re-curl her hair "just one more time" (read: several more times), and we didn't step out the door until ten on the button. And now, because of the sharks, I'm sending her back in. As she quietly reenters the back door, I scrunch myself *into* the spirea bushes so that I, too, am out of sight. My hair tangles in branches and clings to my cheeks while my heart rate shoots straight to cardio zone. The white van trudges by, but I'm so buried in ivory flowers that I doubt I'm seen.

Four minutes later, the phone in my trembling hand becomes a beacon in the dark.

> ISSY: Almost there! Trying to get Maple to chill
>
> EMMY: No worries

What I want to type is "AWAIT MY CUE," but that will set off Issy's anxiety, and that's the last thing I want. It's a Final Fling of Summer party, as she and I and everyone head back to the proverbial grind this coming Monday. We've never gone to a bash like this before, but Issy has been talking about it all month.

"What are you *doing* in there?"

My startle sends filmy petals flying. Issy swipes them from my black tank top as my heart jackhammers away. "Waiting for you, Dr. Stealth. Let's go."

Our sandals flip and flop over hot pavement as the summer-remnant damp amplifies our hair, soaks into our clothes. The sky is completely black, and clouds block the moon. A lunar kind of luck.

We reach our destination in short order, but the house is quiet. Blinds closed. No porch light on.

"She said Friday night, right?" Issy bends over her iPhone.

"Yep. Definitely," I say, but still double-check my texts with Liv, my best friend and brilliant debate partner, on my own phone.

4

Issy looks over her shoulder and from side to side, channeling that "escaped fugitive" energy that comes out when she's anxious. "Wait. Are you sure we should be doing this? What if we get caught?"

I tamp down the urge to roll my eyes. Issy is the queen of half-cooked plans. Her room is a mishmash of partially finished crochet and knitting projects. Then there's the nearly done paint-by-numbers kits, the first pages of a novel she scrawled in a special notebook and never touched again, the basket of clothes that sits near her dresser—clean, but not folded and put away. In our youth she'd once set up a lemonade stand but forgot to bring cups, so she let thirsty neighborhood kids take swigs straight out of the pitcher for a quarter each. This spring she'd decided she was a master gardener and begged Mom to buy her supplies for planting vegetable seedlings, which promptly wilted when Issy forgot to care for them.

All those years ago I'd swept in with a new, backwash-free pitcher of Country Time Pink Lemonade, a bag of Solo cups, and a few bucks' worth of quarters for change. As for the vegetables, I saved most of the seedlings. We're still eating this summer's tomatoes.

Of course, now that we're getting older and I've got a bit of a reputation to uphold, I've had to quit going along with *all* of Issy's schemes. I'm Emmy Crawford, the DC debater to beat. I chew and spit out my opponents' stances like sunflower-seed shells. And I *need* to get to nationals this year. I imagine other kids might choose activities based just on what they love—maybe they play a sport they're only okay at because it gets their blood pumping, or bang around on an instrument even though they'll never make Juilliard. But me? I had to choose something I could be the best at, because when you're the daughter of an actual phenom of a senator, being mediocre isn't an option. As the eldest of three girls, the pressure's even higher. My achievements and "the example I set" are front and center in my parents' eyes, not to mention the eyes of the nation, if we're going to be cliché about it. And since I'm a senior, this is my last shot to be the best, and the best means debate nationals.

But saying no to my sister, on the night of a party she actually *asked* to go to, after years of mostly avoiding groups of people? Not even I'm that big of an asshole. Besides, I'm curious about this party. Well, more specifically, I'm curious about what it feels like to be someone who goes to parties.

Issy pushes into my silence, voice pitching higher. "Seriously, Emmy. What if we get caught?"

"You didn't think about this beforehand?"

Issy's brows stitch together. "I guess not?"

Anxiety is a funny thing. Issy will worry all night about someone saying something mean about her hair and take extra time to make it look perfect, but she'll absolutely forget to worry about legitimate danger until the last second.

I swallow a sigh. "It'll be okay. If we get caught, I'll take the heat."

"If we get caught, it doesn't matter who takes the heat. We'll both be dead meat."

"Nice effort on the poetry, but I'd prefer haiku."

"Shut up. Are you going to knock or what?"

So *now* she wants to be brave.

Correction: she wants *me* to be brave. Typical. I knock.

The door cracks open. One big, familiar brown eye peeks out, and Liv shoos us inside. "You made it!"

"Like we'd miss this," I reply, my voice cool despite my soaked hands and feet—wet from nerves more than the cloying heat.

My eyes bug as we slip over the threshold and Liv slams the door behind us. Twenty or so kids linger in the big front room, some I know from school, some I don't. A couple I've never seen before is on the couch, his hand on her thigh, both giggling as they pass a drink back and forth. Music thumps so loud the floorboards vibrate; a clump of kids dance, holding their red cups up like torches. The whole place reeks of beer.

Issy's gone quiet and stands halfway behind me, like she's trying to disappear. "Hey," I say, nudging her with my shoulder.

"Hey," she says, voice small.

"We can leave if you want." I squeeze her hand.

She looks like she wants to say yes but shakes her head. "We just got here."

"Emmyyyy! Isssyyy! Hey!" A group of our friends swarm us, quick with hugs and fist bumps, thawing a little of my icy worry. Issy's warming up, too—she and Taylor bend over a phone, giggling at a series of text exchanges that Taylor is dramatically reenacting.

"Liv," I say, pulling her aside.

"What?"

7

"I thought this was supposed to be a *small gathering*."

"It is!" she says, throwing both arms out for emphasis.

"This is your idea of small?"

She tucks in her lips, reading my face. "Well. No. But I told our core group, and then someone told like one other person, and then . . . well. You know how it goes."

Actually, I don't. Issy and I don't get out to a lot of events like this. For a multitude of reasons. Can I lose my Georgetown early decision acceptance status if I get caught with beer? Not to mention my family's reputation, always on the line, always my responsibility to uphold. I've got too much going to blow it on some random party. I cross my arms tight, wondering if I should grab Issy and get the hell out of here.

But then I see her. Head thrown back in laughter, no longer trying to disappear. Issy is *glowing*, like she used to in the before times. Like I've feared she never would again, in any public space. My whole body goes tingly, like her happiness is catching.

Liv's arm finds its way around my shoulders. "Relax. You'll be fine." And because I'm hungry to believe her, I convince myself I do. She leads me into the next room, where there is a tall metal thing that she pumps. "A keg," she explains.

"You got a *keg*?"

"Nah, Ramón brought it. His parents had a catering job go south and they had extras."

"Well. I guess it always boils down to who you know," I say, accepting a full cup of beer from Liv.

"To friends in high places!" Liv clinks her plastic against mine and we lift the cups to our mouths. Her chug is greedy, whereas mine is little more than a sip. How something that tastes like mold and sadness became *the* definitive party beverage will never make sense. My stomach grumbles as the liquid sloshes in, and my hand flies first over my gut (*Is it a normal grumble or the bad kind?*) and then to my crossbody bag, where I always, always carry a package of flushable wipes. Since I have a disorder that insists on making my bowels destroy themselves, I always have to be one step ahead. Crohn's disease is stupid, but I am not.

Normal grumble, I decide, relaxing a bit.

Across the room, Issy tastes her beer and cringes but gamely takes another gulp.

The tinkling of high notes turns our heads in unison. "Hey! Yeah, you! Hands off the baby grand!" Liv darts off to shoo kids from her mom's prized possession, and I wander through the rest of the first floor like a stranger in my homeland. Popcorn kernels and Frito crumbs litter the kitchen counters where Liv and I spend afternoons baking cupcakes and dishing about debate. The sturdy antique dining room table has been transformed into a beer pong station, and the den, where Liv and I spread pallets of blankets and sleeping bags when I stay over, is a crush of kids laughing, talking, probably spilling stuff. I hope Liv plans on spending her entire weekend cleaning.

A familiar *something* floats in from the back deck. A solo voice cutting above the crowd noise. And then another, just as loud and articulate. The rhythm and the timbre weave a song I've sung a million times but the context's all wrong. Like when you see your dentist wearing overalls at the grocery store.

Debate isn't supposed to happen at keg parties, is it?

I elbow my way onto the deck. "Health care is a privilege, and we all know it," says a tall, preppy girl with perfectly bobbed blond hair and a Southern twang to her voice—Mary-Kate Greenlee, daughter of Senator Chuck Greenlee of South Carolina. I'm friendly enough with Mary-Kate—the senators' kids always know who the others are—but I do *not* appreciate the hot take she's dishing.

A deeper voice pipes up. "Yeah, it's a privilege as it stands. Only the lucky few get the care they need. But *should* it be like that?"

No, I think, and not just because I'm answering his question. *No*, as in *Please no, not him, not now. No*, as in *Please let me disappear before he sees me*. Ice and steam take turns rolling through my rib cage.

From my position all that's visible is his bottom half, but I know that voice and those signature white Chucks. It's not too late to get away—far, far away. And yet my feet stay rooted to the floor as the debate continues.

Mary-Kate and her flaring nostrils are in full view. "How else could it be? There's no way around it: if we give health care to all, we strip our citizens of their right to liberty. Their right to choose what they do with their money."

"If we don't give health care to all, we strip people of a basic human right—health. And if I'm not mistaken, the phrase is 'life, liberty, and the pursuit of happiness,' in that order. No?"

Without my consent my body takes a step forward. I can't help it—that mouth, that brain, those *principles*, they're my siren song.

For as long as I've known Gabriel Castillo, he's sung me right his way.

Gabe moves across the deck with tense, almost feline grace. I trace him from his Chucks skyward; straight-leg jeans, a white V-neck shirt, and warm brown skin. A shock of thick black hair worn long enough that it sticks out in places. *So soft*, I remember, as all the air leaves my body. *Shit. Shit shit shit.*

Mary-Kate is heavily flushed and opens her mouth to say more, but Gabe holds a palm in her direction. "Let's leave it at that," he says. And he bends down to tie his shoe, an absolute dismissal if I've ever seen one. Mary-Kate storms away as Gabe stands back up to his full height. A horde of testosterone swallows him up in the rituals that only dudes seem to understand, involving chest bumping and complicated high-fiving. Yet if someone blindfolded me and spun me three times pin-the-tail-on-the-donkey style, I'd still be able to find his energy and point right at it.

He emerges from the bro fest and turns my way.

And if ever there was a cue for me to get out of here, it's this.

TWO

Three Reasons to Leave This Party Other Than Gabriel Fucking Castillo

1. Beer sucks
2. My ears are ringing
3. My mom wants to be the president

Three Reasons to Stay at This Party for at Least One More Hour

1. Issy
2. Issy
3. Issy

USUALLY, I'M *MUCH* BETTER AT rebuttals. As it is, my brain has dissolved into something just north of mush. *Why is Gabe here? Why is Gabe* anywhere?

I'd heard of Gabe before I ever saw him. His name was almost mythical in debate circles my sophomore year. *Gabriel Castillo, the one who never loses.* Which might have cowed others, but not me. I went out of my way to find him. I sat in the audience of his matches at tournaments, determined to pick apart his stances and strategy. The only way to beat him was to know how he operated.

He was as quick as everyone said, but not always smooth. A fast-pause-fast pattern of speech; a searching look on his face when his words cut out. But none of this detracted from his effectiveness. If anything, it lent him credibility while also making him more fun to watch. This wasn't a debater who was there to add a line to his college apps. Gabe was so clearly invested. Passionate, all the time. About every word. This plus the lean, rangy cut of his body sent my mouth watering, just like when I smell peanut butter. It was like my body knew it was going to need more moisture because if I got too close, this boy would burn me up.

Still, I avoided casual contact, and for months the only words I ever spoke to him were over a podium. We went toe-to-toe at two different meets—he won the first, I won the second. For the duration of both matches, my heart matched the start-stutter-start of his words.

And then one afternoon there he was, daring to occupy space in my native, non-debate environment. I'd only recently discovered Safe Space, a cozy coffee shop in the Adams Morgan district. He was the very last person I'd expected to see there, bellied up to the counter, ordering a cappuccino. *Safe Space, ha, not anymore!* I'd attempted escape, but too late, he'd already spied me, his grin smacking of recognition and . . . something else. "Ah, the enemy," he'd said.

The skin on every inch of my body had lit up. "Enemy, judge. It's all the same, right? I'd give your last performance a seven out of ten."

His mouth dropped open. "The St. Marcus match? How do you figure?"

And there I went, sailing right into him. I learned this was his Sunday habit—extra debate prep and a treat. He was so *earnest* and worked so hard and god, did that speak to me. I'd never met anyone who cared about debate as much as I did, but finally, here he was. In the form of my most lethal rival.

On three separate occasions we sat at a table in the corner of Safe Space, eating orange scones and sparring and evaluating each other's performances until our mugs ran dry. Our Sunday afternoon meetups were one part challenge, one part dance. All parts forbidden, but that didn't stop me from loving every second or from liking Gabe, altogether more than anyone should like the enemy.

We debated at a tournament once more after that. He bested me, in more ways than one.

And then he was gone.

That was all the way back in the spring of sophomore year. Now after fifteen months of seeing zero traces of him, here he is. It'd feel like magic if it wasn't so terrifying.

I collapse into my favorite cushioned chair out on Liv's screened-in sunroom. It's tucked away enough that none of the other partygoers have found it, thank goodness. I need a moment.

Phone in hand, my thumb hovers long seconds over the "unblock" function on Instagram. Yes, it was *probably* a juvenile move to block Gabe in the first place. Yet when you can no longer trust your brain or your fingers, sometimes you have to utilize primitive skills to protect yourself from . . . yourself. Before I can talk myself out of it, I'm unblocking, clicking, scrolling. I need to try to find out where the hell he's been.

He's still got the profile of a mid-forties dad who doesn't really know how to use Insta. It's all of six posts, five of which were present the last time I looked. But there's one picture here I've never seen. It's Gabe as a little boy, his eyes huge and soulful in his baby-round face, curled up in the lap of a black-haired, tan-skinned woman whose smile is so warm, it radiates through the screen. "Love you, Mami" is the caption, posted on Mother's Day this year.

"Emmy! There you are." The screen door bangs shut behind Liv as she moves into the sunroom, lips drawn into a suspicious pout. "What are you doing?"

I definitely *wasn't* stroking Gabe's childhood face with my thumb. Not after everything that went down last spring. I'm highly selective about who I spend time with—for my own reasons, and because there's always a chance a snapshot of me and whoever could end up blasted onto the internet. Despite Gabe being our fiercest debate competition and someone I probably shouldn't have been dating, I'd deemed him worthy of risk, and my precious time. I had let him in. In complete secrecy, even from Issy and Liv. It stayed that way because the paps never got us, and after, I'd been too ashamed to tell anyone.

There'd been one final text. I'm sorry, Emmy. You're really special, please know that. But I can't see you anymore.

And then he ghosted, leaving my Snapchat missives unread and text messages unanswered, which *stung*. It still stings.

"Nothing," I say to Liv, dropping the phone into my lap.

"Yeah, okay. You might be the best debater on this side of the Potomac, but you're a terrible liar," she replies, pulling up a chair next to mine.

"You must have missed the thing on the deck. *That* was some good debate."

"Oh, I heard about it. Like word of a political throwdown wouldn't fly at a mostly-nerdy-kid party. What happened on the deck was our Super Bowl," says Liv.

"Fair. How's Mary-Kate?"

"She'll be all right. Last I saw her she was letting Aidan Barber kiss it better."

I nearly slide off my cushion. "Aidan? No way." Aidan's the president of our school's environmental activism club and extremely staunch in his liberal stances. "Won't Mary-Kate's mouth, like . . . pollute him or something?"

Liv's curly 'fro bounces with her laughter. "You know, sometimes a damsel-in-distress kink is enough to override better judgment."

The creaking screen door interrupts us. "Finally! I've been looking for you two everywhere. By the way, Liv, I think some guy's passed out on the front staircase." Issy's voice pitches high and fast, usually a sure sign of anxiety. Her cheeks are rosy and her hands are flying as she talks, but she's smiling.

Sparkling.

She might be anxious, but she's also *excited*.

I grin. I guess sticking around wasn't such a bad idea after all.

"Ugh, I'll take care of that later," says Liv.

"I can help! Emmy can, too," offers Issy.

"Is!"

"What? You wouldn't help Liv if she needed us?"

"Yeah, you wouldn't help me if I needed you?" Liv crosses her arms at me.

Leave it to Issy to paint me into a corner in the most benevolent way imaginable. "Fine, sure, whatever. I'm capable of hauling drunk boys out onto the lawn. Anyway, Is, how's the party?"

"It's good. Fun. And speaking of fun, I met someone. I think you'll like him."

Highly doubtful, but I always humor my sister. "Oh yeah?"

"Hold on, I'll go grab him."

My eager smile matches Liv's, who also knows how hard Issy has struggled with anxiety over the years. My sister meeting some rando represents major progress, even if he winds up being a dud.

Issy reappears and this time I have no doubt that the freefall in my gut is the emotional kind, not the Crohn's disease kind. Trailing Issy is Gabe, looking twitchy as hell.

As he should.

Issy shines so hard I could probably see my reflection in her cheeks. "This is Gabe! He just *destroyed* Mary-Kate Greenlee's super gross position on health care."

Gabe flips a one-finger wave. His eyes collide with mine for only the tiniest sliver of time. Long enough to send my heart into a confused sputter.

I should keep my trap shut, but I can't help it. "I heard the deck debate. Six out of ten at best."

"Jeez, Emmy," mutters Issy. Liv eyes me suspiciously.

But Gabe is unflustered, face full of knowing. "You got suggestions on improvement?"

"Finish what you start," I say, wondering if my face is as red as the tips of his ears.

"Wait." Liv cups a hand over her mouth. "Aren't you a St. Jeremiah's kid?"

"Guilty," he replies.

Recognition dawns on Liv's face. "You were in the duo that *killed* me and Emmy at the Centurion debate sophomore year, right?"

Apology and pride war on Gabe's face, and I'd call it cute if I didn't know better. But I've seen this smile before, and it's up to no good. "That was us. Nuclear test banning, right?"

"God, the memory on you. But yeah," says Liv, shaking her head.

"How could I forget *that* day?" says Gabe. He runs the tip of his tongue slowly along his bottom lip. I am appalled by my obscene preoccupation, the way my gaze will *not* unglue itself from his mouth.

Get it fucking together, Emmy!

Since this nightmare *is* happening, I need to get out ahead of it.

18

Even though it's been over a year, I'm still too raw to talk about my history with Gabe with Issy or Liv. Simply put, too humiliating. Way off-brand.

"I don't think we've met offstage. I'm Emmy Crawford."

A shadow of confusion crosses Gabe's face, but he's quick to correct it. Because of course he is. He's nothing if not a smooth liar, and he's caught on to my ruse. "Gabriel Castillo. Gabe, to my friends."

"Well, it's a pleasure, Gabriel." I hold his gaze long enough to send a message but short enough to save myself. Looking right into his face is a dangerous thing.

"Oh, likewise. I've been hoping I'd run into you one of these days."

"Is that so?"

"The only way to defeat the enemy is to *know* the enemy, right?"

Goose bumps of recognition prickle, their tingle starting in my shoulders and wending their way down my body. I'd forgotten how similar we are, Gabe and me. Our two brains always felt like they operated on the same track. How someone who ghosted me can spring back into the picture and immediately make me feel so *seen* is beyond me, but there it is.

Liv's still dubious. "Well, that's cute and all, but I didn't throw this party to be spied on. What are you even doing here, Gabe-from-Jeremiah's?" St. Jeremiah's is a prestigious all-boys school known for its rigorous academics. Their debate team is typically one of the only ones in the city that can keep up with ours. We handled them easily last year, but Gabe wasn't on their team last season; I'm sure of it. There's no way I wouldn't have noticed him, even if our duos never crossed competition paths. I haven't seen Gabe since the spring of our sophomore year.

"I came with Ramón Delgado. Says he's besties with the girl who lives here."

Liv cocks one saucy eyebrow. "I'm the girl who lives here, so I suppose you can stay. *Even* if you're Enemy Number One."

"Assuming you're on the team? I don't remember seeing you last year." The pointed-but-weirdly-desperate-sounding words fly out of my mouth before I have a chance to catch them.

"Yeah, I took my junior year off. I'm back this year."

There's a collective pause. I assume we girls are all awaiting further explanation of his debate hiatus, but when none comes, Liv claps her hands to her pants. "All right, then. See you at the podium, Gabriel."

"I look forward to that, Liv. And Emmy," he says, his nod setting off a predatory glimmer in my direction. My breath hitches, even as my fists clench. I clear my throat and focus on Issy. Her body turns to Gabe like a sunflower cranes to heat, and she pulsates with a new, buzzy energy.

My stomach churns—not with disease. With dread.

Issy is head-over-flip-flops for Gabriel Castillo.

THREE

IT'S JUST AFTER ONE IN the morning when Issy and I creep out Liv's side door.

"Wasn't that the most fun ever?" The Georgetown pavement absorbs Issy's giggle, but still, it's too loud.

"Shhh. Keep it down," I whisper.

She puts her hands over her mouth then talks (loudly) through them anyway. "But seriously, did you have fun?"

"Yeah, it was a good time."

"Then why do you look like we're coming home from a funeral?"

"Just tired. It's way late." And I'm very ready to be in bed with a book or my debate notes or a memory eraser.

"That's part of the fun, though, right? It was *sneaky*. It was . . . *clandestine*."

"You're totally right," I say through a laugh, and it's only a tiny bit forced. Seeing Gabe after so much time tilted my ninety-degree-angle world into something sloppy and undefined, but I don't have the heart to douse Issy's light. It's been forever since she's wanted to do anything but go to school and come home. Probably since her paparazzi incident several summers ago, the catalyst for our family moving from Iowa to DC.

As if somehow reading my thoughts, which I swear sometimes she does, Issy suddenly stops to scope our surroundings. "You didn't see anyone, right? No media?"

I lie because I have to. "Nope. Not tonight."

When we were little, Issy was a showboat. Whereas I was content with a book or some crayons and paper, Issy watched *High School Musical* enough times to memorize every song and dance routine. But sometime around sixth grade, everything changed. That was the year she bit her nails down so far that she had to cover her fingertips in bandages. She'd get keyed up and weepy whenever Mom and Dad were away for an evening or weekend and would obsessively check their locations on her hand-me-down phone. Her daily morning stomachaches were sometimes so bad she would throw up. At the time, I was pissed that she made us late for school so many times. In hindsight I feel sorry for her, especially since now I know how hard it is to have misbehaving guts.

Mom and Dad started Issy in therapy not long after all of that kicked in. During Issy's seventh grade year, some asshole recognized Mom in the therapist's waiting room and surreptitiously snapped her picture. As Mom was a standout, young first-term senator and at the time seeking reelection, her face was a primo one. A prominent conservative pundit picked up the picture and ran with it: "State Senator's Daughter Mentally Ill: If Crawford Can't Help Her Own Child, How Can We Expect Her to Help the Nation?" Issy had a total breakdown after the article went viral, including isolating in her room and refusing to go to school altogether. We muddled through the rest of that school year, and over the summer, we made our cross-country move. Issy finished middle school in DC, I started my high school career at Frida's, and Lucy got into a fancy private elementary school.

Mom and Dad told us the moving plan had been long in the works. Mom was favored to win reelection (which she did), and they wanted our family together all the time, not just the times Mom could manage to get back to Iowa. But still, Issy felt responsible for uprooting our family, and she's never been quite the same. The girl who used to love the stage now wants nothing to do with it. It's like she's convinced she'll publicly and epically fail, no matter how hard I or anyone builds her up. And the threat of paps still gives her the total heebie-jeebies.

"Are you sure there was no one?" She grabs at her bag, like she just needs something to hold on to.

"Positive," I say.

She throws an arm around me and lays her head on my shoulder, hips bumping messily into mine as we walk. "It really was the best party, though, right?"

"The best," I say as I bump her back. Lying gets easier with every breath.

Our back deck door opens to the kitchen, which is mercifully dark. A trickle of relief cuts through my stiff shoulders, because if Mom was up, that's where she'd be. Not even Maple has bothered to click her dog nails into the room, another bonus. Now all we have to do is make it into the hallway and up the stairs—which may still prove tricky with my tipsy sister. I'm mouthing, "Watch the fourth step" when the hall light clicks on.

Mom, in pajama pants and a tank top, saunters into the hallway. "Evening, girls," she says, sipping from the mug she holds between her palms. Her voice is casual, posture relaxed, like she's greeting us after school (which she never does these days, but still). Mom is an expert at unreadability, no doubt learned from all of the hours of prepping for appearances and debating with men who discredit her because of her age and gender. Yet I know Mom well enough that I can *feel* something humming in her, something a stranger wouldn't.

A dark head pops out from behind her. "Hola, chicas," Lucy says. That one little dimple in the top of her right cheek never looked so evil. Maple trails in behind them, yawning hugely.

"What is *Lucy* doing up?" says Issy, incredulous.

"I might ask you the same thing, Isabel," Mom replies, cocking her head.

"Uhhh . . ." Issy turns her big, helpless eyes on me. For the life of her, she looks just like she did one day in seventh grade, post-viral-therapy-reveal, when this kid Elliot Weber started calling her "Crazy Crawford." Lucky for us, that kid's older sister was a friend of mine, and I happened to know he still wet the bed at night. So, he got his.

Mom's a lot harder to derail than Elliot Weber, though. In fact, based on history, there's no way out of tonight's mess but straight through it. "We went to a party," I say.

Mom takes another sip of Jasmine Silver Needle, which she drinks at all hours of the day, so why not at one in the morning? The caffeine apparently doesn't faze her. Or maybe she wanted to stay up tonight once she realized we were gone. Guilt stirs as I imagine her peeking into our rooms and finding empty beds.

"A party," she says, voice monotone, face still placid.

I nod. I'm pretty sure Issy's cowering behind me.

After a couple of blinks, Mom starts toward us until she's right up in my face. She sniffs. "Ah . . . Budweiser, am I right?"

"I think it was Bud Light, actually," says Issy, and she manages to hiccup at exactly that moment. I don't even bother hiding my irritation and let my head flop down.

"Is that beer, Mommy? Don't you have to be twenty-one for that?" Lucy's words are innocent enough, but she's fooling absolutely no one. She *loves* a good fail, particularly when it's mine. I'll remember this next time our resident tiny sadist wants me to take her on the city bus to Target.

"Yes, that's right, Lucy. How about you go back to the den and figure out your next move?" Mom gestures at the dimly lit room.

"I already did. Knight to b7 and you'll be in check."

"Well, then go figure out your next few moves," says Mom.

"I already did. I'm going to beat you in three more turns, unless you don't play well, and then maybe only two more turns." Lucy's unnaturally good at chess. As in, potentially an actual prodigy.

She's already won several tournaments, and she's nine.

Mom takes a long pull of her tea before responding—a non-verbal *give me patience*, though only those of us who know her well would know that. "Okay, just go wait in there for me. Read a book or something."

Lucy sighs, the picture of martyrdom, but drags her slippered feet out of the room.

"Seriously, what *is* she doing up?" I say, and immediately regret it. There's fire right under the surface of Mom's skin.

"She woke up when I came into her bedroom. Which I checked after I left *your* bedrooms. Then she couldn't go back to sleep, and neither could I. Besides, I figured it was only fair. You two were up, so why not her?"

Issy nods. "She's not bad company, right?"

I shoot Issy a look that I hope implies a combination of *Oh my god, what are you saying?* and *Shut the hell up, you aren't helping.*

Mom laughs, and I jump because laughter is *not* the expected response. "I wish I could credit you for being intentionally cheeky, but I think you're probably just a little drunk. Right?"

Issy nods again. "That's right." The girl has no guile. No. Guile.

"Well. I think it's best we talk about this in the morning, when your blood alcohol level is back below the legal limit and little ears aren't within range."

"My little ears don't even care!" Lucy's tinny voice bounces off the hardwood floors.

Mom's mouth levels out. "I rest my case. Up to bed, both of you. I'll save the rest of this discussion for tomorrow."

I expect Mom to go back to Lucy, but instead she follows me and Issy up the stairs, like she's making good and sure we end up in the right place this time. Second shocker: she trails me into my room, closing the door behind her.

Her energy shifts into an even more serious mode as she hands me her phone, which is cued up to a picture of two girls with fantastic, humidity-volumized dark brown hair huddled together on a doorstep, bent over the light of a phone. The snap is dark and grainy, but it's indisputably me and Issy. With a flick of her finger, Mom scrolls to the next picture, an open door, bodies in the entryway and sprawled on the furniture behind it. Liv at the threshold, a red Solo cup in her hand.

I gulp. "Where did you get those?"

"Did you really think, at a party of the children of high-profile politicians, there would be no adults hiding out, keeping watch? And no paparazzi?"

"The paps got us?" With Mom being a favorite for the Democratic presidential nomination and with primary season nearly upon us, she's in the public eye now more than ever. Which means we are, too.

My back teeth grind as my brain goes into autogenerate mode.

Three Potential Taglines for SenatorSlush, a Hot Anonymous Instagram Profile for Political Gossip

1. Crawford Sisters Spend Friday Night on Epic Drinking Bender
2. Emmy and Issy Crawford: Good Girls or Loose Lushes?

3. Not My President: New Photos of Cat Crawford's Daughters Prove She's Ill-Equipped to Lead

Issy will crumble.

"No, it was staff of a friend of ours. Another senator."

My jaw's stronghold loosens.

"It *could* have easily been paparazzi, though."

There's a part of me that wants to defend myself. *Since when did I become responsible for everyone else's well-being?* I'd holler. *I'm so sick of the weight of everyone's shit on my shoulders!*

But there's another part of me, the bigger part, that knows it *is* up to me to keep this family ship afloat. I'm the oldest, the sister with the cool head and fast words, and besides, I've got big dreams of my own that I need to guard.

Before I can make sense of all of that and formulate a response, Mom speaks again. "So, the deal is this: I want to be mad at you."

"So why aren't you?" Enough of this tension, anyway. Elephants in rooms are not my thing.

Her eyes crinkle a little at the corners. "Because when I look at you, I still see a child trying to figure things out. I remember being your age. It wasn't easy, and I lived in a world without paparazzi and primary election polls."

I get caught sneaking back from a party, beer on my breath, *captured on camera,* and Mom, a.k.a. one of the most buzzworthy women in the US, is feeling sorry for me? What is this alternative universe I've landed in?

She's right, though. No matter how much I love debate and

my friends and this life my family has built here in DC, being me isn't always easy. Not like the Iowa days, before public office, Issy's anxiety going rampant, and my stupid Crohn's disease diagnosis. Sometimes, the idea of going back to a simpler life sounds pretty appealing. Nights like tonight, when all I wanted to be was a girl going to a party, instead of a senator's daughter having to choose between freedom and responsibility.

I feel like crying, but I won't. Feels don't get to ooze out of me without permission.

Mom puts her hand under my chin so I'm forced to look at her. "I'm not condoning what you did tonight. It was a questionable choice, and I can think of any number of terrible things that could have happened to you. Or to us. But the truth is that we all make questionable choices from time to time, and I have a feeling you had your reasons."

"Thanks, Mom." I choke on my words, just a little, but keep my eyes dry.

"There will still be consequences, of course."

"Yeah, I figured."

"I can tell you're not drunk like your sister, but you did drink?" Mom holds my face steady.

I nod as well as I can, given her grip.

"It's normal to want to experiment. But you've got to be extra careful, and not just because of the paps. I know this is usually Dad's thing, but I'll cover for him tonight—do you know if beer is okay on your gut?"

Dad's as steady as they come, but his Achilles' heel is our

illnesses. Mine and Issy's. I think it's because they're beyond the scope of his control. No matter how organized he is, or what top doctors our family income and Mom's government health insurance give us access to, or how much he researches ways to be a support at home, sometimes Issy's brain and my body go rogue. "I feel fine. But I only had about half of one cup. I don't like beer very much," I say, shrugging.

"Me neither. I stick to tea, and if we're out for drinks, gin and tonics."

"Um, noted?"

"That's not an invitation. Just tuck that away for someday." She gathers me up then, and I melt into her, my tears pooling only once I'm sure they won't be seen. Even though it's been a while since my second and final pubescent growth spurt, I'm still getting used to being two inches taller than Mom. My arms go on top, hers come up underneath my shoulders. She's tiny in my embrace, which is incongruent with the fact that right now, I feel tiny in hers.

FOUR

THE NEXT MORNING MY BARE foot sets off the fourth-from-the-bottom stair. We've lived here for three years, and my half-awake self still forgets. It creaks and moans like a nauseous cow, and just like every morning, I'm startled. "Fuck you, seriously," I spit under my breath.

But there's another feeling going on today, something that's usually not there. Empathy? *I feel you, old brownstone. I'm cranky, too.*

I'd like to blame a hangover for my state of mind, but it's not that. Ever since the party, I've been reliving one particular ghost from my personal Christmas past, over and over.

Three Memories from a Very Bad Sophomore-Year Debate Tournament Day

    1. A headache so gnarly, it blurred my vision

2. Getting obliterated by my then-secret boyfriend's team
3. A voice mail, which should have been my first clue that more yuck was on the way, because what normal person leaves a voice mail?

That day, the trifecta of bad was enough to send me skittering. Especially after hearing the voice mail, I needed to be *out*, *away*, *alone*, and a stall in the ladies' room was not going to cut it. I bumbled around with tear-filled eyes until I spied a narrow, deserted door in the corner of a hallway. My chest heaved with relief when it opened for me, even if it was a supply closet. It smelled like erasers but was way cleaner than any high school restroom could ever be. Among reams of paper, extra printer cartridges, old computer monitors, and boxes of dry-erase markers, I sank to the floor, pulling my knees to my chest as my breath came too fast and my achy head spun. I didn't *want* the tears, but they showed up anyway. A high-pitched keening cut through the silence, and I got the surprise of my life when I realized the sound was coming from *me*.

And that's about the time the door flew open. The music hit first, insultingly loud, growly guitars and strong backbeats, screeching from Gabe's pocket. His debate team's signature move was showing up to their table with old-school rock music blaring, and apparently he hadn't shut the whole dog-and-pony show down yet.

"Hey. What's wrong? What can I do?" he said.

"Start with turning off that shitty music."

"AC/DC is life, and I won't be taking arguments on that." But still, he silenced his phone.

"Like I want to debate you any more today."

He stretched out beside me, his khaki pants in stark contrast to my black. "Now. Surely you're not crying over us beating you."

I shook my head then clutched it, remembering that swift movements were a no go. "I wish."

"What is it, then?"

The truth was that the voice mail had directed me to check my medical records portal, which had pathology findings from my first colonoscopy, the one I'd been forced to have after months of unexplained anemia and bathroom problems. The results were abnormal across the board. Words like *deep ulceration* and *intestinal edema* and *stricture* had flashed across my phone screen. I didn't know what any of it meant, and not understanding was *not* in the Emmy Crawford wheelhouse. I hardly knew how to put it into words, but for Gabe, I wanted to try. We weren't really anything serious, but I thought maybe we could be. After the debate season.

"A few minutes ago I got some bad news, and it scared me? Like, really scared me?" My truths came out like questions, because they were: *Was I afraid? Was I allowed to feel that?* And then *everything* flooded up, storming my dams. My breathing took off into a new and terrifying rhythm, one I couldn't get a hold of. I gasped and sputtered and I was absolutely mortified that this was happening. With him.

Gabe moved closer and squeezed my hand. "Is it okay if I try to help?"

"How could you help?"

"Would you breathe with me?"

The steady rise and fall of his shoulders were my guide, and after a few minutes, I calmed. And then, for some reason, we ended up spilling things we'd never talked about before.

"Do you pray?" he asked.

"I don't."

"Me neither. But I think maybe there's some kind of force at work. The Universe. It's so big. We're so small."

"Yes," I agreed, though I felt emotionally *huge* right then. I held the Universe inside for a pebble of time in that closet with Gabe.

"I like to think that maybe it's a force that knows more than we do, like what's best for us, even when we don't," he said.

"Honestly, the idea of an entity outside of my control doing things to me? I don't love that," I admitted.

"I feel that. But what if . . . what if sometimes, the Universe takes care of us?"

"I might be able to get behind that if I could see evidence."

His hand was shocking but soft on the curve of my jaw. "This is my proof."

And I was the one who closed the last, tiniest gap between us, not only touched by his words but *hungry* for something other than pain and fear. The kiss might have lasted three or thirty seconds, I'd never know. What I did know in that moment was that yes, maybe the force of the Universe was real.

I don't know if I believe that anymore. Because that was the last time I ever talked to Gabriel Castillo, minus the small talk as we got ourselves together and walked back into the debate tournament fold that day. To be ghosted after all *that* was the most humiliating, painful thing to ever happen to me.

A harsh *crack crack* brings me back to my old crochety brownstone, back to my young crochety self. "Earth to Emmy!" Issy snaps her fingers in front of my face once more. I don't remember wandering into the kitchen, but here I am.

"Oh. Hey. Morning," I grumble.

"And good morning sunshine to you!" says Issy, too chipper by a mile. She flounces to her seat at the kitchen table. A plate of toast and the rest of my family await us.

I make a beeline for the coffee pot, still hot and half-full. "So I guess you're immune to hangovers," I say to Issy as I fill my *NPR DONOR* mug to the brim.

Dad drops the spatula he's using to poke the bacon in the oven. "What's this about hangovers?" he says in his "concerned Dad" voice.

Blood pumps in my ears as I casually panic. Did Mom seriously *not* tell Dad about last night? But Issy's unfazed and Mom removes the newspaper from in front of her face. "That wasn't very nice, Phil."

"Maybe not, but it's hard pulling one over on our Emmy. Gotta take the chances I can get." Dad winks. "Sorry not sorry, kiddo," he adds, now setting the sheet of smoked goodness on top of the stove.

I hip-check him on my way to the bacon, which I grab at and promptly drop. The slice was hot enough to leave a red burn on the tips of my fingers.

Mom clucks her tongue. "Could you try flying a little farther from the sun, just this once?"

"Or maybe just not so close to the cured meats, if we can't get you out of the sky. Also, civilized folks use these things called *forks* and *plates*," Dad adds, shoving one of each into my hands.

I stubbornly pile still-too-hot strips of bacon onto my plate with my fingers, careful not to show how much it hurts.

Dad turns from his cooking, eyeing me mildly. "Are you sure about . . ." And he nods at all the bacon.

I tuck my lips into each other and make a valiant attempt at kinking the firehose of my annoyance, but fail. "It was *one time*, Dad. I've eaten bacon a million times since then." Last summer I'd had a gut incident that involved spending most of the night in the bathroom after eating a half rack of ribs at a neighborhood barbecue. Now my consumption of any pork product makes Dad worry.

"I *doubt* it was a million times. It's only been like four hundred and fifty days since your diagnosis," says Lucy, not looking up from her book.

I turn to the youngest Crawford. "What, you got a copy of my medical records stowed under your bed?"

"Nah, it's just memory. You were diagnosed five days before my eighth birthday, and now I'm nine and a half. Simple math." Lucy doesn't even bother to look up from her Tolstoy.

Having Crohn's disease is already the opposite of cool, but discussing my bowel habits at the breakfast table makes it even worse. Good thing I'm a master of verbal distraction tactics. "Anyway, what's everyone up to today?"

"My brain's cracking on a new song. I think I'll probably hit the guitar after breakfast, because the melody is taking *over*, y'all," says Issy, exuberant in the way only music makes her. In-the-house Issy is an animated, Disney-princess-level human being, and her voice is just as sweet as Anna's or Elsa's. She devours musicals with the ferocity with which I attack debate. I still think stage and performance is where she belongs, but in lieu of all that, she's taken up songwriting.

The thing is that Issy usually only writes music when she's *moved*. I have a sinking feeling about what—or who—might have done that to her last night.

"That's wonderful," says Mom.

"Absolutely," adds Dad. "How's your junior portfolio going, by the way?"

Issy visibly dims. "It's fine."

The media loves to paint me and Issy as total opposites, especially because we're so close in age. When referenced we're shoved together, "EmmyAndIssy," never individuals *except* for when comparisons are being drawn. I'm the smart one, she's the creative one. I'm forward, she's quiet. I'm a statuesque force and she's a petite package, three inches shorter than I. What the media rarely trumpets is how similar we are. We're both sharp, driven, and ambitious. It's just my brain churns out arguments and stances, so things like writing my junior portfolio—a collection of essays on civic duty, cultural competence, and personal growth that's a junior-year requirement at our school—are *fun* for me. But Issy's mind is better at other things, like music and art and caring for people. It doesn't mean she's any less smart, but she often *feels* that way. And the way my dad is obsessed with grades and the things I'm particularly good at doesn't help.

Dad swallows a gulp of coffee. "That doesn't sound good. Emmy, could you maybe spend some time this afternoon helping—"

"I'm *fine*, Dad. I've still got a week before the first drafts are due. And I can do them on my own," Issy growls.

"Of course you can, honey. It's just that we know how strict the grading committee can be." He's left some words unspoken, but the implication is clear. *Issy can do the essays, but Emmy can do them better.* The portfolio factors highly into class ranking and hence how everyone looks on college apps. But I'm not sure it's so vital that Dad needs to wreck Issy over it.

Dad graduated at the tip-top of his law school class, behind only one other person—Mom. It shows.

Mom lays a hand on Dad's sleeve. "Let's remember to let the girls ask for help when they need it, not when *we* think they need it."

"Yeah, Dad," I say, nodding toward my half-eaten bacon.

Dad sits with the composure of the trial lawyer he used to be, before he became Mom's legislative director. "Fine, fine. And you know what, word on the street is that grease and coffee make you smarter, basically essentials for getting life-changing Senate bills passed. Throw in a dash of sleep deprivation to guarantee victory."

He's joking, but also he's not. The dark, saggy circles that live permanently under both of my parents' eyes weren't there before they started working on Mom's health care bill. The bill is a culmination of their "deepest humanistic ideals," to quote the campaign materials. I've never seen them work harder at anything, and that's saying something.

The thing is: They expect *all* of us to work just as hard. At everything. I'm good with that, but Issy's not built like me. She shoves toast around her plate, all her happy music energy gone. Yet she brightens again as her phone dings and she clicks into it. "Emmy, look." It's a Snapchat image—a piece of lined notebook paper with a message written in Sharpie: "So lovely to meet you last night." From Gabe Castillo.

"That's nice of him, isn't it?" Issy's face is so shiny and hopeful.

"Yeah," I mumble through the piece of bacon I've shoved into my mouth.

Then *my* phone sounds off, and I want to ignore it but find I can't. It's two red messages from a name that's remained in my Snapchat friends list for months and months with no activity. Handwritten notes for me this time. "Let's try again." "Coffee, the usual place?"

And immediately I wish I'd left Gabe unread.

FIVE

LATER ON SATURDAY AFTERNOON, MAPLE and I lounge under the canopy of Issy's bed as she picks at her guitar. Her room is the most beautiful mess. Mismatched-yet-surprisingly-coordinating furniture in various wood finishes and styles, all selected by Issy from antique stores and thrift shops. Art prints and fabrics everywhere. Guitars rest in one corner; an easel in another. It's all a stark contrast to my bright, neutral room—comfortable, but generic. Issy's curated chaos is indisputably cozy and so *her*.

"That's good," I say, interrupting her most recent plucking. "What you did right there. The chord progression?" I'm not sure I'm using the right musical terms, but I'm trying. Issy's about the only one I allow myself to sound uneducated around.

She strums a few beats again. "This?"

"Yeah, that. I like that."

"It *is* the chord progression," she says, marking something up on her staff paper notebook. "And thanks." She plays it again, humming over it, then jots more down. "Not like I have anything else to do."

Three Punishments for *Clandestine* Party Attendance
1. Phones in iPhone jail for the rest of the weekend and each evening after school this week
2. Issy and I have to meal plan, prep, and make dinners Monday, Wednesday, and Friday nights
3. Lucy's gleeful face, as the dinner stuff was her idea

Salty as I am about the phone thing, maybe it will give Issy a push to work a little harder on her school projects. It's probably wishful thinking. Issy doesn't even have a desk. Instead, she keeps her stuff on a rolling cart, which she wheels over to her bed when she wants to work. The cart currently overflows with loose papers, a couple of poetry texts, empty cans of LaCroix (which I personally think tastes like fruit ghosts). I catch a snippet of what appears to be an essay on cultural identity, with words slashed out, scribbled over, and a big X scrawled over the whole of it.

"Is?"

"Mmm?" she asks, over a new chord experiment.

I speak tentatively, which, as a rule, I don't. I'm always breaking rules for Issy. "Be honest. How are the portfolio essays going?"

She blows a caramel strand of hair out of her face and throws the kind of look she reserves only for me, one that involves the shooting of hot lava. "I can handle them."

"You should write about how you started that GoFundMe for Leah's family, when her mom got cancer." When Issy learned that our friend's family was paying out of pocket for all the ancillary things needed for intensive cancer treatment—food, hotels, gas money, lost work wages—she sprang into immediate action. My parents want to prevent situations like this from happening by improving health care policy—useful, but a heady and detached approach if you think about it. But Issy? She goes directly to the source of the hurt.

"I already thought of that," Issy replies.

"Great! And you could—"

"Emmy." Her tone holds a warning.

"Sorry. I'll back off," I promise.

Issy lays the guitar in its stand and stretches. "I think that's enough guitar for today. Let's go for a walk."

"Why not a run?"

Ten minutes later, the trio of us—Issy, me, Maple—pound our usual route from our house to Wisconsin Avenue toward the Potomac. Since Issy's with me, I keep the pace a couple notches slower than my usual. Issy's a more-than-competent runner, but even she struggles to keep up with me.

"Not gonna lie," Issy pants, "I don't think partying is great for endurance."

"You don't say?"

"Thank god we're almost there."

Two blocks later and we're tying Maple's leash to the bike rack outside of Baked and Wired, the best coffee and pastry shop in Georgetown. Issy and I have an understanding that all runs include a pit stop here. We enter the little storefront, veering off in our customary directions: Issy goes left for the sweets and I go right for the caffeine. Before I turn my back I watch Issy steel herself, taking one deep breath and blowing it out, before she steps up to the counter. It's her ritual for self-calming in a public place.

Ten minutes later, I'm back outside with one dirty chai and one black coffee, Issy and Maple waiting at a small table. All that's left of Maple's Pupcake is a chewed-up wrapper. Issy has better manners and has resisted digging in without me. I know without looking that the untouched white box nearest her holds the Chocolate CakeCup of Doom, and mine will reveal Pretty Bitchin' (a.k.a. chocolate cake with peanut butter frosting). I've eaten so many of these, but it's somehow just as amazing as the very first time.

I hand the dirty chai to Issy as I swing my legs over the bench to join her, the roasty-salty peanut butter smell finding me even before I pop open the lid. Crumbs scatter into my lap with my first giant bite. Even though it grosses out my clean-freak sensibilities a little, I let Maple lick them right off my legs as they land. There's a lot I'll tolerate in the name of someone else's joy. (For the record, the tiny amount of chocolate in these crumbs will only make Maple happy, not hurt her. Thanks, Google.)

Today isn't unlike the first time Issy and I sat outside Baked and Wired, three summers ago. We were thirteen and fourteen, brand-new to DC, and running seemed like a worldly, mature thing to do. But it wasn't only the cool factor we were looking for. Issy and

I had free rein over our rural-ish Iowa town, allowed to bike to the pool and hang with our friends almost wherever and whenever we wanted. After Issy's therapy attendance went public via internet, and especially after the move, Issy and I lost a lot of that freedom. Running was one line on a very small roster of activities that Mom and Dad decided was okay for us to do by ourselves in DC, at first. By the end of that summer the Crawford sisters were very fit Baked and Wired regulars, which is no small feat to pull off at the same time.

"What's on your agenda for the rest of today?" I say, washing down another huge bite of CakeCup with a slug of coffee.

"Agenda. Ha. Not all of us are built like the always-on-a-schedule Emmy Crawford."

"You're pretty spicy for a girl with a hangover."

"If this is as bad as a hangover gets, I could handle being a closet drinker." She wipes her mouth daintily.

I snort. "Yeah, because you really *nailed* the art of discreet drunkenness last night."

She makes the same face she does when she bites into the lemon that comes with her glass of water in restaurants—which is a thing she always, always does and always, always regrets.

Maple goes feral and starts lunging at neighboring tables' Cake-Cups, so we leave, this time walking. We used to run home after eating, but then one time Issy threw up and we swore: never again would we waste such delectable goodness for the sake of fitness.

"So," says Issy, in a tone of voice that I know is fake-casual, "what's your take on Gabe Castillo?"

Just hearing his name sends cold fingers through me, squeezing my windpipe. I can't remember the last time Issy expressed romantic interest in anyone other than a Marvel superhero or the main character in a Jane Austen adaptation, so I hate to squash this. But it seems all kinds of wrong to encourage her to pursue Gabe. I choose my words carefully. "He's infamous."

"Infamous?"

"He's a hellishly good debater—people *still* talk about some of his matches, even though he wasn't even on the debate scene last year. I think he's only lost once, ever."

"Was it to you?"

"Well, yeah."

"But you've lost more than one match over the years."

"Duh."

Issy's eyes widen. "Does that mean he's better than you?"

"I'm sure *he* thinks he is."

"That's a pretty negative take on someone you don't even know."

And here it is, my golden opportunity to come clean. But gold's only worth the value we assign to it. I'm not going to tell her, because I'm not telling *anyone*. "I know *of* him."

It could be true. Maybe I only ever knew *of* Gabe. I think of the cold closet floor.

The bricks of Georgetown's streets are extra red in this morning's light, and our quiet is extra loud. What stretches between Issy and me is different than our usual comfortable silences. And yet we're still so in sync that an observer would only be able to hear one set of steps on the pavement.

Issy breaks our pause. "I think Gabe seems cool. And like, not dude-bro cool, like smart-cool. The kind we like. Maybe we can hang out with him sometime."

God, Issy's going to break my heart. Or I'm going to break hers. "I wouldn't count on anything from him. Probably too busy fighting off debate groupies."

And of course *that's* not a thing, but Issy's face suggests she thinks it *is* and she's not a fan. I'm terrible, but I'm going to go ahead and let her believe. Just like I let her keep believing in Santa Claus, for three full years after I'd figured out the truth.

Our footsteps slow, then stagger. *Crunch, crunch . . . wait wait crunch.* So many slaps on the pavement, now.

Issy and I have fallen out of stride.

SIX

FINALLY, AUGUST RIPENS INTO SEPTEMBER. Though DC's leaves are still greener than I think they should be by the official start of autumn, my debate team has no problem shifting for the season. Our colors deepen from smart to smarter. From quick to quicker. If you've got an argument, we've got a better one.

The last Saturday of September brings the first major debate tournament of the season, and hallelujah! This is basically my Christmas, except better, because the only awkward gifting required is the smile I'll give my opponents as I verbally annihilate them.

My team makes an *entrance* at Mount Genesis, the host school. By tacit understanding, we leave our sunglasses on until we're through the front doors, like hot FBI agents bursting onto the scene in a crime drama. At my left shoulder, Liv towers over me in her three-inch pumps, head set straight, her kinky curls huge and glorious. With her neutral lipstick and minimal gold jewelry, she's tasteful and timelessly beautiful in a way that's intimidating to strangers—*especially* opponents. On the other side of Liv is Taylor, whose head comes up no higher than Liv's shoulders, but her petite frame is the perfect disguise for what she really is—sharp as her stilettos and as mean as a bee-stung bull. And at my right hand is John, our golden boy. Literally: gleaming honey wheat hair, bluebell eyes, white polo shirt, and perfectly, utterly crisp chinos. He's almost imperturbable, but I know his soft spot: Issy Crawford. He's pined away for my sister for years, and she's clueless.

Liv, Taylor, John, and I are the "varsity" squad. John's the head, I'm the heart, Liv's the soul, and Taylor's the claws. Preston, our student manager, is the legs. He trails with a cart of resource materials, our extra emergency laptops (#firstworldproblems), notebooks, snacks, and a cooler of water bottles.

Confident as I am, my hands tremble as we walk the halls of Mount Genesis. It could be that three full cups of coffee weren't the smartest choice for a debate day, but I need all systems go and I didn't sleep well last night. Good thing I'm not *also* taking Prednisone, the steroid my Crohn's disease doctor prescribed at my last appointment. That stuff makes me jittery as fuck and wrecks my sleep. I shoved the full bottle under my bathroom sink, where hopefully Dad doesn't find it.

"You good?" says Liv, nodding at my shaky struggle to get my sunglasses tucked into my bag.

"Fine," I say because of course I am. It takes more than a little too much caffeine to disrupt my debate flow.

She toys with the tiny rainbow charm dangling from her necklace. "I really wish today's topic could've been trade and the economy. We were strong on that in prep." Today's topic is *Education is becoming costlier, but the quality is not improving.*

"Health care reform would've been even better," I say, thinking of all I've learned from the creation of Mom's bill.

John jogs to catch up with us. "Yes to trade, but I'm happy we dodged health care. It's so controversial right now."

"They're all controversial, Wood. That's kind of the point of debate." Which I can't believe I have to say to him.

"There's controversy and then there's *controversy.* Some of us have a hard time staying *convincingly* impartial on that topic," he says, looking pointedly at me. My heart rate soars to new extremes, and I clutch the strap of my bag so tightly that my whole arm vibrates. But just before I open my mouth, I shove anything that could be construed as *emotion* away, down deep deep deep. I will not prove John's point for him.

"Topic doesn't matter. We can dominate on any of them." And I say it all in the cool, calm demeanor I've been working so hard on for the past three years. I'm going to need every iota of chill if we're going to win regionals, which we must. Last year, we missed it by one match, and boy, did the press *love* to watch me lose. My black blazer and stormy face graced SenatorSlush and a few other outlets for several days after. "Senator's Daughter: Almost a Champion" was the headline that cut the deepest.

If I would have practiced in the mirror one more hour, stayed up late one more time, maybe I would've carried us to victory.

This time I will.

My stomach lurches in a way I know is the *bad* way. Part of having Crohn's disease is always, always knowing where the bathroom is, and I dart to the one I clocked on our way in. Quietly, and on my own. The fact that I have Crohn's disease isn't a secret, but I don't go around shouting about my symptoms and struggles, either. I have absolutely nothing to be ashamed of—not even poop stuff, I can't help that—and also *I* know damn well that Crohn's doesn't detract from my talent or drive. I just don't want it to become all of how people see me, as in, "that girl debater with Crohn's disease." I need to be Emmy Crawford, the one to fear. As far as I know my disease isn't "public" information, and I feel like it should be my call whether or not I ever want it to be. Just like Issy's anxiety should have been for Issy, only she had that right stolen from her.

I exit the bathroom just in time to witness Toomey, our coach, scuttling back over to my team's cluster after registering us. He has short legs and a mustache so big that sometimes I fear his neck must be tired from holding it up. Papers fall from the messy stack he's holding under one arm; he's also toting a coffee mug, phone, and various writing utensils. Basically, he's the kind of person who toes that fine line between genius and madness.

Nose buried in what remains of his papers, Toomey bumps into John and reels back, spluttering. "Pardon me!"

"You got the skinny on today?" John prompts him.

"Right, yes, of course. Emmy and Liv are in room 110 all day.

John and Taylor start in room 115 and rotate. Are you all ready?"

Liv and Taylor give curt nods. "Always," says John, through a mouthful of fruit. Tiny banana chunks spray out of his mouth, undercutting his credibility just a tad.

"Let me get you a schedule," Toomey says, rumpling through the hopeless mess in his hands while also managing to drop his coffee mug. After he bids us all good luck, we scatter, leaving poor Preston to mop coffee off the tile floor.

The hallways are marked with neon arrows and bold lettered signs, which Liv and I follow in lockstep. The click of my heels on tile, the nervous hum of other debaters, Liv's last-minute review ramble of our three-pronged argument strategy—this is all *right*. It's mine. Debate is the closest I ever feel to flying, but it's also my harbor.

Liv and I find room 110 without difficulty. Our first opposing team is already inside, milling around the tables at the front. Electric guitar squeals from a phone speaker, causing a baseball bat of dread to thwack me right across my middle. And Gabe's smile imparts mischief and fondness and all the words he kept from me for fifteen months.

I breathe. I center. It doesn't matter who Liv and I are debating. We've got this.

Only we didn't have much of *anything*, not while facing Gabe and his partner, who sounds like he eats *Webster's Dictionary* for every meal and regurgitates it for public enjoyment.

After the match I sit staring at the table, wondering what just happened. And though Liv and I could lip service each other all we want, *They just wanted it more* or *Any team can win on any given day depending on circumstances*, we both know the truth. We didn't just get beat, we got *destroyed*.

"I'm going to take a minute," Liv says, pushing out from the table and booking it into the hall. I want to go after her, but my legs aren't ready. My feet are anvils at the end of adrenaline-soaked thighs and calves.

"*You* were formidable," says a voice that would be pleasant if it hadn't just eviscerated my stances. I look up into the face of Gabe's partner. He is tallish and brown-skinned, his hair a shorter version of Liv's shiny coils.

"Were we?" I manage, my mouth souring with the taste of that much crow.

"You were. Truly. It's an honor to finally meet you, Emmy Crawford. Your name's been coming up all the time lately."

"Don't believe everything you read online." Last week, a major news source ran a story, "Emmy, Issy, and Lucy Crawford: The Next First Daughters?" It was a cute and mostly complimentary piece, although not fact-checked in the least. They had Issy as the chess star and me as the musician and said almost nothing of Lucy, which she pouted about for hours. (Meaning the media got that wrong, too. It's Issy who'd rather go unnoticed.)

His smile is cordial but his eyes gleam and shift, like he knows something I don't. "I get my news from the *Times* and Reddit, and I haven't seen your face splashed all over those. Yet."

He must mean he's been hearing of me on the debate front, then.

"Well. Anyway. Pleasure to meet you, too . . ." I've already forgotten his name.

"Aaron Vanderford."

A few minutes of small talk follows. Yes, my mom is Cat Crawford. Aaron wants to get into politics someday. Do I? (I answer honestly, which is to say: maybe.) He tells everyone his favorite food is beef Wellington but he has a secret affinity for McDonald's chicken nuggets. I tell him I love the strawberry shakes from there, but it's not a secret.

Three Things My Traitor Libido Suddenly Appreciates in Aaron Vanderford
1. A laugh that makes me want to laugh along
2. High cheekbones, as if carved out of bronze
3. Impeccable grammar, which is hot

He's smiling at something I said when I discover my legs work again. I stand and pull an ankle toward my backside, stretching.

"You a little tight?"

"Yeah. I'm kind of not used to losing."

"So I hear. What an honor to be the team that took down the best in DC."

"Congrats. I guess." I switch legs, enjoying the loosening of my thigh muscles, even as my jaw goes rigid.

Aaron's gaze skims the outline of my body. "You're just as ferocious as everyone said. Don't know if I'd want to tangle with you again." The way *tangle* rolls off his tongue saturates it with sexy double meanings. Now *that's* verbal talent.

I'm on the verge of blushing and my own verbal talent has gone into hibernation. Rather than give Aaron the pleasure of hearing me stammer, I sit quietly. A portrait of poise, camouflaging my rumpled mind.

He leans in closer, conspiratorial. "So, are you ever going to get that coffee with Gabe?"

Utter whiplash. Gabe has reached out via Snapchat two more times since his original request to meet. I've opened both but blew them off. It's like the old saying goes: Fool me once, shame on you. Fool me twice, shame on me. And Emmy Crawford is nobody's fool.

I find my voice. "How do *you* know about that?"

"We're teammates. We talk."

"So, is your nosiness an errand for him? Or for you?"

"Both," he says, looking proud of his command of English.

"Hmph."

"Oh, come now. I just heard you using all *kinds* of words; I know you can do better than that."

I glare.

"Well, if you won't meet Gabe for coffee, how about grabbing a milkshake with me?"

"Why would I?"

"Easy. Me and you, we're cut from the same cloth."

"What does *that* mean?"

"I've got a bigwig parent, too. My dad's the president of George Washington University." And he awaits my fawning.

Which does not come. "Okay?"

There's a pause, because finally I've thrown *him* off-center. But then he does a whole-body fidget, like a wet puppy shaking his fur out, and he's right back at it. "Anyway, you can trust me. I might be able to understand you in ways Gabe never could."

A familiar, oily feeling starts at my top and slides its way down. "How do you figure?"

Aaron worries his shirt cuff button. "You and me, we're bound to have similar backgrounds."

I raise my eyebrows, still not understanding.

"You know. Pedigree, and all that. Trust fund babies," he says.

"So you and I are the same because our parents have money?"

"That's not what I meant."

"Except it was."

I wait for him to show a little humility, but no. He *grins*. "Think of it more like compatibility. Duty calls," he says, glancing at the clock behind me. "Until next time, Emmy Crawford."

Completely lost for words, *again*, I gape at Aaron's back as he gathers his things and walks away. Why my rebel eyes want to watch him leave when he is exactly everything I don't need is a mystery.

My heart is still pounding furiously when Gabe steps over to my table. "I give your performance a ten out of ten. You were excellent."

"You flatter me. Five out of ten at best."

"I'd never flatter you. Also, I'm stoked to see you're alive after all." The amount of eye contact he's toting is overwhelming.

55

"Proof of life," I offer, rearranging my notebook and pens.

"Thank goodness. Was starting to worry, since you never answer my Snaps."

"Yeah, how does that feel?"

He bites his top lip with his bottom teeth. "That's fair. But like I said, can we try again? I think we can work this out."

"I wasn't aware there was anything to work out."

I was aiming to punch, but it doesn't land. "Oh, come on, Emmy. We both know better."

Just as quick as always, which sends dual zings of annoyance and desire straight through my already-upset stomach. I am *not* in the headspace for this, not after getting crushed and letting down my team and the topsy-turvy exchange with Aaron. "This is literally the worst time for this conversation," I manage, though my throat is thick in a way that's pissing me off.

"I know. You're right. But ever since running into you at that party, I've been *feeling* things. I'll tell you what things, if you give me a chance."

When I say nothing, he pushes on. "I . . . Well, all those months ago I thought I'd done my math right, but the equation changes when I'm close enough to smell your shampoo and see your scar. I still remember how you got that, by the way."

My hand flies to the crest of my cheekbone, where the faint evidence of an elementary school scuffle still lives. I want to ask what cruel arithmetic made him subtract me from his life, but I won't. Gabe doesn't get to feel things *now*. I felt and felt and *felt* for months with no idea what'd gone wrong, until the gaping wound crusted over into a nasty scar. For him to show up out of nowhere and reopen all that? It just isn't fair. "How am I supposed to trust you? After what you did?"

"I'll earn it back. I'll explain myself. Please."

There are reasons upon reasons why I should get up and walk away. Gabe as a debater is *the* major obstacle between me and my desperate hope for nationals. And then there's Issy, who's been casually Snapping with him and who's made a habit of (loudly, dramatically) extolling his virtues at least two or three times a week.

There's also the way he stomped my heart into the cold cement floor of a supply closet.

And yet my next words come flying out before I've even committed to saying them. "Okay. Coffee, next week."

Mom and Dad were right. Flying too close to the sun will always be my specialty.

SEVEN

A SERIES OF SNAPS THAT I actually respond to leads me back to Safe Space Coffee, which I've avoided entirely since spring of sophomore year. Running into Gabe in person while he simultaneously ignored my texts and Snaps was too humiliating a possibility to even consider.

Dad says that on time is ten minutes early, so I show up at 1:50 on Sunday afternoon. The smells of espresso and the yellowed pages from the small lending library in the back hit me first. I'd missed them and the cacophony of pride flags, "RESIST" posters, and colorful hand-painted murals on the walls.

Immediately upon entering, I home in on our table, a corner two-top that's always chilly, since it catches drafts from the storefront window and is also right under an air-conditioning vent. But Gabe doesn't look cold. He scrawls feverishly across one page of a banged-up notebook, chewing on what is no doubt an orange scone, cappuccino still steaming beside him. Dark hair falls across his face, and I want to rake it with my fingers. My body screams for it: *I didn't get enough!* Memories of the last time Gabe and I were alone flood back, and I wrap my arms around my trunk. He might be warm enough, but I'm freezing.

And the table, formerly *ours?* It's his now. One more thing I lost when he peaced out. As if he can feel my hesitation from across the room, he looks up. My bones dissolve in the way I've never been able to fight off, not when it comes to Gabe. His smile is tentative but sunny, and there's no stopping the small one I give him in return.

I scrub the happiness off my face. He's going to have to work for it.

I slither through tightly packed café tables, my face carefully in check. It's a weird sensation, a form of déjà vu, to sit across from him after so many months. The books-and-coffee smell. The slick, grainy wood under my hands. Low voices and the whirring of the espresso machine. It all automatically takes me back to times I leaned so far forward while waxing philosophical that I probably spit in Gabe's face.

"Hi," he says, almost a question.

"Hey," I say, fiddling with my hoodie string.

"You want some?" he asks, pushing his plate of half-eaten orange scone toward me.

I love those scones, but I don't think I can bear to eat one. It would hurt too much. I shake my head with such force that hair whips me in the face.

"You're nervous."

"What did you expect?" What I don't say: *Yes, and also I'm guilty AF, because now my sister is into you and what the hell am I supposed to do with that?*

His chair legs slide back a bit. "Fair enough."

I rub my biceps like I'm cold, which I am, but that's not why I cover myself. I'm too raw, too exposed. I need a shield.

"Emmy? I swear I won't bite."

It's not your bite I'm scared of.

His clasped hands rest on the table, face a pleasant blank. It rankles me that he gets to be this calm. But I suppose that's the privilege of being the one who disappears rather than the one left behind. Something hot stirs behind my sternum and it isn't lust. I didn't come here to *lose*.

"Why are we here, Gabe?"

Finally he gives a little of himself away. His jaw tightens and his Adam's apple bobs hard in his neck. "Because I couldn't not see you anymore."

I cross my arms tighter, like they can restrain my racing heart. "That's nine-out-of-ten-level cryptic."

"I think it's pretty clear."

"I don't. Do you mean we're going to be running into each other at debate now? Or do you mean . . ." I can't bring myself to say the rest.

"The latter."

There's a part of me that is stupidly, desperately *joyous* to hear him say it. And then there's the other part of me. "Well, that's just *great* that *now* you *can't not* see me. You've seemed perfectly capable of not seeing me, for *months*."

His lips press together, but his eyes are wide and sorry. "I know. That was shitty."

"Yeah. It was."

For the briefest of seconds I wish we could hit rewind. Go back to sophomore spring, Gabe throwing hot-button debate topics at me just to watch me "spit fire," as he called it.

And he'd throw flames right back. Round and round we'd go until we both burned. And he was *good*. Which under any other circumstance would have felt like a threat, but with Gabe, it was fun. And more—a challenge. Chemistry. No matter how heated I got, he never shied away or took advantage, not even the time I got so worked up about women's reproductive rights that angry tears leaked down my face. I'd never felt that kind of freedom with anyone.

Even though we'd just spent a few lingering afternoons flirting in the nerdiest possible way, I'd trusted him. Enough to share more of myself, things I'd never shared with *anyone*, over tears in a tiny, cold closet. And that's where I went wrong. It pains me to admit it, but his sudden absence *broke* me.

To be sitting across from new-old Gabriel Castillo, still the enemy, *still* making my heart riot, is fucking terrible and also fucking amazing.

"Do you have any idea how it felt? For you to just be . . . gone?" I say it to the table. I kind of can't believe I'm saying it at all.

"I might. I hated not talking to you."

"Then *why*?"

He leans his mouth into his hand, which is propped via elbow on the table. I know this look—he's searching for the right words. Real-time Gabe is reminiscent of his sanctioned-debate self, who looks to an audience like he's stringing his stances together on the spot. Only right now it's not part of a credibility strategy, he really *is* trying to build a case. For himself. For his shocking exit from my life.

I'm equal parts dread and curiosity as I wait. I remember, from before, that this might take a little time. Coffee shop Gabe is a little messier than debate tournament Gabe, but no less choosy about his words.

Finally, he sits up straight again. "Emmy. I really want to talk to you about why I . . . went away. Long story short, there's been a lot going on in my life over the past year. But it's very hard for me to talk about. And I need to make sure you're . . ."

"What?"

"That what I have to say sits okay with you, I guess."

My brow wrinkles as his sad eyes hold mine for one, two, infinity seconds. "Okay. I hear you." I hear his face, at least.

"Thanks. I think I need to ease into all of this. Can we do small talk this time?"

A scoff shoots past my lips. It's not very empathetic, but my compassion is still kind of on empty when it comes to Gabe. "All right. How 'bout that weather?"

A little eye roll, which has the accidental side effect of showing off his unfairly beautiful lashes. "I want to be an asshole, but I

62

asked for this, so here we go. I like fall. I like the smell of burn-pile leaves and shorter days and all the pumpkin stuff. I wish it would cool off, though. It's *fall* and I'm tired of sweating."

"Four out of ten on your transition. But truth. I'm ready for hoodies."

"I think I earned at *least* a five on details alone, but yeah, me too. But I see you've broken one out for the occasion."

"Had to be prepared for the cold table."

"Good memory," he says, grinning.

"Excellent memory, actually. I rarely forget anything important."

"Me neither," he says, his foot nudging mine under the table in a way that is clearly not accidental.

I'd forgotten how forward he could occasionally be—something I'd really liked about him. Before. But now I jump away, startled, and my cheeks burn. I shove my face into my coffee, willing the pounding all over my body to *slow the fuck down.*

"That hoodie looks new," he says. "College visit?"

"Yes." I run an absent hand over the bulldog face on my blue-and-gray Georgetown full-zip. "I got in, early decision."

"That's awesome! I visited there, too. It's great," he says, then frowns.

"Yeah, that looks like the face of a man just *smitten*," I say, then hold back a blush because *why* did I say it like that?

"It's complicated, me and Georgetown. Me and college in general."

"Seems to be your calling card. Complicated relationships." I chomp my jaw down so hard and fast that I draw blood from the side of my tongue.

The smile he gives me is sweet-sad. "Guilty again."

We spend an hour and a half at Safe Space, which feels more and more normal as the minutes tick away. Gabe and I slip into old rhythms, familiar cadences. We talk a little debate, not much. We share our current favorite songs and who we think will win the Super Bowl this winter. I'm fully aware that we're skimming the surface, but it's not as irritating as I thought it would be. It's more like getting back behind the driver's wheel after a bad accident—or so I imagine. I don't drive.

Before I leave, I agree to eat the last tiny bite of Gabe's scone.

His small talk idea might not have been terrible after all.

I head back to the family brownstone late afternoon. Issy's in the middle of losing a game of chess to Lucy at the dining room table. Studiously, I avoid looking at the corner of faded Victorian floral carpet that's pulled up, revealing the dingy but original hardwood floor underneath. I *know* that having the floor in this room redone is "good for resale value" and "will really improve the aesthetic of the space" (phrases borrowed from Dad and Mom, respectively). Issy is thrilled beyond belief about this development, because Issy loves an improvement project like I love labeling and alphabetizing my debate binders. As for me, though, I'd just rather *not* with the gross, exposed, undone floor in its current state.

My phone dings as I enter the room, and it's a text from Gabe.

GABE: I can't even put words to how amazing it was to hang

with you today. And I'm not bad at words. Please tell
me we're doing this again next Sunday.

"Who're you chatting up?" Issy asks, eyes never leaving the
game board. She's such a good sport, a.k.a. a glutton for punish-
ment. She's never once beaten Lucy, yet she almost always agrees
to play. Me, I stay the hell away from the chessboard when Lucy's
on the other side.

"Check," says Lucy, moving her bishop across the board.

I shift in my seat, doing my best to keep my face nonchalant. I
can't shake the image of Issy at that party last month, in full bloom,
and all because she finally met a boy. "Oh, just Liv. We're gonna
meet up and do some debate stuff tomorrow." The lie rolls off my
tongue with so much ease that it feels gross. I dive into the book
I've brought to the room with me, hoping a distraction will wash
my guilt away.

There's a long pause in the chess game, but finally the clack of
wood on wood as Issy makes her move, and Lucy's swift pounce
of a follow-up.

"Checkmate," Lucy says.

It's hard to say which sister's playing Issy worse.

EIGHT

SUNDAY NIGHT IS HOMEMADE PIZZA night in the Crawford house, a tradition that used to include my grandparents. Back in the Iowa days, Grandma's job was the cheese and Grandpa insisted on overseeing the veggies. "When you've got not one but *two* sous chefs. What a life," Dad joked, every single week.

My grandparents used to be real. Now they're little more than pictures over our mantel, pixelated faces on FaceTime from time to time. As a little kid I'd have never believed anyone who told me we'd move so many miles away from them, because as far as I was concerned, they were as much a part of my family as Issy or Lucy. I ache when I hold the past up to the present.

The day Mom and Dad told us we were moving to DC, everything I loved flashed through my mind, like it was all already in the rearview mirror. Goodbye, Grandma and Grandpa. Goodbye, friends I'd had since kindergarten. Goodbye, softball team.

Goodbye, house; goodbye, favorite little ice cream shop, Field of Creams. My chest caved with pain, but I sat like a stone, because it was Issy who needed the space to fall apart. She needed my parents more. She always will.

I suppose all of this is the price you pay for politics. We've paid in full for Mom.

A package of pepperoni skitters across the counter and smacks into my black North Face T-shirt. "Um. You rang?" I say to the littlest Crawford.

A scowling Lucy has Canadian bacon clutched in her fist, ready to toss that, too. "I can't get the bags open."

"Oh really? Miss I Don't Need Help With Anything Ever needs . . . what's that? Help?"

Her scowl deepens. "You don't have to be a jerk about it."

Issy grabs the pepperoni, wordlessly using a pair of scissors to slice open the top. She's having an "Issy's world" kind of afternoon, humming under her breath and drifting about the house with a vague expression, replying to things said to her with "Sure" and "Hmm?"

Three Potential Meanings of an "Issy's World" Day
1. She's in the middle of writing a song
2. She's plotting a craft or improvement project
3. She's highly anxious

Sometimes it's all three at once. When I sit and really try to imagine living on the inside of Issy's brain, it makes *me* anxious. From what she's told me, it's a lot like her room in her head, colorful and cluttered and chaotic. A beautiful disaster.

I'll stick to numbered lists and black-and-white, thanks so much.

Issy hands the pepperoni back to Lucy, who smiles up at her with far more admiration than I ever get from Lucy. Issy is very clearly Lucy's favorite, but Issy earned it. An example: two years ago, Issy slipped up and told Mom what Lucy got her for Christmas. Issy cried. *Cried*. For the record, I laughed. It was probably a dick move, but I couldn't help it.

If I'm being perfectly honest, sometimes Issy is so pure that I want to hate her. But of course I can't. She's Issy, *my* Issy, and *we* are one of the only things from my Iowa life that stayed constant here in DC.

Until now. I haven't told her I met up with Gabe. Or how halfway through our time, his hand lingered on my thigh, and my rib cage thudded like I was about to take flight. Also unmentioned: one of the best hugs of my life, including the press of his hands into the lowest part of my back, pushing our hips together and making everything south of my navel go weak. I'd forgotten that's how it always was, how it apparently *still* is, when it comes to Gabe.

I shouldn't be seeing anyone. *Especially* not now. Debate dominance, perfect grades, maintaining friendships, dodging the paparazzi for my privacy and for Issy's mental health and for my mom's dreams—this is my life, and it's all more important than romance. Not to mention that if I were to date anyone, it should *not* be my biggest debate rival. It should also not be the first person who's managed to turn Issy's head in forever.

But the truth is that I'm not sure there *is* an enter/exit system when it comes to me and Gabe. We were, and then we weren't, and now that I've let him back in it feels very much like we *are*, again.

And I say none of this to Issy. Our *we* feels more like a *she and I* than ever and it's my fault. Worse, she has no idea.

"There," says Issy, now finished lopping the tops off all the meat and cheese packages. I'm manhandling the rolling pin and preparing pans, as I'm the dough rock star of the house.

"Thank you, my sweet Isabel," says Mom, elbow deep in bell peppers and onions, which Dad will later encourage me not to eat because one time I had a bad gut reaction to onions. In movies, some characters keep lists of enemies they plan to seek revenge on. Philip Crawford's list is any food that has ever hurt me.

"Yes, thank you, sweetest, dearest Isabel," I say, batting my eyelashes at her, trying to recover some sense that I can be *normal* even if nothing inside me is.

Issy hurls a slice of pepperoni, clearly intending to nail me right between the eyes, but I'm quick and dodge it. It bounces off my right shoulder; Maple happily swipes the spoils off the white tile floor.

Mom's phone is tuned to live TV and propped up on the counter. The face of a senator friend of hers fills the screen, headlines rolling across it. "Democrat Sinks in the Polls after Disclosing an Abortion in Her Teen Years." Mom shakes her head. "Can you believe this, Phil?"

Dad grimaces. "Unfortunately, yes."

"Jen values transparency and integrity. That's why she shared. Her whole demographic *supports* abortion rights!"

"Supposedly," says Dad, who is browning ground beef on the

stovetop. "I respect what she's trying to do. Honestly. She has my vote."

Quietly, I watch pundits dissect this articulate, accomplished woman, but I've already seen so many versions of this. They've done it to my mom. They've done it to me, to Issy. There's no right way to be a girl or woman, not when the political media gets involved. But I've been taking notes for years, and I do what I can to keep myself safe. When you project perfection, there's less to tear apart.

"Hey, Mommy, didn't another senator go after you on TV like that? That one time?" Lucy, precocious as always.

Mom huffs. "One time. I wish."

"That *one* time, though. Where he was talking about me. The tall guy, bald and with big black glasses?"

And now we all follow. When Mom was running for reelection, she and a prominent Republican, Senator Livers of Florida, went on a pundit's evening show to talk issues. Livers had been *brutal*, going after Mom's choice to run for office with Lucy still so young. One of his attacks became a soundbite, perfect for posting and reposting on socials forever, with whatever your personal stance on the matter is. It still pops up, every now and again.

"Ah, my moment with Senator Livers. Lucy, did you know that now he and I are working together on my health care reform bill?"

"*What?*" Lucy is aghast. "After what he said?"

It'd surprised us all, when Livers reached across the aisle to cosponsor the bill with Mom. And Mom needs Republican votes, so she grabbed that hand and held on. They get along now. We were invited to the Livers' Easter brunch last year, even. (We didn't go, but still.)

"He's apologized for hitting me below the belt like that, and I forgave him."

I toss a handful of mozzarella into my mouth. "Is that forgiveness, or politics?"

"Both, kiddo. It can be both. Here's a tip you might want to hold on to, though: forgiveness is as much for you as it is for the other person. It feels good to let go of grudges, like ten-pound sacks of flour lifting off your shoulders."

Which sounds both way too easy and way too hard, all at the same time.

"So, Emmy," says Dad, talking over his shoulder. "What's the over/under on you making nationals this year?"

I've shared bits and pieces of my recent debate experiences with him, but we haven't had a chance to go in-depth. Dad's missed a lot of family meals lately. Both parents have, though they take turns doing it. The health care bill is looming *and* Mom's preparing to officially announce her bid for president. These projects are their babies every bit as much as I am, and to admit that gives me dual pangs of sadness and pride. I'm just like them, loving my work as much as I love my people. And it's no secret that they're grooming me to follow in their political footsteps. I only hope I can live up to their expectations and those of the entire world watching me. "I'd say the odds are in our favor."

"Per usual," says Issy, now opening a can of high-fructose-corn-syrup-free tomato sauce, which is the kind that's easiest on my gut.

Lucy launches herself by her bony wrists into the center of the island. "FYI, she lost one already this year." If there's one thing that gets my youngest sister excited, it's scooping folks with the latest news. And this is her favorite kind: an Emmy Fails special.

"How did you know that?" My fingernails sink into my palms, cutting deep.

"Heard you Facetiming with Liv."

"You little sneak."

Lucy shrugs. "You never know what kind of intel you're going to need."

Three surprised faces swivel toward me, which gives me squirmy feelings. "Emmy? Really? You lost?" Mom sets down her knife.

I flex and release my fingers, trying not to notice the stinging divots in my palms. "I know this is hard to believe, but I'm not a machine. I'm fallible."

"But you didn't say anything! We always just . . ." Dad trails off.

"I know. You always assume I won." I knead the dough like it has personally offended me.

"Because you haven't lost in . . . ever!" Issy looks genuinely horrified, far more than anyone should. This isn't breaking news.

"That's not true. I definitely lost more than a few my sophomore year. And I lost at the end of last season."

"What, once?" says Issy.

"Yeah. Once. The regional tournament? I'm sure you all remember how I blew my shot at nationals." A pizza pan clangs against the counter as I throw a dough ball onto it.

"I don't know if I'd call that 'blowing your shot.' You debated well, it's just the other team was better that day." Mom, always the pragmatist.

Dad ruffles my hair in that Dad-ish way that does not take frizz or styling into account. "Agreed, kiddo. So as for this recent loss, you must have rubbed elbows with greatness. Who got you?"

Oh, damn. There were layers of reasons why I didn't share the news of my recent defeat with the family.

"The team from St. Jeremiah's," I say as I smooth my hair back down.

"Jeremiah's?" Issy's voice flies so high and loud that Maple's ears perk. "Gabe's team?"

I pour all my focus into getting dough evenly rolled out across the bottom of one of the pans. "Yep."

"You *debated* Gabe and you didn't say anything?" Issy is a model of emotional expression. The shock, the horror, the incredulousness.

"Guess it slipped my mind," I say.

"Who's Gabe?" say Mom and Dad, in unison, with the same intonation. We all break in laughter, and so does the tension in the room.

Issy's face goes full-on glowy, just like at Liv's party. "He's a guy we met a few weeks ago. At that party we weren't supposed to be at," she says, but her sunny eyes, which are currently blasting me with all the UV they've got, do the *real* talking. *Did you say anything to him about me? How did he look? Please make this happen for me, Emmy.*

Mom and Dad exchange a look, their smug faces mirroring each other. It must be fun, being an adult, knowing everything.

73

An hour later finds me at my desk, Issy sitting at the foot of my bed, having an impromptu solo jam session—in my room, for some reason. I'm at my desk, reviewing arguments for our team's next debate topic, contemplating getting a head start on the AP Government and Politics paper that's due next week.

Her song's coming together. It's a tighter version of the project she's been plucking around on for a couple of weeks. If only Issy could write essays like she writes music. She *did* get her junior portfolio draft done by its due date, but the gush of the bathroom sink at 3:00 a.m. the night before told me what it cost her.

"That's sounding good, Is."

"Thanks," she says, still a little vague. She'd sharpened after my big Gabe-debate-defeat-reveal, then slunk back into her inner world. Maybe her mind is her safest space—at least, when it's not attacking her.

Many minutes, chords, and words later, Issy lays the guitar across my bed. "Hey. I've been thinking about something."

I turn away from my laptop, rubbing my stinging eyes. "What's that?"

"I think—" There's a tremor in her voice, which I've heard many times, but never when it's just us. My palms go clammy. "I think I'm ready to try some new things?"

My shoulders almost hit the ground with the force of my relief. "Like what?"

"Well. I was thinking about . . . maybe dating? Like going on real dates?" Most of my sister's previous "relationships" have involved a lot of texting or Snapping, exchanging bashful looks at school, and an inevitable fizzle, because it's hard to keep a relationship going when you struggle to go out in public. Given this, I *love* Issy's new idea.

In principle.

Which doesn't stop my insides from balking. I know where she's going with his.

"More power to you," I say, because I do *not* want to say, *Who do you have in mind?* For the first time in my life, I understand the meaning of that stupid old saying *Ignorance is bliss.*

"You don't seem excited. Do you think I'm not ready?"

"No! I mean, it's not that." I swallow, going on a deep dive for the right words. "It's just the world sometimes isn't very kind to tender hearts." I remember the senator on TV being criticized for her personal choices. And handing my softest self to a boy in a closet.

She twirls a lock of hair around her index finger. "I get that. But I think maybe my heart's not changing, so maybe I need to change around it. You know?"

I take a second to absorb that one, because whoa. "How did you get so smart?"

A framed picture of us on our porch swing in Iowa sits on my dresser. Matching smiles against the same dark brown hair (hers is longer and she leans into our natural wave, whereas I straighten mine), same light olive skin, but Issy's just that much shorter, softer, and, I've always thought, sparklier. I envied her easy charm when we were younger.

"Probably from basking in your presence," she says, her voice sarcastically sweet.

"Shut up."

"Never. One more thing, by the way."

"What's that?"

She fidgets with her guitar strap, working *very hard* to look uber casual and failing. Chill is just not part of our genetic package. "Maybe you should also think about dating. Like, really dating."

I force a chuckle, even as her words gut me. "Why? You know I've got bigger fish to fry."

"I know you do. And honestly you can keep grinding away at all the serious stuff and be single forever if you want and I'll never judge you, because I think you're great just the way you are. It's just that sometimes . . . well, sometimes I think you don't *let* yourself hang out with anyone, even though maybe you want to."

I grab a blanket from my bed and throw it around my shoulders. I'm freezing all of a sudden, and also feeling the need for something between me and Issy.

Because maybe I'm not the actress I think I am.

NINE

MID-OCTOBER BRINGS ALL THE THINGS Gabe said he liked about his favorite season. The smoky tang of burning leaves. Earlier sunsets. Pumpkin spice lattes and bread mixes and candles. Yet falling temperatures and squash-dominated menus aren't the only changes in my life this autumn. Every afternoon at Safe Space, every shared bite of orange scone, has cleaved new cracks in my armor, places where joy can leak in. And today it's soaking in like I'm a sponge and it's water, and I nearly run to the table where Gabe awaits me. Sometimes Liv or Taylor will drop comments about the people they're talking to, like *I'm getting bored* or *We're supposed to hang out tonight, but I don't really feel like going.* Though Gabe and I are *not* dating—or so I keep telling myself, despite the fact that this is our sixth meet-up in three weeks—I can't imagine ever feeling bored or even ambivalent about him. Every time we see each other, it gets better. *We* get better. I've always been into his wit and passion, but peeking out around his edges is a playfulness that complements all the earnest. It's new to me, and endearing, and I am definitely in trouble.

Which is why a low undercurrent of dread also haunts me every time I see Gabe. And it's not just about the debate rival stuff. Issy still doesn't know what I've been up to, and I can't seem to bring myself to tell her. *I will*, I think. *Not yet.* I push the guilt back and away, which leaves room for me to notice the other tension in my space. The air between me and Gabe is always charged but today it's saturated with energy, and potential for more. It's there in his teasing-not-teasing words and his too-long glances and the sink of his dimples.

How weird that my heart thuds the same way, blood laced with the same adrenaline, whether I'm excited or anxious.

Or maybe it's the caffeine doing a number on my heart. Every time I get flustered, I gulp my coffee, and that's how I drain an entire mug within ten minutes. We're both onto round two when Gabe's cappuccino leaves a whisper of steamed milk on his nose. "Here," I say as I lean across the table to swipe it away with my hand. Without thinking. Without asking.

His tongue slips across pink lips. "You want a taste?"

"Thanks, but no." And RIP, my dignity, as my face has to be at least as red as Gabe's American University hoodie.

"Let me know when you change your mind."

When. Presumptuous for sure, but that doesn't stop my knees from squeezing together.

I haven't let him kiss me, not once in all the times we've met up lately. This much is just like the sophomore-year days in Safe Space—I'm always vigilant, wary of paparazzi infiltration. Still, we've held hands on top of the table. Below it, our feet have tangled so much that our legs got involved. I've *thought* about kissing him, almost every minute of every encounter we've had.

And yet I know what it's like to kiss Gabe. If I settle into that, there's no turning back.

And I desperately need the space to turn back. Beyond Issy's crush and also debate nationals, there's another reason I keep Gabe at café-table distance. I still don't understand where he *went* for months upon months. It's not like he had any obligation to me. But after what I'd shared with him, I thought we were more. Or would be.

The confusion leaves a sour taste in my mouth that goes beyond coffee dregs. Maybe I'm tired of not knowing.

"Hey," I say, fiddling with the handle of my now-empty mug.

"Ready to sample?" He waggles his brows in a way that's supposed to make me laugh, but I can't. The wheel of emotions is spinning and lands dead in the middle of *hurt*.

"I like this. I like *us*." Saying so is enormously difficult, and I'm surprised I get the words out at all.

"I like us, too." He reaches for me, but I pull back.

I temporarily banish Issy from my mind. I love her, but I need a moment that's just for me. "Why weren't we *us* all along, then? Where did you go?"

He's been tight-lipped about his absence, and I haven't pushed him. We've had fun these past few weeks, the banter and flirting and footsie more than enough to keep me giving away my precious study hours. It's almost like I've been trying to separate Gabe into halves—the part of him who's here, and the part of him who didn't say a word to me for fifteen months—and I only let myself interact with the first of those.

But he *is* whole, and I need to know.

He inhales deeply and releases it slow. Repeats. "I do still owe you an explanation. I think it's probably time."

Three Statistics Regarding Gabriel Castillo
1. 50%: The odds that what Gabe tells me deepens my hurt (which means I'd have all the evidence I'd need to leave him behind forever)
2. 75%: The odds that not seeing Gabe would clear up most of my internal conflict
3. 100%: The odds that not seeing Gabe again would break my heart

In sum, the statistics do not lead me to any meaningful conclusions on what I want to happen here. And it's weird for me to not know what I want. To just not *know*, generally.

One last deep breath before he launches. "Right about the time I stopped talking to you, my mom got sick. Really sick."

I suck air through my teeth as if I'd been burned.

TEN

GUILT STORMS MY BLOODSTREAM, THIS time from a completely new angle. For so long I'd painted Gabe as the villain of our story.

God, I hated being wrong.

Still, I needed to know *how* wrong. "What do you mean, sick?"

He's still here, looking out the window, but he's also far away. Maybe watching a movie in his mind like Issy says she does, or seeing the next several moves like Lucy does, or making mental lists like I do. And then, he's back. "Sick as in majorly mentally ill. Sometimes I think that's even harder to talk about than physical illness. Like if I said she had cancer, everyone would know what that was. But when I say 'mental illness,' people balk."

Not me. "I'm comfortable talking about mental illness. I've . . . been around it."

He squints, like he doesn't believe me. "You been around an illness so bad that the person couldn't live at home?"

"Your mom lives . . . elsewhere?"

I take Gabe's silence as a *yes* and push on. "My understanding is that it's good for people with mental health problems to live with supports. Why isn't she with you?"

"Believe me, I'd do *anything* to have Mom home again. If only it was that easy."

"Isn't it, though? I mean, there are medications and therapy and—"

"Emmy, do you *really* think I don't know about medications and therapy? About CBT and behavioral modification, about SSRIs and antipsychotics, injectables versus pills? Do you think I haven't spent hours of my life Googling every possible thing to help?"

"I'm sorry." I pull back, sheepish.

He scrubs a hand down his face. "It's okay. I'm getting worked up. This is *hard* to talk about."

"I get it. I really do want to know more, though. If you're willing. You keep talking, and I'll shut up."

He heaves a massive sigh, wearier than any seventeen-year-old should ever be. "Okay. I'll try. It probably works best to start all the way at the beginning. I was born in Texas. Mom and I lived basically right next door to my grandparents, who had immigrated from Mexico in the eighties. They were *everything* to me when I was little—like two extra parents. And then they both died the same year, when I was seven."

I absorb that like a gut punch, thinking of how my grandparents were part of every childhood memory, none of my teen ones.

"With them gone, Mom decided to move us to DC. Her older sister was already here—that's Mari."

"Do you still have any family in Mexico?"

"Oh yeah, great-aunts and uncles and cousins. We keep in touch for sure—social media and stuff—but it's a lot harder to get to Mexico from DC than it was from Texas. And money got a lot tighter for me and Mom after we moved here. My dad not contributing anymore was a huge financial hit. Hard to see when I was little, easier to understand now."

I feel my brows scrunching. "Why did your dad stop helping?"

Gabe takes another deep breath. "I've learned a lot of hard things about my dad over the years. The big one was that Mom was his mistress, and we were his second family. He has a wife and three kids who are all older than me. Before she and I left Texas, she ended things with him, and then I guess he took that as his cue to end things with *me*. I haven't seen or talked to him since we moved here."

"God. I'm sorry."

"Not that we have to rank order these things, but losing my grandparents was worse. They were my constants. Dad was always in and out when I was little. There for a few days, gone for a bunch, then back for a weekend, that kind of thing. But yeah, it was still shitty when he was just *gone* gone and I didn't really get why."

I try to fathom my dad, my *dad*, there one day and gone the next. It's painful even in my imagination.

"It's been . . . I've had a strange life, I think. Not in terms of all people in the world—lots of people have lived something like this, I'm sure. But compared to most of the Jeremiah's crowd, I stick out. Which is part of why I don't like talking about it."

I could never fully understand what it's like, being through what he had. But with the presidential candidate mom and the paparazzi problem and the chronic illness, I did understand his reserve. It's hard to share things that people might not understand.

"We rented a place not far from Mari, and our new neighborhood was amazing. Like, right away, the people who knew Mari treated us like family—sharing meals, giving tips on best ways to get around the city, stuff like that. And they've always been able to see what I'm *really* about. Like, somehow Mari's friend Jerilyn knew this angry, mouthy eight-year-old needed a channel for energy, and so she walked me to storytime at the library every Saturday. I got obsessed with books, and learning, and I figured out that building a good argument for the things I wanted got me further than throwing fits."

"Ah, the seeds of a master debater were planted."

He smiles. "Yes. I became the kid who won all the public school spelling bees, blew through grade-level assignments and asked for more, lived at the library in my free time—and it was the librarian who told me about Jeremiah's and the option of testing into a scholarship spot. Mom worked her tail off at her bookkeeping job, but a one-parent middle-class income is just not enough for tuition there."

I nod, silently ashamed that I'd never once thought about how my parents paid for Frida's.

"So when I started high school, I was okay and we were okay. Good, even. And then everything went off the rails."

Gabe's hands ball up into fists. I slide my hand across the table and cover one of them. I can't force the tension out of him, but I can remind him I'm here.

"The fall of my freshman year, Mom told me one of the business owners she worked for was following her. Said he was tracking her car when she went out for groceries and was taking pictures of her receipts so that he'd know exactly what she'd bought. Later, she started thinking he had tiny cameras installed in our house, so he could keep tabs on her all the time.

"At first I believed her. But I wanted to see for myself, so a few times I followed Mom around and kept a lookout for Mr. Mendoza, the business owner she was accusing. I never saw him. I tossed our house for cameras. I even confronted Mr. Mendoza at his store. He looked at me like I'd lost my mind. I was pissed at first, but then it hit me—he wasn't lying, and it wasn't my mind that wasn't working right. It was Mom's."

Gabe's voice has gone soft and scratchy. I squeeze his still-tight fist.

"When I tried to reason with Mom, she'd get so mad at me. 'I have proof!' she'd say. But the pictures on her phone were of *nothing*. They were like . . . furniture. A cupboard door. A window. It didn't matter, though. The more I tried to show her the truth, the more agitated she got."

Gabe tells the story so well, so vividly, that it unfolds inside me like it's my own memory. Fear on his face as he pleads with his mother. I remember times during Issy's anxiety attacks when I'd said things like "No one is looking at you!" "No one cares if you blow an audition, just *try*!" And she'd said, "It's not like anxiety is logical, Emmy. You can't beat it out of me like that." I can't relate to the illness Gabe saw in his mother, but I can relate to the desperation of wanting to *fix it*.

"For a while Mom was sort of okay. She could work and go to my school events and cook and see her friends. But then her brain would get stuck on Mr. Mendoza. She'd lock herself in the bathroom because she was convinced that was the only room in the apartment with no cameras. Near the end of sophomore year, about the time you and I met, things got really bad. She started thinking more people were watching her. And when I tried to bring her back to reality, she accused *me* of being a spy for them, and I have to tell you, Emmy . . . that broke me."

I swallow the ball of sludge in my throat and rub my thumb across the dark but soft hair on his forearm. "It all sounds so sudden. Unexpected."

"Mostly it was. In hindsight, I can think of past times Mom had weird ideas. Someone at work was talking about her, and once a friend's husband was part of some kind of conspiracy. But I was little and I believed what she said. Why wouldn't I? It all looks different with older lenses. I've tried so hard to understand the when, and also the why and the how. Mom's doctors said that sometimes, mental illness just happens. Even without a clear traumatic event or cause."

I nod, knowing that my tenacious brain would have done

exactly the same, in his shoes—gone searching for answers. Accepting that there weren't any sounded like my worst nightmare.

"And nothing helped?" Issy's therapy has been her lifeline.

"Like I said, I spent hours Googling mental health problems and medications and therapies. Mom refused to do any of it. She insisted she didn't have a problem, and that *I* was the problem, I was the one not seeing what she was seeing. I was confused and stuck and so I went to therapy myself—Jeremiah's has a social worker who does that with students. Pretty quickly the social worker told me she was very worried about Mom, from what I was telling her, and then the school got involved because they were concerned for my safety. It was a whole thing."

"It sounds awful." I can't believe he didn't tell me this was going on, back in sophomore year. I could've been there for him. Yet *now* is not the time to re-center on me.

"Yeah, it was. I mean, therapy wasn't awful—I still go sometimes—but the situation was hard. Mom was *furious* and tried to have me pulled from school. I panicked, because school is my happy place and things are mostly normal and predictable there. That's when I brought Mari in. She'd thought something was up with Mom for a long time and took the school's concern as her cue to take over, at least with the practical stuff. She got my mom to her first psychiatrist appointment and her first meeting with a therapist. But Mom hates therapy and isn't good about taking meds. How do you convince someone who thinks she is absolutely fine that she is *not* fine?"

I shake my head, full of sadness.

"By the summer after sophomore year, Mom was spending most of the day in our bathroom. She wasn't eating because she thought our food was all poisoned. She wasn't sleeping because she thought someone would take pictures of her in bed. Mari and I spent so many nights trying anything we thought could help Mom—special foods, music. One time a priest came over, even though we're not really religious. Nothing worked, but hospitals wouldn't keep her because she wasn't a *clear* harm to herself. That didn't happen until one of her voices told her she was better off dead and started giving her specific ideas . . . I won't go into it."

"Oh, Gabe." Tears pinch at my eyes. "That's so much."

"Yeah. After *those* voices, she did go to a hospital. They told us she has schizophrenia. Which is . . . a complicated disorder. One of the hardest things is that it's incurable. Treatable, but it will never go away. And Mom's has gotten progressively worse, with really no indication it's going to turn around."

Which is a statement that lands like an anvil. Incurable illnesses *are* hard to sit with. I know that better than anyone.

"After the first hospitalization, Mom was stable enough to come home. We drove through the pharmacy to pick up her meds after she discharged. Mom heard Mari and I fumbling through the process of figuring out what meds were covered by insurance and how much out-of-pocket costs were going to be for everything—which was a lot, because insurance wasn't covering much. Mom got super anxious. And guilty. And I'm not sure if this is why, but two days after coming home, she started refusing to take the meds altogether.

"The second hospitalization, we got connected with a case-worker, and she recommended that Mari become Mom's power of attorney—which meant Mari would assume medical decision-making for Mom—and also my legal guardian. During the third hospitalization, I moved in with Mari, and thank god for that. I'm still in my neighborhood and living with someone who loves me. I get to go to my same school with my same friends. I'm really not sure what would have happened to me if not for her."

"And your mom? Where is she?"

He sighs again, heavily. "The plan was for all of us to live together. We tried bringing her home, to Mari's, but she got worse almost immediately. She refused meds, spent all day curled up in the bathroom again; the whole thing started over. We realized she needed help beyond what we could do for her, so we started looking into other places for her to live. Even with a caseworker helping us, it took *months* to get it all lined up. The first half of my junior year was kind of a nightmare."

My head spins with the details. "But . . . I don't understand. Why did it take so long?" Issy has always had exactly what she needed, right away. She needed a therapist, we found one. She needed medications, a doctor wrote a prescription, and we pick them up at CVS every month. Mental health care always seemed so straightforward, a lot like my treatment for Crohn's disease. We got a doctor, he ran the tests, I got a diagnosis, I get what I need.

His fists clench tighter. "Money. And fucking health insurance, *again*. I'm still learning about how all of it works, but I know way more now than I did three years ago. Mom had a private plan for us that she paid for on her own, but I guess it was basically only there for a catastrophic situation."

"Isn't *this* a catastrophe?"

"You'd think, but not according to the health insurance system. First, it wouldn't pay for the medications her doctors were prescribing, so we had to go with less-than-perfect meds. Maybe she'd be better by now if she had the best ones? I might never know."

Again I shake my head, because I have no words for how unfair this is.

"And then the insurance wouldn't cover any of the facilities her doctors were recommending. Do you have any idea what residential mental health care costs, out of pocket?"

I've never had to think about the financial realities of Issy's care. Or mine. I don't even know what kind of health insurance we have, let alone how it works. "No."

"Hundreds of dollars a day. And Mom's caseworker thought she'd need this kind of care for at least a month and possibly a lot longer. There was no way we could pay for it." Gabe smashes his lips together, and I don't know if he's angry or fighting off tears. Or both.

And just like that, I get *why* my parents are so doggedly committed to health care reform, even though it drains them, and even despite the many political obstacles they come up against. It's *this*, and situations like it. I've always cognitively understood, but now my blood hums with a deeper recognition.

"What did you do?" I say, quietly.

"A lawyer helped us file disability paperwork for Mom. Now

she has a kind of public coverage that will pay for certain meds and certain facilities—but not the best ones, and not the ones Mom's doctor recommended. Currently she lives in a supervised group home, which is sort of like a halfway house but for people with SPMI—severe and persistent mental illness. It's . . ." He slumps in his chair. "It's safer for her there, but it's a sad place. Our old apartment was clean and sunny and comfortable. Her current room only has a one tiny window, and she shares it with a woman who is terrified of the shower, so it *smells* in there, and . . ." I hear the tremble of his chin even before I see it. "It's just so degrading, Emmy," he whispers.

The thought of anyone going through this—the loss of one's home, one's identity, one's ability to take care of herself—is horror-worthy, but to know that maybe people with more money or better insurance land in a better position? Infuriating.

And the fact this all happened to Gabe's mom—and to *Gabe*—tears me up.

"I'm so, so sorry," I say, taking one cold hand into both of mine.

"She's alive and I get to see her, so that's something. But she's so different now, even on her good days. She's not my mom anymore."

These words need space, and we let them ring, our sniffles the only interruption.

Three Things That Are Suddenly Very Loud
    1. The squeal of the radiator
    2. Every single clink of silverware on plates

3. The sloppy chewing of the middle-aged couple sitting at the nearest table

The usually cozy space of our coffee shop has gone claustrophobic. Gabe's bouncing right knee matches the anxious energy that pumps in my bloodstream. And for some reason my head flashes back to his sparse Instagram. His five generic posts and then one recent, that picture of him and his mother. "Love you, Mami."

Can a heart implode just from sadness? Ask mine.

ELEVEN

THOUGH GABE'S HUGE SELF-DISCLOSURE LEAVES me emotionally reeling, life moves on. I have no choice but to move with it, including dealing with my own incurable illness. The following Wednesday I walk myself out of school right after lunch, shoulders dragging with how much I *do not* want to go where I'm going.

Dad picks me up where he always does when either Issy or I have to leave in the middle of the school day—the special side exit, which a corridor of trees and bushes shields from the street and foot traffic. We're not the only high-profile kids who go to Frida's.

Thirty minutes later I'm parked in Dr. Dalke's office, exam table paper crackling under me as I squirm. My nurse, Jo, peppers me with the usual questions.

"How are you feeling?"

"About the same as I have been."

"And your energy level?"

"I'm able to do what I need to."

"Appetite?"

"Ask Baked and Wired about my appetite."

Jo laughs, and I know I'm winning. "I'll go get Dr. Dalke and he'll go over your recent labs with you." Jo's one of my favorite people on earth, which makes my evasive maneuvers feel that much worse. But since Dad insisted on coming into my gastroenterology appointment with me, I have no choice. I'm way too close to regionals to let anything get in the way, and if I'm *too* honest about my rogue bowel, I'm screwed. Dad's doing something on his phone during Jo's exam, but I still feel him trying to read me. I might have fooled Jo, but Dad's a tougher sell.

Dr. Dalke sweeps into the room, tall and pale and brooding, his dark-rimmed glasses slipping down his nose a little. Mom says he's a "snack," but I think he looks like a nerdy vampire. He's also very kind. "So, Emmy. Jo says you're feeling okay."

"Yep."

He clicks around on his computer. "I wish your labs agreed."

"Huh," I say, picking at my jeans.

Dad gets up to peer over Dr. Dalke's shoulder. "Hemoglobin low. She's anemic," he says. Because when I got Crohn's disease, Mom and Dad became amateur doctors, using WebMD and various Medline articles to understand every single thing about my illness.

"A little. The ones I'm more worried about are these," Dr. Dalke says, pointing at the screen. "CRP elevated, ESR also up."

I hate it when I can't keep up, and it's worse when the words *directly apply to me*. "And that means?"

"C-reactive protein and erythrocyte sedimentation rate are markers of inflammation. The higher the scores are, the more likely your inflammatory disease is active."

"Okay. What do we do?" Behind Dad's blank face is worry.

"Well, these labs aren't ideal, but they also aren't the worst I've seen. Before we get too worked up, let's review. Emmy, have you been taking your daily medications as instructed?"

"Um, the Imuran? Yes." Mostly. On nights I pass out without washing my face, I forget, as I keep my pills by the bathroom sink. But that only happens sometimes. No more than twice a week. Three at most.

"And the prednisone taper—did you do that in August?"

Paper tears beneath me. "Yeah." Hopefully one full-on lie doesn't make me an awful person.

Dr. Dalke clicks away on his computer before rolling his chair over to face me. "Okay, then. My suggestion is that for now we stay the course, but I want to recheck your labs in a month. If they're still looking like this, we'll probably need to consider a regimen shift. Which would also require diagnostic testing."

I grasp the destroyed exam table paper and rip another slow, straight line. "And that means . . ."

"Another scope, unfortunately."

Yeah, I am *not* getting a colonoscopy prior to regionals. The procedure itself isn't a huge deal, but the day before is brutal. No food. Only clear liquids. And you have to drink this stuff that makes your bowels clear *completely* and it's just as appalling as it sounds. I'm usually wiped out for a few days after a scope. Which I do *not* have time for this fall.

"Well. Let's cross that bridge if we come to it," says Dad, pressing his mouth into a line.

"Sure, sure. I also want Emmy to try another prednisone taper, starting today. I'll have the prescription called in to your pharmacy within the hour."

I'm not doing it, but I don't say anything. Two complete lies is probably past the threshold of redeemability.

"Let's give you a look," says Dr. Dalke. "May I?"

He always asks before he touches my body, and he is now the standard I hold all doctors to. I lay back on the table; he does the usual exam. I can't help but flinch when he pushes in on the lower left part of my stomach.

"Does this hurt?" he asks, pressing again.

"Not really," I manage, through gritted teeth.

He now looks suspicious. "Prednisone taper. Make sure you're taking the Imuran. I'll see you in one month."

One month and one week from today is regionals.

I nod. "You bet."

I've officially lost track of my number of lies.

TWELVE

A WEEK AFTER OUR LAST coffee date finds me and Gabe back at
Safe Space—a welcome distraction after the doctor appointment
that did not go as I'd hoped. I expected that we'd fall back into
our normal pattern, but we don't. Our conversation is stilted and
surface-y, like we're both a little scared to go back into the depths
of the prior Sunday. The tension is like a cord pulled taut between
us, threatening to snap.

I've brought tight spots that I'm well aware of. The Issy spot,
and the *OMG you're a debate traitor* spot, which are feeling even sorer
now that I'm admitting to myself how much I enjoy being with
Gabe. But there's another thing. Something about Gabe's disclosure at our last meeting has been nagging at internal places I can't
yet name. Places that are dusty from misuse yet also pulsating like
festering wounds. I wish they'd stay buried.

He shifts and stretches, like he's had enough of this and would rather be elsewhere. Disappointment strangles me until he says, "Hey. You up for a little walk?"

"Totally."

He looks as relieved as I feel.

Leaves crunch beneath our sneakers and sharp autumn wind whips my hair in all directions. Gabe smiles as we fall into step, and a parade of hot things lights up my midsection when he takes my hand. We pass restaurants and bodegas, barbershops and bars, until Gabe steers us up an impressive set of cement stairs.

Black letters above a bank of windows proclaim the place to be Mount Pleasant Branch Library. Gabe pushes through the door with the confidence of a regular, and the old-paper smell immediately mellows me. The thing about libraries is that they're almost the same, no matter which one you visit, city to city. The hushed murmur of voices and electronics. Tall shelves bulging with knowledge and wonder. Even the fluorescent lights. I soak in the comfort of being here. I'm home. Gabe being here with me is like adding a perfect cup of coffee to a rain-and-a-book kind of day. The walk, our hands suspended between us, and now a library—it's transforming my tension to a pleasant stretch. A sweet anticipation. My sidelong glance at Gabe shows a mirror, the corners of his mouth curving up. We're both library kids, safe here. Safe together.

I follow him upstairs and through corridors until the tables shrink to pint-size, and the shelves are lower slung. It's a little disconcerting, like I'm Alice down the rabbit hole.

But it's just the children's section. Gabe leads us into one of two small alcoves. Circus murals cover its walls: pigs riding bicycles, monkeys making a pyramid, a hippopotamus on a horse, like the fever dream of a child in a past era. He lowers himself to the floor and I follow suit, landing so close that our thighs touch. So close that I can smell his skin. When he smiles I swear I hear the stretch of his delicious, full lips across his teeth. I'm forcibly reminded of that time in the storage closet, so long ago now but still so fresh in my memory.

We're sitting so close, and still we aren't close enough. He's so . . . *here*. When we're together, he's all presence. I drape an ankle across his, and he laces our fingers together, and I wonder how we ever went fifteen months without seeing each other. *I shouldn't, I shouldn't*, but equally, I should. He and I have wasted so much time. And if there's anything I hate, it's inefficiency.

We haven't spoken. We don't need to. All the words and feelings hang between us like the dust motes hovering in front of the big picture window. I wonder if he feels it, too, how much this is like *before*. I turn; his eyes blaze with things we haven't said out loud but are *saying* anyway. *I'm tired of wasting time, too*, they say. They scream.

I nod my silent consent and his hand is under my chin, lifting my mouth to his, and *oh god, oh god*, why did we go so long? Not wanting to feel this good every single day defies logic. His kisses are sincere yet urgent, and my free hand tangles in his hair, so hungry to feel more of him. For once I don't fight the burning that's taken over. If my future is ashes, this is the way to go.

A child's giggle snaps me back to rationality. Two tiny kids grab picture books off nearby shelves. I pull my mouth away but can't bring myself to disconnect completely, instead bracing my forehead against Gabe's. "Well," I say, breathlessly.

"Well, indeed. You are *the* best distraction." He still smolders, and not going in for more is a little torturous.

But, *children's section*. "Noted. I have another, less pornographic distraction that you might like, *and* which stands less chance of getting us kicked out," I say, now opening the flap of my bag.

Gabe snorts. "Better be good."

I brandish my secret weapon, which is an orange scone from Safe Space. He emits a soft groan. "I thought they were gone today."

"They were. I bought the last one."

"How dare you. Were you planning on sharing?"

"Maybe." The truth is that I've taken to surreptitiously buying my own orange scone at the counter. I love them, but what I like more is thinking of him while I eat them alone, in the privacy of my own room. Where no one can read the *want* on my face. It only has a little to do with pastries.

He removes the cellophane with care. "I don't think food is technically allowed in the library."

"Nothing we've done so far today is probably allowed in the library."

"Truth."

I usually like rules, but Gabe wakes something up in me. He crooks his finger and I lean in, allowing him to feed me a bite of buttery-citrusy goodness. He takes a taste of his own and we enjoy together, not breaking eye contact. Something about the exchange is maybe more charged and intimate than the kissing, and I find myself having to look down at my knees. In hindsight I see how this has all been a long time coming, but it still feels fast.

Not to mention the Issy factor. My stomach cramps around the scone.

I scoot away, just a little. "I need to cool down or I'm going to make some truly questionable choices."

He grins. "Fair enough. Let's talk."

"Let's. It's arguably what we do best."

"I don't know, better than . . . ?"

And he kisses me again.

"Okay. You're right. We're good at that, too," I say, my hands still clutching his.

"Mmm. Yes. But to save you from your questionable choices, how about you tell me something about your life? Since I sort of dropped the hardest thing about mine on you last week."

My breath catches. His suggestion isn't any safer for me than kissing him. But I can try. "What do you want to know?"

He chews and swallows before speaking again. "Well, you probably get asked this all the time, but what's it like to have a mom who could be the next president?"

Three Types of People Who Ask That Question
1. The Social Climbers
2. Media/paparazzi, duh
3. Those who genuinely give a shit about my experiences

I've learned the intonation of the question matters. A certain edge to the voice, bordering on sarcastic, and I understand it's a

#1—the asker really only wants to stand next to a girl who's been photographed for *People* magazine. The #2's are obvious and often shouty. A softer, more level timbre, though, one where the question has a genuine lift at the end—that's the rare #3. Gabe is that.

"It's . . . weird? Don't get me wrong, I'm excited for Mom. I think she'd make a great president. And if she does end up on the ticket, I'll be proud to vote for her. Finally! I've been waiting my whole life to be age of majority."

"You're such a dork," he says as he boops my nose. "But yeah, I'm not gonna lie, I'm also excited to vote. I'll do my research, but maybe I'll cast one for your mom, too."

"Hopefully the paparazzi don't wet themselves over my trip to the polling booth," I say, for the first time wondering if maybe I should consider an absentee ballot.

"Ah, wow. I hadn't thought about that aspect of political life."

"It sucks. For some reason the paps are *obsessed* with me and Issy. It's mostly inconvenient and embarrassing for me, but it's really kind of fucked Issy up."

"Really? How so?"

I start to answer, but a squiggly jolt in my stomach reminds me that saying more would be a betrayal of her privacy, the very thing she dreads. "It's just been a lot for her. Also, moving across the country for Mom's job changed our whole life. But I guess maybe you can relate to that."

He nods. "Yeah. It's not easy, leaving behind everyone and everything you knew. Starting over."

Suddenly my eyes sting because *yeah*, it was a lot, and sometimes

I forget how much I gave up in the process. The tire swing and quiet streets and sheer *ease* of my smallish childhood community. My friends, right when friends were becoming my everything. My grandparents, whose absence I feel like a missing heart ventricle. More than a move, it's been a complete reinvention of the Crawford family. And despite how the media shines us up, it hasn't all been good. "It's not," I say, swallowing hard.

I thought I'd done a commendable job keeping my feels tucked in, but still, Gabe squeezes my hand, like he knows. Even with my face turned down, he manages to *see* me. He doesn't shy away, not like that time after the closet. Hope and fear and guilt take turns thumping my heart.

He throws me a lifeline via subject change. "What else? There's been more to your life than paparazzi tangles and the move."

Sure, there's been Issy's mental health meltdown, my Crohn's disease diagnosis. There's been Mom and Dad softly arguing behind their bedroom door over schools for Lucy, evening plans, and what the next several years of our collective lives are supposed to look like. Dinner table political strategy talks and primary poll postulating, because even when Mom and Dad are trying to keep the mood light, they can't help it. Their vision for serving our country is what they live and breathe. But I'm not ready to say any of this out loud. "We volunteer as a family once a month. We've got this wood sign thing above our mantel that says 'Give Abundantly,' and Mom and Dad are really into actually living by that. This month we're going to sort clothes at a place that puts together essentials for kids going into foster care."

"Wow, I love that. It's so wholesome."

And it is, but I cringe, realizing I'm handing him exactly the stuff we are media-trained to say during interviews. Surface stuff. But before Gabe ghosted, I shared too much with him and I really, really don't want to do that again. Somewhere between the inner-inner me and the safe-outside me there's got to be something that matches his level but still keeps me safe. "You know, there's this thing that started bothering me, a few months into living here. Everyone assumes it's fucking awesome to be a senator's kid. Like it's all I've ever wanted for *my* life. But it's not, you know? It's not just the move that sucks. It's all of it."

"All of it?"

"Well, a lot of it. The forced-smile photo shoots. Needing to think about what I'm wearing and saying and doing, every minute of every day, because some media person could always be watching. My parents talk politics *constantly*."

"But they support you and your sisters' activities, yes?"

"Of course, but they're also a big part of why I do debate. I mean, I love it, but also it's something I'm really good at. I make *them* look good."

Gabe strokes his chin. "It's interesting, how our parents influence so many aspects of our lives. I went back to debate for my senior year because of my mom, too. I need to get my mind off the doom and gloom sometimes. And honestly, it feels like a thing I can control, even when I totally can't with Mom. No argument I crafted was good enough for the insurance companies, but they're sure as hell good enough to win debate matches."

"I'm not gonna lie—I like the control thing, too."

"You don't say."

I spare him a smile. "It's like that for my sisters, too—control plus appearances. Every chess match Lucy wins is a victory for her *and* for my parents."

"And Issy?"

My teeth grit, hearing her name from the mouth I just kissed. "She won't even try the things she loves. Because of the visibility." I drum my fingers against my thighs, knowing I need to shut down the Issy talk and probably this topic altogether. But it feels good to say the words out loud, and I'm not ready to stop. "The whole political family thing is almost too much sometimes. I don't even know if I really want Mom to be president, truth be told. I'll vote for her, but . . . in a lot of ways, being a first kid will kind of ruin my life."

Gabe's face goes stricken and now I *know* I've said too much. *Why* does being with Gabe always make me go full-on turncoat? I slap my free hand over my mouth. "Wait. I don't mean that. Not really." I yank my other hand out of Gabe's, now feeling altogether too close.

"It's okay, Emmy."

"Please. I . . . wasn't thinking."

"It's *okay*. Whether you mean what you said or don't, it's between you and me. Your words are always safe with me."

My body is still hot and nauseous, but my pulse slows under Gabe's softness. He's safe. The sharp of my shoulder blades dulls against the wall. "Thank you," I whisper.

Gabe rubs at his jeans. "Parent stuff is tricky. I love my mom. I'll always love her, even if she's not *her* anymore. What's harder maybe even than accepting she's gone is accepting parts of *me* are gone. Maybe you'll be able to relate to this."

"What do you mean?"

"With every year that passes, it's like a little more of what made me *me* has slipped away. When I was little, I thought I'd be able to do anything I wanted, when I grew up. And now . . ." He takes a deep breath. "I'm on my way to growing up and I see the limits. Money limits. Time limits. Mom limits. I'm going to need to stay close to DC for the rest of my life, because someone needs to look after Mom."

I think of the activities I am and am not allowed to do, because of cross-country moves and political aspirations and paparazzi. Pieces of me that I've tossed aside for the sake of my family. Girls I am not allowed to be.

A dull ache in my stomach wants me off this topic. *He's about to yank something loose*, says my intuition. And still I say, "But I thought your mom was in residential care? Doesn't that mean someone is always looking after her?"

He scoffs. "Oh yeah, sure, she's safe enough. I guess. But no one who's a part of the system is going to take care of Mom and advocate for her the way I will. And I still want to bring her home, to live with me. Now and forever, she's going to come first, Emmy."

My insides are shaking, a whole-body earthquake that I'm not sure I can prevent much longer. If only I could figure out *why*.

He goes on. "This is what I mean: the Mom thing has taken

parts of me. I'll never be *carefree*. I'll never not have someone to worry about. And I'll never stop searching for better coverage, better treatment, better *everything* for her. I can't keep seeing her constantly sick. Hooked up to IVs when she won't take her meds by mouth, in that awful place that strips her of dignity. I can't *stand* it. It breaks me, because I *love* her and this isn't fair."

Gabe's voice is cracking with emotion and my own smashed-down feelings are surging up. They storm my carefully held walls and I fall apart. I am an avalanche. And I finally understand.

Much as I constantly deny it to myself and the world, I'm sick. Incurably. I need regular treatment. If my current medications for Crohn's disease fail I'll need IV therapy. The medicines are called biologics, and my doctors say if I start them, I'll probably need them for the rest of my life. I, too, am quickly and slowly losing the carefree parts of myself, and I'll always have someone's health to worry about—mine.

The last rocks of my personal avalanche collapse on me. *It breaks me*, he said, *because I love her*. Gabe has already lost so much. I can't have him giving up anything else to look after another sick person. I won't ask him to impose yet another limit on his life, yet if he falls for me, that's exactly what would happen to him.

So I can't let him fall.

And I can never, ever show him my sickness.

I don't know if I can open myself up wide enough to share this part of myself, anyway. Crohn's disease is mine to know about and mine to take care of.

My aching heart is a vacuum, gobbling everything into its

vortex. I pull my knees to my chest, an attempt to keep myself to-gether. *Just like that day in the closet. This will be another last.* And then I hold tight and breathe. Breathe. I will close up. I *am* closing up. I will batten down these grief hatches because I must. It's better for Issy, anyway. And for debate. And for Gabe, of course.

He's looking at me like he knows. Because somehow, he always does. "Emmy?"

"I can't do this."

"Can't do what?" I hear rather than see him sit up straighter. I'll probably never forget the sound of me breaking two hearts at once, the very specific *zip* of denim rubbing against industrial carpet.

"This. You and me. It's too much."

"Wait, what? A few minutes ago we were fine! Ten out of ten. Remember this?" Before I can think or speak or act his lips press into mine. They smack of desperation and taste like orange, and I can't help it, I kiss him. And god, do I kiss him, because I know it's the last time. Gabe deserves someone who can be his comfort, not someone with the kinds of problems that will weigh him down further. And would he resent me, if he saw that I have every treat-ment and medication available to me and his mom doesn't? Yet another reason he can never *know* me, not all the way.

I'm *this* close to heaving, gasping sobs, but I can't. I won't.

This time when I pull away, it's for real. I'm getting out of this, for him but also for me. *Issy, too,* I realize, as my brain slowly takes the reins back from my heart. "I have to go."

"Emmy, wait. Look, I know this is all a lot, but I thought ex-plaining about my mom would help? I thought . . . I thought this time it'd be okay?"

He's wrong about what's going on in me, but I can't find the words to explain. I shake my head as I blink too quickly, trying to keep my eyes dry.

"Talk to me. We can figure it out, together," he pleads.

If I look him full in the face, it's game over for me. Gabe isn't the only one who breaks when he sees someone in pain. I focus on my bag, and my shoes, and anywhere but him as I push myself onto my feet. "This isn't going to work. We aren't right for each other."

"Wait, please wait. I'm so confused. How can you say something that feels so right . . . is wrong?"

My eyes bore into the carpet. "It just is."

I want to see how my words hit, but equally I don't, and I all but run out of the alcove, out of Mount Pleasant Branch Library. Away from everything I should never have allowed myself to want.

THIRTEEN

THE NIGHT IS RESTLESS, ONE of those where you lie there for hours but never feel like you're actually sleeping. Tears camp behind my eyes, a huge tangle of emotion underneath them. But every time something tries to surface, I sit up in bed, rub my cheeks, pinch my thighs—not enough to hurt myself, only enough to feel something other than loss.

The digital bedside clock becomes my red-lit nemesis—12:47, 2:15, 3:28.

In the course of my lifetime as a sister, a daughter, and a debater, I've said a lot of dumb things. Sentences that have kept me up like this. Arguments replayed over and over. I'll obsess over unsaid things, only to come up with the perfect wording about eight hours too late. But still, I don't think any of my words have ever haunted me more than *We aren't right for each other.*

Too bad there's no upcoming tournament for liars. I'm getting a lot of practice.

There's comfort in knowing I won't have to look Liv or John or Taylor in the face and tell them I've been seeing our biggest rival. They'll never have to assume I'm choosing him over them. And then there's the whole matter of Issy's crush on Gabe. Although a wave of nausea rolls through me when I consider the two of them *together*, I still choose this. I'd choose my misery a hundred times over hurting Issy.

Yet this perfectly rational line of thinking doesn't help me sleep, and at 5:29 a.m. I give up. Running clothes live slung over my desk chair, so I throw those on, lace up my shoes, and grab my phone.

Hope flares as I hit the foyer landing and tug a hoodie over my head. I'm about to be in my most peaceful place. The rhythm of my soles pounding pavement, the cool, damp air cutting through my sweater, fresh beats blaring in my earbuds. Safety in familiarity, a taste of oblivion. This run will hand me almost everything I need. My runner's adrenaline surges as I pull the heavy door open.

White lights flash, flash, flash to the tune of something snapping, temporarily blinding me. Hands thrown instinctively in front of my face, I cower and blink, trying to make sense of the scene in my front lawn. A fuzzy black thing is shoved into my chin by a lady wearing too much lipstick. She's saying something, but I can't get any of it to make sense.

Cameras. Microphones. At least a dozen white vans are parked in *our* driveway, in the street, up the street. News people and paps swarm.

"Miss Crawford! Emmy!" they shout, over and over and over. Though some part of me realizes they're saying my name, that they want *me*, another part of me balks and denies. *No. This is not happening.* "Can you comment on the Instagram post?" one reporter yells, her voice a screech above the rest.

The question jars all of me into the moment. Much as I'd rather it wasn't, this *is* happening, but I'm trained for it. The whole family is. And thank god it's me they got, not Issy. "No comment."

A short, squat man wearing a flannel and a worn Red Sox ball cap pushes his way to the front. He's got the nerve to come up the first two stairs of our front entry, which is enough to tell me he works for one of the sleazier outlets. "C'mon, babe, we know *you've* got something to say."

Red-hot anger seizes my veins, but I stick with my training. Mostly. He's invaded my personal space, so I step right back into his. "No. Comment." I spit the words down into his face, as I'm a good three inches taller than he is.

The voices and flashes surge on, relentless. It feels like giving up, but I've got no other choice—I go back in the house and slam my back against the door, like some primal part of me is prepping for the battering ram. Chest heaving, I reach into my leggings pocket for my phone. It takes my shaking hands multiple tries to click into the one app I really need.

The Instagram picture is Mom at the podium during her last victory speech, chin high and face proud, but blurry. It's me, Issy, and Lucy, standing behind her, who are in focus. The picture isn't new to me—it's long been a media darling, used whenever they cover me or my sisters. It's the caption that's damning. "Sassy Crawford daughter says she hopes her mother, presidential hopeful Catalina Crawford, loses the election. #senatorslush"

I might throw up.

Usually these fiascos are the press's fault. Solely theirs. But this particular time, I'm the one who threw Mom and Dad and all of us to the sharks. Well, me and a certain someone who *absolutely is wrong for me after all*. Despite the way I left things, I am absolutely stunned that he would do this to me.

The fourth step creaks. "Emmy? What are you doing?" Mom's in her bathrobe, hair swept back with a wide headband. Wearing a small, calm smile, which I'm about to wipe off her face.

"Paparazzi. They're out there."

Mom blanches. In a move that shocks me, she turns and yells up the stairs. "Philip! Kids! I need you!"

Within seconds, Dad, Issy, and Lucy stumble down the staircase, a testament to how deeply wrong it is to hear distress in Mom's voice. Dad's hair is sticking straight up in the back; Issy's shirt's on backward. Lucy doesn't even look awake, and she burrows her head into Dad's side as they all converge on the landing.

Mom's too-pale face turns to my father. "The media, out on the doorstep. Any insight?"

"I don't have the foggiest idea." Like a comic strip father, Dad scratches his head.

My guts churn and my hands go sweaty. "I know why they're here."

"Emmy, honey. You don't have to hold the door like that," Dad says, his hand an anchor on my shoulder.

"I . . . know," I say, voice shaking in a way I wish it wouldn't. "It's like I know but my body doesn't agree with me."

He tugs me gently away and into his arms. "I've got you. And if any of those assholes break in, I'll sue them all to kingdom come."

I go a little soft around the edges and bury my face against him. He smells like our bedsheets and the Old Spice deodorant he's always worn, which for some reason makes my eyes leak. He squeezes me tighter as I try to hide my tears, sinking my face deeper into his warm pajama shirt.

"Are you okay?" Dad whispers.

I don't have time for a breakdown. I need to find a way to fix the mess I've caused. I nod into his shoulder, then force myself through one massive breath. And another.

A padding of springy footsteps makes toward the foyer, where a small bay window opens to the front of the house. Lucy has her hand on the curtain when Mom catches her arm and carries her back to the foot of the stairs. "This isn't the time, Lucy," says Mom.

"I just wanted to see the paparazzi! They never try to talk to *me*!" Leave it to Lucy to want *more* paparazzi attention.

"Em. You said you know why they're here?" Issy's not clutching her knees or rocking, her usual panic attack position. She's steady and looking at me with pity, which makes me want to squirm.

I step away from Dad and shove my hands into the kangaroo pockets of my hoodie so no one can see they still shake. "It's SenatorSlush."

Issy whips out her phone, scrolling on hyperdrive until she goes completely still, shocked face lit up in the fluorescent light. She looks up at me for a hairsbreadth of a second before reading the caption out loud and showing all of us another picture that went up seconds ago: me on our doorstep, toe-to-toe with the short paparazzo. The caption reads, "Emmy Crawford stands her ground."

Well. That could be worse.

Mom's shoulders droop but the corners of her mouth turn up. Relief? Hurt? What did I do to my mom? "Okay. This isn't a crisis. We can deal with this," she says. The lines around her eyes are deep today.

It's only a matter of time until the words that need saying come tumbling out of me. Dad's attorney hawk eyes are already casing the room, reading faces. The moment he lights on me, I'm a goner.

"It was me," says Issy. "I'm the one who said it."

I immediately choke and start coughing. Then I can't stop. Lucy thumps me on the back a few times, because there's nothing like a socially sanctioned opportunity to whack your mean older sister. My stomach is roiling, churning with the ferocity of a mid-Pacific whirlpool, and I instinctively know I'm going to be spending a majority of my day in the bathroom. Crohn's isn't a stress-caused disease. Yet in my case, stress has never done my gut any favors. My doctor calls it "an exacerbating factor" and tried to prescribe me something for "nerves," a suggestion I immediately dismissed. I'm not at all against that kind of medication—it's done wonders for Issy—but the last thing my parents need is another set of medications to pick up and later harass me about taking. Also, I'm one hundred percent certain that I'm going to get a handle on all this; I just haven't figured out how yet.

I've only got a few minutes until I'll need to hit the bathroom, so now's the time to seize control of this situation and say my piece. I can't let Issy take the fall for me, obviously. For some reason I start to raise my hand—like a five-year-old—but Issy ever so subtly shakes her head. My hand falls as confessions die in my mouth.

Issy lifts her chin. "The other night I was venting. About just . . . everything. To friends I thought I could trust." Her eyes drop as she winds a molasses curl around one of her fingers. "But they misquoted me. What I said was that being a first kid wouldn't be my first choice, not that I wanted you to lose." Of course Issy has found a way to soften my harsh, albeit misquoted words. She's the curve to my edges, always.

The pause that follows her confession is loud. Full.

Then Dad crosses the room to riffle Issy's already-tousled hair. "Well. We can't fault you for having feelings. And for seeking support."

Mom is perfectly still and completely buttoned up for one, two, three beats before gathering Issy into her arms. "I know our life isn't an easy one. I get it. And I understand needing friends to talk to, but you know you can talk to us, too. Right?"

Over Issy's shoulder, my mom's face is blissful, full of love. But the moment she opens her eyes and they find mine, I know that she *knows* and that her invitation to talk wasn't really for Issy.

Issy pulls out of the embrace. "I'm sorry. To both of you. To everyone. I should have been more discreet."

"This, too, shall pass," says Dad, retying his bathrobe and walking toward the kitchen. "No point in standing around in the hallway. I'll make us all French toast."

"You're not going to work today?" My voice comes out all squeaky when I'm incredulous.

"Maybe. Maybe not. I wonder how long paps will wait outside for a story like this?"

Mom crosses her arms. "You want to try to wait them out?"

"Why not? I'll call Reese and see what she thinks, but honestly, we could use a day off."

We all look at him like he's just announced his conversion to the Flat Earth movement. Not the part about calling Reese, Mom's campaign manager, because they're always calling Reese. It's the *day off* part that shocks us all. "You're just going to . . . stay home? *Both* of you?" says Lucy, and her obvious confusion makes me a little sad. I remember Snow Day Dad, Softball Coach Mom, back when they had "let's go grab Froyo after school" schedules. Lucy will likely never see those sides of our parents.

"Yep! And you, too!" he says, pulling Lucy off toward the kitchen. She screeches in joy as her slippered feet slide across wood beams, Mom trailing.

And then it's just me and my full-of-surprises sister at the foot of the stairs.

"Why did you do that?" I whisper-yell.

"Remember that time I broke Mom's family heirloom vase and I started hyperventilating, so you told her you did it? And the time I threw up at our first DC slumber party and you cleaned it up yourself so that no one would know?"

I nod, because of course I remember. For a long time, I've seen myself as Issy's anxiety goalie. I don't save every shot, but I do catch a lot of them.

"It's not that I don't appreciate all of that, Emmy. I do. I've . . . needed you. So much. But I thought maybe this time, *you* needed *me*."

I'm reduced to a pillar of salt, frozen in time and unable to take my eyes off this person who used to be Issy. "I don't know what to say, Is."

"How about 'thank you.' That's what you say when someone helps you out."

I wouldn't know.

"Thank you. Truly." I worry the string of my hoodie. "I just hope the fallout from this isn't terrible. How big of news can this post be, really? Local? National?"

Time will tell. And there's probably nothing I can do until we have damage to survey.

Nothing, that is, except for these three things:

1. Find Gabriel Castillo
2. Stab him with my eyes
3. Finish him off with my words

FOURTEEN

I STEP OVER THE THRESHOLD of Toomey's classroom thirteen minutes early (on time for me) and a deep, cleansing exhale falls out of me. When running's not available, debate practice is the next best thing. Here, I know exactly where I stand—at the top.

And I need this today.

Not that yesterday didn't turn out okay in its own right. My family spent the day holed up at home, safe behind closed curtains and silenced ringers. Lucy finally got a taste of Snow Day Parents, even if it was due to a publicity snafu instead of a blizzard. It was board games and junk food, and I only spent about a quarter of the time in the bathroom contending with my nerve-frazzled bowels, which could have been worse.

Before I went to bed I checked my unread texts and Snaps—mostly variations of "OMG r u okay" and "paparazzi suck, ignore them." Gabe has Snapped walls of text—explanations and excuses, which I mostly skim then delete so I don't have to keep looking at them. They are all bullshit. Finally he sends a sad face selfie with the words "I'm sorry."

As if two words and a blurry picture are enough to make up for what he did to me. Again.

Despite the okayness of Paparazzi Snow Day, walking back into school today felt weird and raw. I'm trained on how to handle the press. Not so much on peers in the wake of a pseudo-scandal. As expected, the halls have been buzzing with the Crawford sister gossip. Throughout the day the weight of nosy stares crawled heavy down my backbone. The temptation to scream a confession was real, both for the catharsis factor *and* because that's how Tony Wagner took care of things after his senator dad got caught sending dick pics to an aide. The school's whispers became a roar, and Tony finally shouted something in the middle of an assembly about how his dad's bad decisions didn't have anything to do with him. Shortly after that, people mostly shut up.

I *crave* the satisfaction of shutting them up. But I made a promise to my parents and to Reese to keep my lips zipped, so I will.

The first thing I see in Toomey's classroom is a huge printout photo taped to the whiteboard. It's me in my running clothes, shouting down into the face of the vertically challenged paparazzo. Someone has written in Sharpie caps, "GLAD YOU'RE ON OUR SIDE." The cackle slips out of me in breathless relief, because someone has taken the elephant out of the room for me. The whole gang's already assembled around our training table: Liv, John, Taylor, Preston, and even Toomey, who is perennially late.

"We thought maybe you'd need a few minutes. Before we got started," says Liv, sliding a peanut butter cookie across the table. Liv has respected my request to not talk about the SenatorSlush episode, but the cookies show me she's thinking about me.

I shove the cookie into my mouth unceremoniously. I'm touched by everyone's kindness, but still don't really want to rehash the last forty-eight hours.

"How's Issy handling all this, by the way?" John asks, oh so casual. Like he hasn't been smitten for years.

"She's okay."

He grabs a cookie and eats half of it in one bite. "Studies show that social support moderates the relationship between stressful events and poor outcomes, like bouts of anxiety or depression. So consider this your social support."

Leave it to John to come at a personal life disaster with *research*, and to spit little chunks of cookie alongside his knowledge. The way his jaw chomps reminds me of Gabe taking down a scone. Familiarity and rage roll through me, wave after powerful wave. Stupid, stupid me. Vulnerability fails me, every time. *Just like before, brainiac. When will you learn?*

My lips go quivery at the edges. *No.* I will not let this situation best me. I breathe until my mouth is back under control, then smile as brightly as I can muster. "I'm okay. Truly. Let's just have a normal practice."

Taylor sits up straighter, like she's been waiting for this invitation all along. "That's what I said you'd want, just normal, but no one ever listens to me."

Liv scoffs. "Yeah, you've got a *really* tough time being heard,

Taylor." Taylor's the student body president, founder and secretary of our school's AAPI student alliance, and last spring she also sang the lead in the school's production of *Les Mis*. She is the opposite of a shrinking violet.

"Whatever. Toomey, what've you got for us?" Taylor taps a bloodred fingernail on the table, impatient.

Anytime Toomey's asked something he *absolutely knows*, he forgets he knows anything at all. Flustered, he shuffles some papers and cracks open his planner. "Right. Oh, yes. This weekend is the All City Debate Exhibition!"

I stifle a groan. Today I'm aching for a major, substantive, juicy issue to sink my teeth into. Something that will use up the entirety of my brain capacity so I have no room to think about anything else. Instead we have the "fun" All City Expo to prep for. Talk about poor timing.

Toomey scans a crumpled sheet he's unearthed from his stuffed briefcase. "As a reminder, the expectation is brief, one-on-one, extemporaneous debates. You'll each be seeded based on your win/loss record to date. The top debaters will be on the Big Stage—in the auditorium—near the end of the day. Since all of you have stellar records, you should expect to be among the last to go."

"Similar topics to last year?" says John, laying into a third cookie.

"Yes. Broad stuff. Examples they're listing are: school uniforms should be the norm, every high school student should have to take a performing arts course, people should embrace vegetarianism."

"Fluff," I say, melting hopelessly into my chair.

"These debates *are* intended to be entertaining. Consider yourself an after-dinner speaker, only in debate format. Don't hesitate to be witty and make the audience laugh. This is your big chance to ham it up."

And my big chance to look like a no-fun stiff in front of a crowd. I win debates with my brain and preparation, not with *charm*. I'm about to let loose a string of useless complaints when my brain stampedes me.

Three Pieces of Damning Logic
1. Gabe and Vanderford are undefeated
2. Liv and I have only been beaten once—by Gabe and Vanderford
3. No one else in the city has come close to touching the dominance level of our two teams

I let my head hang low as I realize what's about to happen. This day has bested me after all.

FIFTEEN

FROM MY HARD WOODEN SEAT in the back of the auditorium, I watch John mount the stage and adjust his collar. He looks like Apollo in his pristine white shirt. I've got a feeling he's about to take his opponent to task, and I will revel in it.

At least I'm going to try to revel in it. I've been sitting here for the greater part of two hours, awaiting my turn in isolation. My bowel has decided to go rogue, so a seat near the bathroom is a must, but the part about *avoiding everyone for as long as possible* was a free-will choice. My skin's damp but also cold, a gross and uncomfortable combination that has given way to chattering teeth. I am officially everything in the world I thought I'd never be. Nervous. Weak. And all because of a boy.

My fall from badassery started several hours ago. Upon our arrival at the debate site, Liv grabbed the list of the day's matchups from Toomey's hands. "Taylor, you're up against some guy from Oliver Heights. And John's against a girl from there. Emmy and I debated them already this season and they're good. I mean, not as good as we were, obviously, but good."

"Amen," said Taylor.

"Focus. Who do we have?" I attempted to get a peek at the list over Liv's shoulder, but not even tiptoes made me tall enough for that.

"Hey, relax. This is a no-stakes debate, remember? You're gonna be fine. We both will." Liv folded the paper and shoved it into her pocket, which should have been my first clue that *fine* wasn't on the agenda.

"Liv," I said, my shrill voice a warning.

"For what it's worth, we're the number two seeded team in the city."

"One seed lower than we should be," I grumbled.

"We'll come through when it counts. I know it."

"When it counts?" Liv's uncharacteristic vagueness trampled what was left of my chill, and I snatched the tournament schedule from her pocket.

A quick scan was all it took. My head fell into my hands.

John tugged a strand of my hair. "Oooohhh, the great Emmy Crawford is . . . what? Scared?"

"I. Am. *Not*. Scared."

John's smirk was a taunt. I'd never had such vivid fantasies of punching a debate peer.

Liv refolded the list and removed it from sight. "Look, this is fine. I've got Aaron Vanderford—he's a show-off, but I can handle that. And Emmy's got Gabriel Castillo."

"Wait, was this the team that *stomped* you two a few weeks back?" Taylor cocked her head as she tapped her teeth with one long, manicured nail.

"Ugh, *yes*, who else could even come close to touching us?" I said.

Taylor snickered. "We've learned a lot of shit from debate, but not humility. I'm good with that."

I turned to Liv, desperate. "Trade me."

"Umm . . . I mean, I kind of want to take on Aaron. You know, keep learning and growing through new experiences? His vocab will challenge me."

"I also want that!" The whole team flinched as echoes of my voice ricocheted off the grimy cinder block walls. "Okay, John, will *you* trade me?"

I might as well have suggested we streak naked across the stage. "Why?"

"Just . . . please. Please." I leaned in close, gazing up at him from under my lashes. Being a damsel in distress *usually* wasn't my thing, but I wasn't above giving it a whirl. For a good cause.

John blinked once. Twice. I held my breath, willing him to say, *No problem, Emmy.* "We can't do that. Assignments are assignments."

Because I am the *wrong* Crawford sister to coax Prince Charming out of John.

And all this is what sent me to my self-imposed exile in the back of the auditorium. Mom and Dad arrived between matches from the opposite side of the room and the seas parted for them, everyone anxious to shake hands with the woman who could very well be the next president. Though I'm stoked my parents both found time to come watch me, I can't bring myself to go to them. Or to Issy and Lucy, who came with them. Instead, I stay in my seat, destroy my cuticles with my index fingernails, and seethe. I had no idea a person could stew for this long. Props to me for uncovering a hidden talent.

Thank goodness it's almost time for Debate Emmy to make her appearance. But even now, on the cusp of clicking my heels up the wooden stairs and onto the stage, I vacillate between wanting to hide and wanting to tear Gabe apart. How I'm supposed to look him in the face at all is beyond me. And somehow I've got to manage it on a stage, in front of my friends, family, the paparazzi, and thus the world. The *only* way through is to banish my feels. They missed the memo, though, and they're still popping out of me all over the place—my goose-bumped skin, my shaking hands, my angry stomach.

Taylor's up. She *destroys* her opponent, quick-paced and lethal, and she does it with a smile. Liv is next. She mounts the stage and shakes Aaron's hand with the grace of a foreign princess. A less savvy competitor might relax right now, but Liv is a swan, a beautiful but dangerous thing. Vanderford's jawline works double time in his angular face, letting me know he's not underestimating her.

While the bestie dukes it out with Vanderford, I drift to the stairs at stage right, where the on-deck debaters are expected to wait. I keep my eyes on Liv, but Gabe's so close now, my bookend at stage left.

Though it takes exactly one hundred percent of my willpower, I act like he isn't there.

And then we're onstage together, introduced as the "Grand Finale" matchup. The moderator draws the topic from a large glass bowl and clears her throat. "Comprehensive sexual education should be a required class for all high school students," she says, and it's obvious she's pressing down a smile.

A blush threatens. *Don't. DON'T. Not here, not now. Not in front of Mom and Dad and ruthless Lucy and phone cameras and especially not Gabe.* I almost yelp as my index nail finally slices through my right thumb cuticle.

"Ms. Crawford, you will begin, arguing the affirmative. Mr. Castillo, you have the opposition. Your ninety-second prep time begins . . . now."

I force the audience's titters and my own internal noise out of my head and furiously scribble down as many cogent ideas as I can, mostly for my opening argument. Going first is a disadvantage when the debate is extemporaneous. Gabe will have time to think about his opening remarks during mine and adjust his stance accordingly.

"Ms. Crawford, the floor's to you. You have ninety seconds." The moderator sits behind a digital stopwatch counting down the total debate time, as well as a panel of multicolored lights: green for good to go, yellow for almost out of time, red for shut the hell up.

The green light blazes on.

"First of all, a sincere thank-you to Sonderson High for hosting this event, and to all the friends, family, and other guests who came out to support high school debate. Gabriel, I look forward to debating this topic with you.

"In an ideal world, a nation would be able to trust its citizens—all its citizens—to do the right thing. To take care of themselves and others. To vote. To work, to earn, to self-govern their behaviors so they don't hurt themselves or anyone else. We could leave comprehensive sexual education out of the school curriculum if we could count on the following things to happen: one, parents and guardians would take the lead in teaching their children about sex; two, our youth would learn and internalize those teachings; and three, youth would consistently act on those teachings. However, we all know the world we live in is far from perfect, and that our people are just as flawed. Not all caregivers are equipped or interested in having those kinds of conversations with their kids, leaving some with a precarious knowledge gap that could greatly affect their health. For this reason, among others, provision of sexual education to all high-school-age youth is a physical and moral imperative. We need comprehensive sexual education to increase the chances that our youth make sound sexual choices. It is the caring and responsible thing, for the health of our nation, to do this."
I finish just as my yellow light turns red.

I gaze out into the audience, garnering a wink from Liv and a fist pump from Taylor. John's eyes aren't on me at all. They're not even on the stage. They're glued to a seat two rows ahead of him, where Issy sits between my parents. Bless him, he's got it bad. My life would be a million times easier if she liked him back.

But, of course, Issy is oblivious to John's admiration. She shoots me a playful thumbs-up, but her eyes drift to Gabe, her face awash with an indiscernible emotion. Something beyond curiosity. Something that says, *You are the most interesting person in the room.* If she knew he was the cause of our family Instagram spectacle, she'd realize that he is interesting for far more nefarious reasons. But I can't tell her. There's no scenario that safely lets me break this news. I'd have to come clean about my meetups with Gabe, and it would be a one-two punch to Issy's gut: her sister is a liar, her love interest is a d-bag. And how could I pick up her pieces if I'm the one who breaks her? The only viable answer is to keep Issy in the dark on who Gabe really is and hope like hell he doesn't hurt her, too.

"Mr. Castillo, your opening comments."

And then I have to look at him, because that's what you do in debate. Generally in these situations I use my eyes like teeth, sinking them into the flesh of my opponent. Letting them know that I see and I'm not afraid.

But today I see and I *am* afraid, though not of losing. I'm terrified of feeling anything other than anger. As my eyes trace the sharp lines of his jaw, the curve of his upper lip, they are once again teeth, but not the killing kind.

I need them to be the killing kind. Internally, I sharpen my canines.

"To reiterate what Emmy already said: thank you, Sonderson High, for all your hard work today, and thank you, everyone, for being here to support us. Also, a heads-up: I've debated Emmy before, and it was the most I've ever sweat in my life. You're all in for a treat."

The audience laughs, and even I can't stifle my smile. I wonder when he'd sweat more: during our formal debate, or during one of our many meetups at Safe Space. My shirt was drenched every time I left that coffee shop. Not that any of that matters anymore.

Gabe's carriage shifts into full-force debate mode. He's about to bring it, even at this stupid exhibition. And honestly, it's better this way. At least the intellectual pursuit of it all will be distracting.

My body clenches. I feel my heartbeat in my sore thumb cuticles.

"In the unforgettable words of Patrick Henry, 'Give me liberty, or give me death.' Henry knew the value of liberty, having lived in the time of England's oppressive control over the nation he so loved, our United States. It would seem in our modern day and age, sometimes we forget the power and the importance of liberty.

"Our Declaration of Independence states our three unalienable rights are life, liberty, and the pursuit of happiness. Isn't it the case that we must place citizens' decisions in the hands of the citizens in order to uphold their unalienable right to liberty? Is it not the hallmark of a free country that we *must* trust our citizens, whether or not they are indeed trustworthy? Requiring schools to teach comprehensive sex education strips citizens of their right to liberty. Though this type of education may be important, it should not be required."

Gabe is *impressively* good at crafting an argument, even one that's out of line with his personal politics. Sex ed had come up during a few of our Safe Space conversations—for, um, reasons—and I know he supports it.

"Ms. Crawford, your rebuttal."

"I agree with Gabriel that liberty is important, and that sometimes the value of liberty can get lost in the shuffle of modern life. However, Gabriel also mentioned the other two unalienable rights: life and the pursuit of happiness. Forgive me if I'm missing something, but it seems to me that an unplanned pregnancy or contracting a sexually transmitted infection aren't exactly happy or life-affirming events. Comprehensive sex education can help prevent these."

"Isn't pregnancy the actual definition of life-affirming?" Smugness only makes Gabe prettier. And I know he's doing his job as a debater, but this conservative stance on *life* is weird coming out of his mouth. Like when you think you're eating an M&M and it's actually a Skittle.

I grind my teeth. "I'm alluding to the quality of the life of a young mother who hadn't intended to become pregnant. Or a young father."

"Isn't it possible that in some circumstances, an unplanned pregnancy brings joy to new parents? Either biological or adoptive?"

"Maybe, but I've never known anyone who felt overjoyed about getting chlamydia."

The audience chuckles and I allow myself to make full eye contact with Gabe. His face is pink-over-brown, his eyes sparkling with barely suppressed glee. He's enjoying this.

Who am I kidding? So am I. It was exactly the thing I needed but didn't know I needed—a chance to obliterate the one who betrayed my trust and hurt my family.

Gabe squares his shoulders. "Fair enough. But let's not forget that requiring formal sex education represents a burden for the schools. They'd need to hire and train staff, allocate classroom resources, purchase curriculum. Where do you propose schools get the funding for this?"

"With its ability to provide students with powerful preventative information they might not otherwise have, sex ed could fall under the larger umbrella of physical education, and schools have been funding PE for decades. I propose schools broaden the definition of PE to include comprehensive sexual education."

"Well, I personally cringe at the idea of sitting through a lecture about sex with Coach Furman, but maybe other schools would fare better." The cluster of the audience that must be from St. Jeremiah's hoots and hollers as Gabe mugs in their direction, the rest of the crowd laughing along. Then he *leans* up against the podium, going full-on casual. As if it were just us again, back at Safe Space. "Do you think that all students make good sexual decisions as a result of sex education?"

My body automatically cranes toward him. "No. This kind of education increases the chance that more students make good sexual choices, but of course people can have all the right information and still make a bad choice."

"You don't say." There's a long, pointed pause, and I realize he's talking about *me*. The sheer hypocrisy is astounding. He has no room to come after *my* choices.

But he presses on. "Schools would have to sacrifice funds and resources but with no assurance of the outcomes they seek."

"People have to make calls like that all the time," I spit. "I mean, schools do. All anyone can go on is the best data they have at any given moment."

"You put a lot of emphasis on data," he says, then runs his tongue over his bottom lip and squints.

A zing of something like *want* flies through me, but I don't have time for that. "Yes, I do. What would *you* emphasize as an alternative?"

He *puts his hand over his heart.* Like he's saying the effing Pledge of Allegiance. "Trust."

Trust. *Trust?* From the boy who spilled my unedited thoughts about my family to *everyone in the world*? "Trust. Yeah, okay. The thing is, people need objective information to be able to make informed decisions about *who* to trust."

"I agree, but sometimes people say all the right things, and still they are far from what we think they are." He tugs at his collar. "And, um, data. Data, too. Data can lie."

"And here is where we agree, Gabriel. Data *can* lie. People *can* represent themselves as something they aren't." I shower my microphone with the force of my point.

The moderator's trying to wave us down, but I hardly notice. Gabe eclipses everything.

"So if we agree, what are we doing? Should we call it a day? Skip off into the sunset, pleased that people *and* schools get to make their own choices in the ways they see fit?" Gabe grins like he's got me.

But he never did.

I grip the wheel of rationality. "We are talking about two different things. Maybe there's a place for *unfounded* trust in other types of decisions, but making a call on whether or not to fund sex education isn't one of them. And, while we're on this topic, wouldn't you say that's one objective *of* this type of education? Giving students data in the form of factual information so they can use it, rather than pure emotion, to guide their sexual decision-making?"

"Ah, if we were all as responsible as, say, someone like you, Emmy, we wouldn't need to train students not to listen to their hearts. They'd do it naturally."

Ouch.

The moderator now flails wildly. The red light couldn't get any redder, but I don't care. No one gets away with taking cheap shots at me.

"And if we were all as reckless as, say, someone like Gabe, as he is *so* deftly demonstrating on this stage, comprehensive sex education in and of itself wouldn't be enough to save people from themselves. We'd need to add an entire class on impulse control."

"Hmph. If we never act on our emotions, we miss all the best parts of life," Gabe says.

"If *all we do* is act on emotions, we could royally mess up our lives. And the lives of others. Sometimes things that *feel* right in a moment are *wrong* in the long run."

There's a pause and I know he's remembering the library, too. The kisses and the disclosure and my final exit. "Feelings are never wrong," he insists, but quieter than before.

The moderator abandons her waving and defaults to a helpless, silent plea. I take pity—on her, on me, on anyone still paying attention to us—and go in for the kill. "If every student acted on every emotional impulse, we'd have an epidemic of STI transmission and unplanned pregnancies. Comprehensive sex education won't stop all instances of these things happening, but it can give students a fighting chance. Sex ed is important. It's worth the financial sacrifice. And arguing against it is arguing against the holistic well-being of our country."

"I'm not arguing that sexual education isn't important or helpful. But I stand by my original point: schools should not be *required* to teach it. Making a requirement of sexual education strips our citizens of their right to liberty. To autonomy. To making the choices they see fit for themselves and owning their own destinies."

The moderator leaps out of her chair. "Err, well done, Ms. Crawford, Mr. Castillo! A . . . spirited . . . debate to end our evening!" She turns to the audience, hands held wide in front of her. "Thank you all for coming! Please have a safe drive home."

The auditorium is dead silent for several ticks, but finally someone starts clapping—Issy, applauding enthusiastically. Mom and Dad join her, though I can see even from here that they are exchanging a *look*. The crowd joins in with a bare minimum of polite applause, and I can't say I blame them.

I risk one last glance at Gabe. His face says either *I want to kill you* or *I want to kiss you*, and I am *very* invested in never finding out which.

SIXTEEN

Three People I'd Least Like to Interact with Right Now

1. Everyone
2. Gabriel Castillo
3. See above

I STUMBLE QUICKLY AWAY FROM the podium and into the pitch dark of the unlit backstage, seeking the cold of a metal doorknob. One toppled chair and two hard shin-bangs later, I find what I think is a door—and voilà, it is. Air leaves my lungs in a strangled whoosh as I step into a sunny hallway. I have no idea where I am, but anywhere *away* is better.

"Fancy meeting a girl like you in a place like this."

I slump in defeat, because there he is with his white Chucks and stupid/cute/sweaty face. "You took the back exit, too." My voice is dull, weak, like I used up the very last of my vocal cord juice onstage.

"Of course. This was my best chance of catching you alone. I didn't think you would head straight out into the crowd after that dumpster fire. Three out of ten for both of us, I'd say."

"Speaking of, what the *hell* was that? I get that these debates are meant to be recreational, but holy shit, Gabe. This was supposed to be like dinner-party-level entertainment, not a full-blown circus."

"Yeah, only *someone wrong for you* would bring the monkey, the giraffes, and let's not forget the clowns. Guilty as charged."

And yet *I'm* the one who feels guilty as he throws the last non-debate thing I said to him back in my face. But he does not deserve my pity, not after the whole SenatorSlush mess. "Funny, you don't look remorseful at all," I say.

"I'm not."

"So you *can* be honest, when you want to be."

His face scrunches in such authentic pain, I almost buy it. "I'm honest almost all the time."

A part of me doesn't want to waste my time responding. But then the words are all right there, falling, *pouring* out of me. "Almost-all-the-time is kind of a shitty record when it comes to honesty, though, isn't it? Because if you were one hundred percent trustworthy, my family wouldn't have had to live through yet another media debacle. How could you? I mean, maybe you were pissed that I didn't want to see you anymore, but that? Jesus, Gabe. That was a cruel kind of revenge."

He shakes his head and opens his mouth to defend himself, but

I'm not done. "I would never have expected that from you, not even at your angriest. You promised my words were safe with you. You *hurt* me. You hurt us." My body is a lava lamp, black rage bubbling up and then sinking back down, over and over and over.

"If you would just read your Snaps—"

"There's *nothing* that excuses what you did."

He emits something between a huff and a sigh. "Fine. But you hurt me, too. Peacing out on me in the library like that. After everything we'd shared with each other."

"Are you saying I deserved you sharing my most personal disclosures with the world? That's a solid zero-out-of-ten-level stance."

"What? No!"

"Then *why*? I *trusted* you." And I can't help it, my bottom lip starts trembling and my nose runs. I swipe a lone tear from my cheek.

His mouth hangs open. "Are you crying?"

"What kind of question is that? Obviously I'm crying." I sniff back bigger sobs.

"But you . . . never break."

I expect disgust but instead he looks . . . curious? Intrigued? Proving once and for fucking all that this is all I am to him, a curiosity. A sideshow. "That's not true. You've seen me in bigger feels." And it's those big feels that turn me into deadweight, too heavy to haul around. Easy to leave behind. I should have learned the first time, after my massive overshare, sophomore spring.

"I suppose I have. Just not anytime recently."

I reach up and pull at the ends of my hair, hard, because maybe physical pain that matches the emotional will be a comfort? It isn't. I should've known; my cuticles already sting from my earlier decimation. "Anyway, I won't let you sidestep your bullshit behavior to focus on *that*."

He holds his hands up. "Okay, okay. Fair. Just give me five minutes and I swear I can explain—"

"There you are!" Issy's midi-length peasant skirt billows around her calves, giving her an epic movie-star entrance that I'm certain she's not trying for but achieves anyway. Her fashion sense is enviable, not to mention the sheer sweetness of her, which is obvious even from feet away. I'm in my typical all-black ensemble, and her white-and-yellow is coming at us like sunshine cutting through a storm. My teeth grate as I sneak a look at Gabe, waiting for his inevitable jaw drop when he sees my lovely sister.

He's looking at me, still. It's like Issy isn't even on his Doppler.

Liv's a few steps behind Issy. Her eyes flip between me and Gabe, which makes me immediately twitchy.

"Well! That was . . . a different kind of debate, huh, Emmy?" Issy links her arm through mine, even as she beams at Gabe.

"Sure was," I say.

Liv leans in close to my other side. "What the hell?" she whispers.

I shoot her a *not now* look and she gives a tiny nod of understanding, but I'm probably going to have some explaining to do later. Which means lying. But I'm getting good at that, it seems.

"Anyway," my sister says, barreling on, "I was thinking about the party at Liv's and how much fun that was, and wouldn't it be great if we could all hang out again? Me and you and Liv and Gabe, too? Maybe next Saturday?"

Ah, Issy's working on another of her grand schemes. That explains the pink across every inch of her face, the twirl-twirl-twirl of her index finger in her hair.

"I've got a family thing next weekend," says Liv, looking truly remorseful.

"What's this about Saturday?" Our heads collectively turn to the boy whose saunter channels all the privilege he loves to wave around. "I'm Aaron Vanderford, by the way," he says to Issy.

"Oh! Hi, Aaron. I'm Emmy's sister, Issy Crawford. Um. Well, we were talking about getting together, but if Liv can't make it . . ." Her mile-a-minute speech slows and quiets, her confidence draining away in real time.

And I can't let that happen. Issy is *talking*, to near-strangers, in public. She is planning social events! This is incredible progress. I open my mouth to save her, but Gabe does it for me. "It sounds like fun, Issy," he says, and she immediately brightens.

A trickle of blood escapes one of my thumbs, and I shove it into my mouth.

"Why don't you all do next Saturday, and I'll catch you the next time," says Liv.

"Sure, why not? I've got a few ideas." Vanderford's grin is *full* of them. And other things. I move backward as surreptitiously as I can in blocky heels.

"Great! I'll need all the help I can get, coming up with fun places to take a group," says Issy.

Gabe clears his throat. "Sorry to be a buzzkill, but I'm noticing our fourth has yet to agree to this plan."

"Emmy?" My sister's wide brown eyes flutter to mine. In them I see our childhood, and her future, and myself. This is just like the time I wanted to adopt a retired greyhound. We went to the shelter to meet him, but we went home with our beagle mix Maple instead. Issy saw her and it was love at first sniff. And when Issy read on Maple's bio that she'd been dumped on a roadside and left to die before she was taken in by the shelter, that was it.

I never stood a chance at what I wanted—then or now. But I'll do what I must to keep my sister shiny.

"I'm in," I say, tasting blood.

SEVENTEEN

THE EVENING OF MY NIGHTMARE scenario group date arrives, and I've never wished so hard for a fast-forward button. But because that's not a thing, I'm moving in real time, my joints screaming as I lower myself into the back seat of Aaron's canary-yellow racing-striped Camaro. Though I'd like to believe my pain is left over from yesterday's run, I know it's not. Joint pain is one of the telltale signs of Crohn's flare-up activity. Yet the last thing I need right now is another doctor's appointment or lab draw or whatever, not right in the midst of my most important season. So, I'm pushing through. My body *and* my unresolved Gabe feelings can all wait.

In direct contrast, Issy's emotions are spilling out of her from every angle. She had an "Issy's world" kind of afternoon, but the anxious energy that often trails her like a personal rain cloud isn't there today. I think maybe she's happy.

Gabe, I think. She's excited to see him. Dread coats my gut like tar.

The Camaro engine purrs and Issy *squeals*, more evidence of her exploding feels. "This car is *amazing*," she says, running a hand over the smooth leather of her seat.

Aaron grins and fusses with the collar of his bomber jacket, trying to look like he's not checking himself out in the rearview mirror (but he totally is). "So the Crawford girls are auto mavens?"

I scoff. "No."

"But we *are* Transformers kids. And I *love* Bumblebee," insists Issy. "Who's your favorite again, Emmy?"

"Optimus Prime," I admit. Why go for the showboat when the cool, knowledgeable leader is *right there*?

Gabe sits close enough that warmth brushes my ear. "I also prefer Optimus, for what it's worth." Because the gods and Issy's can-I-please-sit-in-the-front level of short skirt conspired against me, I'm knee to knee in a tiny back seat with Gabe, his denim sliding against mine. The cinnamon on his breath flashes me back to the coffee shop, the library, and further back yet. To all the Gabes I knew and thought I'd know in the future.

I lean as far away from him as I can.

Ten minutes later, Aaron manages a slick parallel parking job next to a brick building with neon signs and grimy windows.

"This looks sketchy," I comment.

"It's fine, Emmy. Live a little," says Issy.

I am nonplussed.

A chalkboard tripod sign is propped up by the door. "All Ages

Night! Karaoke like a rock star." Aaron reaches for the handle.

I catch the swinging door with my foot and kick it shut again.

"No. No way." If I was wearing heels, they'd be dug in so hard that they'd be making holes in the cement right now.

Issy clamps my upper arm and leans in like a coach giving a pep talk. "I know this isn't really your thing, Emmy."

"I didn't know it was *your* thing!"

"Well. It hasn't been. But maybe . . . it could be, now?" She lifts onto her toes and yet again, Issy wins.

Karaoke is situated in the basement of the bar, which is perfect for an activity so tacky. The air is mildewy and sticks to my skin, and it's so loud I can't think coherent thoughts. Ten bucks says an ultra-violet lamp would reveal ungodly fluids on the once-gray carpet. We end up in a four-top booth, me and Gabe across from Vanderford and Issy.

Aaron catches my eye and winks. "How's it going over there?"

"Fine."

"Bullshit."

"How do you figure?"

"You look like you're at a funeral."

My hand, which has been picking at a loose thread on my tank top, freezes. "You're just seeing what you want to see."

Aaron shrugs, unruffled. "Doubt it."

"Besides, aren't there more interesting things to pay attention to than the state of my body?"

This lights him up like street lanterns at dusk. "Absolutely not."

145

Gabe tugs his coat off with a violence that shakes our whole side of the table. Ah, he's pissed, and you know what? Good. Let's see how angry I can make him.

I force a smile at Aaron from under my lashes, biting my lip coyly. "Well, then."

Surprise looks good on Aaron, I'll give him that. The shock oozing out of Issy is less enjoyable, but in a minute she'll be so focused on Gabe that she won't notice me at all.

Aaron bounces back, and his return smolder is the kind usually reserved for pre-bedroom scenes in movies. Every particle of me wants to look away, but I won't disrupt the moment. I need this all to seem *authentic*. Mercifully, Aaron switches gears. "So, what are we singing?"

Gabe shoves a thick binder in Aaron's direction. "You gonna be able to? Sans liquid courage?"

"Oh yeah. I'm good. Just scream loud for me, girls," Aaron replies.

"If you *do* need liquid assistance, I've got you." And my darling sister reaches into her bag and brandishes four mini bottles of Fireball whiskey. Just flaunts them right out there in the open. Even though Issy doesn't know how close we were to being paparazzied that night at Liv's, she surely has better sense than *this*. We *just* made it out the other side of a scandal.

I swipe the bottles into my purse before she has a chance to No Guile us into further calamity. "Where did you even get these?"

Issy shrugs. "I have my ways."

Aaron's eyebrows land somewhere dangerously close to his hairline. "Jesus."

"Yeah, holy ghost indeed," I agree. Who *is* this sister of mine?

Aaron jots his song choice on a slip of paper. "I'll pass, and I left my flask at home. Figured keeping you two as squeaky-clean as possible is probably for the best, given the recent media thing. Right?" He's totally earning his right to be flirted with.

"I guess," says Issy, but she looks deflated. Mildly pouty, even.

"You can do this, you know. Without liquor," says Gabe, now sliding the song binder to her.

Even in the dim bar, I can see the color rising in Issy's cheeks. Tentatively, she leafs through laminated pages, eventually scribbling on another scrap of paper and shoving it into Aaron's hand. "Here, take it before I chicken out."

And this is the move that keeps me from going outside for some air and quiet. I can't leave her now.

A few songs tick by before the karaoke host is calling for Aaron. His slither to the front, the Ray-Bans he slides on, the way he hits every beat like he wrote Michael Jackson's "Billie Jean" himself—he is the definition of confidence. He doesn't even miss the falsetto "eee!" parts, pelvis thrusting with each one.

And yet he's actually . . . *good*. Rabid applause and girl-screaming fill the bar, and his grin is contagious.

Even I catch it. "Wow, Aaron," I say, impressed despite myself. And, if I'm being honest, my body's gone warm in ways that have little to do with the crowded space.

"What'd you expect? Off-key howling?" He bats me playfully, but a chill starts at the place he touches, traveling down my arm, into my trunk, and what the fuck is happening?

Issy looks at least as confused as I am. But isn't this exactly what she wants? For me to *enjoy* dating?

The karaoke host booms, "Jane! Jane Doe, you're up!"

"That's me." Issy wedges her index fingernail between her teeth.

I gently tug her hand away. "Jane Doe?"

"It's the best I could do under pressure."

"Well, come on then, Jane." I hope my smile is encouraging, even as my stomach twists on her behalf. The last time Issy attempted a public performance—tryouts for the school musical, sophomore year—she made it as far as the audition stage and bolted. Now, her cheeks fade, her hands tremble, and she closes her eyes around a huge, stuttering inhale.

I brace for a panic attack. All the signs are there: the shaking, the sweaty forehead, the quiet. My pep talk is practiced, waiting for me. *It's okay, let's just breathe. You'll get it next time. No one else saw you. We all still think you're great and like you just the same, right, boys? We can go home if you want.*

But Issy's exhale is slow and smooth. She grasps the table, which steadies her hands. "Okay. I'm ready. I'm going to do it."

I blink, my reassuring words going dry in my throat.

She grimaces. "It's a duet, though. *Please* tell me one of you boys knows 'Shallow.'"

A duet was a smart choice for reentry to performance life, even if she hadn't quite thought of enlisting her partner ahead of time. Typical Issy: big idea, forgotten details. And of *course* Issy would pick something from *A Star Is Born*, which, oddly, is one of her comfort movies.

Aaron's face goes comically blank, but Gabe smiles. "Issy goes Gaga," he says, and takes her hand. Onstage, the lights cut shadows into Gabe's biceps, the hollows of Issy's cheeks, and the weave of their fingers, still holding on to each other. The first lines are Gabe's. He brings the microphone close to his mouth, hitting the melody with ease.

Aaron clambers into the booth beside me. "Break it down for me, Crawford 1. You prefer Gabe's singing, or mine?"

It's hard to verbally strategize when your heart is onstage. And yet I must. I've never backed down from any challenge ever. "Gabe's voice is like vanilla ice cream. It's basic but flavorful."

"And what does my voice taste like?"

"Hmm. Bananas foster. You know, the kind of thing a waiter sets on fire at the table?"

Aaron snorts. "Pick your poison, then—plain Jane or flambé?"

"Depends on the night."

He whistles through his teeth. "Such equanimity."

No clue what that means, but I'm not going to ask him. I'm pulled back to the singers, as Issy's turn has arrived. Everything about her—her perfect beachy waves, her red polka-dotted dress, her extra-long lashes—screams *starlet*.

But her first lines are so tentative that they're hard to hear. Gabe pushes the microphone toward her lips and the next line cuts something beautiful through this dank basement, Issy's voice both shy and sultry. The crowd can hear her talent and encourages her, which stretches Issy's smile. By the time she hits the big diva-worthy chorus, she's fully immersed, pushing the notes all the way up from her stomach and just *killing* it. My eyes mist a little because wow, this is absolutely where my sister belongs.

"Damn," says Aaron.

"Yeah," I agree.

"They look good together, don't they?"

Though Issy is clearly the star being born tonight, Gabe is doing his part to carry the duet. His face is full of wonder. Full of Issy. The glaze over my eyes transforms into something *else* and before I can overthink it, I pull a mini bottle of liquor from the safety of my bag. I finish it in four greedy gulps.

"Oooookay, Crawford 1. What're we doing?"

I pull out a second bottle and chug that one, too. "You want one?"

"Thought you'd never ask." I note every sinew of his throat as he easily drains his bottle. "Split the last one?"

And we do.

The singers return to our table hand in hand, victorious. I can't possibly be under the influence yet, but still Issy's lovesick face hurts less than I thought it would. *I did something I wanted, for* me. Oh well if that something was cheap cinnamon liquor.

We inhale greasy fries and onion rings out of red plastic baskets as the performances rage on. Slowly, and then all at once, my body goes heavy. I flop back into my seat, my smile now very real. "Let's see that binder."

"Um. What?" Issy laughs as her eyes trace the now-relaxed lines of my body. "Are you okay?"

"Fine," I say, grabbing the song list myself. I scribble my choice onto a slip of paper and thrust it in Aaron's face. "Here."

"And what should I do with this?"

"Take it up to the person."

"You? You want to sing?" Aaron's laughing at me, and I do *not* appreciate this.

Sure, I'm no Issy. I'm the plain blue jeans to her cherry red dress, and the straight line to her curves. If she was a sparkle, I'd be a sword. But swords can glimmer just as well as shiny pretty things.

"Yes, I do," I growl.

"Well, I'd never stand in the way of Crawford 1 on a mission," Aaron says.

As we await my turn, the bar gets hazier. The outlines of heads and trunks bend and bleed, seeping into each other. My words weigh more even as my body feels lighter, but the biggest gift? I don't care. Issy and Gabe are giggling and saying god-knows-what into each other's ears and it's fine. I'm fine. This whole night is just peachy.

A balmy hand slides over my already hot fingers. "Hey. You okay?" Gabe.

I snatch my hand away. "Never better."

"Annnnnddd I'm looking for Gwen! Gwen Stefani, you're up!" The karaoke guy's voice titters as I stand up.

It's brighter onstage than I thought it would be. Much brighter than it ever is from behind the debate podium. And suddenly I'm freezing. My hands and feet have almost lost feeling.

I sway, I think just a little, as Karaoke Dude shoves a microphone in my face. Squaring my feet, I squint up at the screen. It goes black, then blue, then my song title ("I Knew You Were

Trouble") appears in some cheesy font. The opening guitar riff sounds fake and canned, but it's familiar enough. I can do this. And the song's perfect because it applies to any of the parties sitting at my table.

An elbow jabs me in my side. "Hey. Girlie. You missed your cue."

What? No.

Sure enough, the song is rolling across the screen and the words I'm supposed to be singing are lighting up. And I'm not singing. Damn.

I make a spiral hand gesture, which to me *obviously* signals, "Play it again." But Karaoke Dude only stares.

"Start it over!" I yell over the music.

Still with the face. Maybe it's revulsion, maybe it's sympathy, maybe it's both, it's hard to tell. It's dark in here. And the edges of everything are soft.

Finally, he starts the thing over. The lyrics pop up on screen black, and then they're turning white, white, white . . .

"Girlie! You missed the beginning again! You sure you know what you're doing?"

I step closer, to maximize the impact of yelling in his face. "Of course I know what I'm doing! And don't call me 'girlie.' Start it again."

"Look, girlie, I—"

A hand closes on the side of my waist. "What's the problem, folks?" Issy.

"*Gwen's* having a little trouble," says Karaoke Dude, now rifling through the tiny sheets of paper with song requests. He must be about to boot me off this stage if he's already looking for his next singer.

"Hey, Emmy, wait over there." Issy motions to stage right, and I do what I'm told. She's up in Karaoke Dude's business, hovering over his computer screen. A few moments later they fist bump, Karaoke Dude looking pacified.

"What's going on?" I stumble, over what I don't know, but Issy grabs my arm and pulls me upright. "Do I need to get off the stage?"

"Emmy, there are phone cameras pointed at you. If I haul you offstage now, it's going to be one kind of media tagline. But if we slay this song, it'll be another. You understand?" Issy squeezes my hand. Automatically, I squeeze back.

"Yes."

"Trust me, we're going to be fine. But be ready, because this one has *zero* lead-in."

A familiar laugh booms over the speakers, and I realize she's right.

Issy and I used to think it was so fun and *retro* to use Mom's ancient stereo system and full case of CDs, which she'd had since high school and for some reason refused to ever get rid of, even after iTunes and Spotify moved into the mainstream. Issy and I spent many summers playing Mom's old music over and over, memorizing lines and creating moves to go with them. One of our very favorite songs was "Wannabe" by the Spice Girls.

Which is what's playing now. Issy kicks it off, taking the first two lines, then I sing the next two, not needing the screen, not needing anything but to be nine years old again. I close my eyes and I'm there, body thumping in time to the music in our living room in Iowa. We sing the chorus together, Issy being musically savvy enough to take a harmony while I stay down on the melody. Second verse, Issy bounce-walks and I go the opposite way, now putting a hand on my knee and jutting my shoulders in, and out, and in. Our old choreography is all coming back via muscle memory.

Now for the part of "Wannabe" that some might call rap. Issy and I lock eyes. *Take it*, she says, without having to say it.

It's weird how I can't remember what I had for breakfast but I can remember every word, every pause, every rhyme of this song I haven't heard in years. I finish the rap and the crowd goes bonkers, both women and men literally screaming for me. Now *that's* something you don't get on the debate stage, no matter how witty and articulate you are.

Better yet, I'm thinking of nothing, nothing, nothing but the here and now. There's no worry about my dumb disease or whatever's going to happen with Gabe or debate or school or making sure everything is a-okay with Issy and the rest of my family. There's just this *glow*.

Issy and I launch back into the chorus, now grooving freely around the stage. We finish the song to deafening applause and cheers, Issy wrapping my still-cold body in her warm, solid arms.

EIGHTEEN

Three People in Favor of Leaving the Bar After My Spectacular Karaoke Debut
1. Issy
2. Aaron
3. Gabe

I'M THE LONE DISSENTER, STILL riding that "Wannabe" performance high and wanting to bask a minute. Me. Bask.

But public basking is not my destiny, not this evening. Issy yanks me out of the bar, into the crisp autumn night. And it's quiet. So quiet. No summer locusts, they're all frozen and gone to ground. No birds, they're asleep. The only noise is my ringing ears, because damn that bar was loud.

Aaron tosses the Camaro keys to Gabe.

"What the fuck, dude?" Gabe jingles the keys in surprise.

"I, uh, indulged in the Fireball with Crawford 1."

Gabe's lips press together in disapproval, but he opens the driver's door anyway, pulling the front seat forward so I can clamber in behind it. Aaron squeezes in next to me, his lanky extra inches a tight fit. Probably any other time I'd dodge his less-than-subtle advances, but tonight I'm grateful for his attention, his humor, even his ridiculous vocab. But most of all, I like the way he takes the sting out of what's happening with Gabe and Issy.

The purr of the car is soothing, and my head's so heavy that I let it loll on Aaron's shoulder. He rests his hand on my thigh, and I grasp for it, the shock of that lodging somewhere in a distant, quiet part of my brain. In the front seat, Gabe and Issy talk but say almost nothing, so very, very different from the zing of Gabe's and my Safe Space conversations. Is this their usual? I don't even know what to hope for.

The car stills in front of our house, and then Gabe's right there, offering me a hand. Our skin collides and I'm startled by the glorious, blinding light that corresponds. I like clean lines and clear stances and three-point arguments that wrap everything up. This jolt makes no sense. It's wrong.

But he gets back into the car. With my sister. I know exactly what her sweet, eager little face looks like without having to see it.

Aaron helps me up our front steps unnecessarily—I'm buzzed, not sloppy—then clutches both of my hands. "I know this isn't how it's supposed to go," he says.

"How what's supposed to go?"

He pauses, the tip of his tongue sliding around the inside of his cheek. He's especially hot when he's being thoughtful, and *again, what the fuck.* "I mean, it seems like you're focused on what you want in life, but right now that's not romance."

I nod.

"But you're amazing," he says.

"Amazing? Why?" My words are sharp now. What sobered me up faster: the autumn breeze, or Aaron?

He bites his lip, his head dipping bashfully toward the ground. *So* not Aaron-like. "Every time I think I have you figured out, you surprise me."

"How so?"

"Well, it's like this. Issy's response to the night was predictable. She really wanted to go to that bar, and she seemed to have her reasons. She committed, she faced her demons, she did the thing. But you *hate* karaoke. Even the idea of it. Right?"

"Essentially."

"Still, you got up and *performed* and it was really something."

"Really something, huh? What a compliment."

"I can do better. Emmy, you sizzled up there. You might have been a little drunk, and I think spite was involved . . . but god, it was beguiling."

And then I'm kissing him, the remnants of Fireball and watermelon gum a splashy combination on my tongue. Say what you want about Aaron, but he called me sizzling *and* beguiling and kissing him was the right follow-up. Also: kissing Aaron turns out to not be half bad. Not even a quarter bad. Not . . . bad. At all. Good, you might even say.

He cups my face as he draws away. "You taste like a booze factory."

"You too." I let my forehead dip against his.

"Text you in the morning?" The pads of his fingers against my neck are soft, and my whole body is throbbing.

"Sure. Be safe on your way home."

"It's cute that we started the night with you trying to bolt and ended it with you concerned for my safety."

"Oh, shut it. Let's not ruin the moment."

He holds up his hand in defeat as he jogs to his car. Issy meets him halfway up the walk, says good night, continues toward me. Her face is a moonbeam.

"Well. That was . . . fun?" she says.

"Yes. Surprisingly," I reply.

And for once I'm not even lying.

NINETEEN

ISSY AND I *DO* FLAG the attention of SenatorSlush once again, but this time the press is mostly positive. Dim shots of us with microphones in front of our mouths, dropped low into our knees as we broke out our moves with shining cheeks and toothy smiles. A grainy video capturing part of a chorus and my debut as a rapper also goes up. We don't sound half bad, and the world agrees.

Issy is oddly *pumped* about this development. "We look cute, Emmy!" Her toast has gone cold on the breakfast table as she intensely scours socials. With the rest of the family at Lucy's chess tournament, it's just her and me this morning.

"You always look cute, Is. I've been saying that for years."

Several gulps of the coffee are the entirety of my breakfast today. Two little bottles of Fireball aren't enough to cause a full-blown hangover, but I've already spent some quality time on the toilet, and I'm not sure if the liquor or the bar food or the nerves or all of it was the culprit.

My Snapchat notification clicks. Aaron's Bitmoji and mine together on a parasail. "Let's hang sometime," says the neon block text.

EMMY: LOL. You use Bitmojis

AARON: All the cool kids are doing it

EMMY: So that means *you* need to?

AARON: Ah, there's that stodgy-mom-like Emmy I thought I
knew. Bring back karaoke Emmy

EMMY: Karaoke Emmy is on hiatus due to reasons

AARON: Ahhhh. Hangover?

EMMY: Tiny one

AARON: Bet I could kiss it better

Across the table, Issy laughs. "You got some spicy pics queued up over there? You're as red as my strawberry jam."

I clear my throat and take another lifeline sip of coffee. "Debate stuff. You know how I get about certain topics," I say, coolly as I can.

My thumbs tap my phone screen lightly as I consider my response. Aaron's smarmy as hell but if I didn't mind his company while tipsy, maybe I could find it in myself to enjoy him sans Fireball. And if this Issy and Gabe thing *is* happening, a little diversion wouldn't hurt.

He sends another Bitmoji, just him, holding a bouquet of flowers.

AARON: Seriously though. Can we hang out? Kissing
optional

EMMY: Yeah. I think we can do that

No acting required for the smile as I type it.

As a November twenty-first baby, my birthday always falls some-where the week before Thanksgiving—sometimes several days before, sometimes the *day* before, but I'm forever one day shy of my birthday being right on the holiday. Regardless, my day usually gets a little bit lost in the chaos of Thanksgiving-week festivities. This year it's worse than ever, as the media sharks have been *invited into our home* to film a "Thanksgiving with the Crawfords" special. Only three candidates on either side of the ticket were chosen by CBS for this "opportunity," and Reese says it's widely known that these things boost polling numbers, especially among more cen-trist Democrats—which my mom desperately needs to win over, per Reese.

That's right, the always-smart Cat and Philip Crawford have made the illustrious choice to spend the best, most relaxing holiday of the year with the enemy.

I guess this runs in the family.

Though I spend the daytime hours of my birthday with Liv and Issy and infinite reruns of *Supernatural*, I spend the evening with Aaron Vanderford. We meet at a McDonald's in Trinidad for chicken nuggets, fries, and strawberry shakes. He peppers me with questions about the holiday special, which is mostly annoying, and then starts in with a bunch of stories from his childhood—European vacations, yachts his family has owned, his sister's celebrated career in debate during her high school years. I get the feeling this is all meant to impress me, but it's falling flat. I steer the conversation back to current events, and *that's* where the magic happens. We scrap, we get heated, we can barely wait for the other to stop talking before we blast back with our rebuttals.

Now this Saturday night reminds me of coffee shop Sunday afternoons with Gabe. I take a very slow, intentional slurp of ice cream. *Strawberry. Orange is all in the past.*

It turns out I didn't need artificial fruit to keep me centered—Aaron whiplashes me to the present a few minutes later. "You're maybe getting a little *too* emotional, don't you think?" he comments as I finish delivering my stance on Medicare-for-all.

My chair screeches against the floor as I push away. "That's a seriously misogynistic take."

"Nah, I would've made the same criticism of a dude."

"Doubt it," I say, shoving the last of our shared fries into my mouth. Gabe would never have accused me of being *too emotional* about a stance.

McDonald's wraps fairly quickly after that, and we don't talk at all on the way back to his car. Once there, he opens his door but motions for *me* to take the driver's seat. Me.

"Here, you can drive him."

"You do understand your car doesn't actually have a gender."

"Sure he does. He's Bumblebee, and he wants you to drive."

"No." Aaron has once again managed to hit me in a soft spot. Unless I come up with some baller excuse, I'm going to have to tell him something that I'm not especially proud of.

Aaron's tongue swipes across his bottom lip, which I notice

altogether more than I want to. "Look. The other night Issy let it slip that you don't know how to drive."

No fucking guile. "I *do* know how! I took driver's ed back in Iowa, right before we moved to DC."

"Uh-huh. So you were what, fifteen?"

The corners of my mouth pinch down. "Fourteen."

"And how many times have you been behind the wheel since?"

I cross my arms. "None."

"I rest my case."

"So, what, you're going to teach me to drive?"

"I'm going to reacquaint you."

"Why?"

He splays his hands widely. "It's among the best of the trappings of teen life. Driving."

"Trappings?" A laugh bubbles out of me. "Jesus, Aaron."

"Don't hate me for my vocab."

"Not sure if I can help it, but I think I can manage hate-lite."

"Good enough." Aaron's face shifts from jokey to something like sympathetic. Or condescending. Maybe it's both. "Issy seemed to think you're . . . uhh . . . intimidated. By driving."

"I. Am. Not."

But I am. A little bit. I wouldn't call it intimidation as much as I would Complete and Utter Embarrassment That Renders Me Incapable of Getting Behind the Wheel. Did you know it's technically a federal offense to tamper with any mail receptacle? I learned that on my last day of driver's ed. The day I backed into a mailbox. And it turned out to be the *principal's mailbox.* I vowed to never

163

drive again, which ended up being easy after we moved to a big city with mass transit systems. Most of my peers in DC don't have cars, so I don't stick out here. It's perfect.

It *was* perfect. Then cue Issy.

"Is it at *all* possible that you're only bringing this up now because it makes you feel powerful, and you maybe didn't feel that way when I came after you for being chauvinistic?"

"Mmm, *chauvinistic* is such a nice big word. Talk dirty to me, Emmy."

I stamp my foot, but a laugh flies out anyway. "C'mon, Aaron!"

"Fine, fine, maybe I'm offering the lesson to restore myself to big-strong-man status. But maybe it'd also be good for you. Let me be solicitous."

Because he can't not talk like a crossword puzzle, apparently. I grit my teeth around having to ask, "And that means?"

"Considerate."

"Why can't you just say *considerate*?"

"Why can't you just accept my help?"

I suck in a deep breath before I speak again. "Tell you what. I don't love surprises so I'm not doing a driving lesson today. But I promise I'll try it another time."

"Pinky promise?" He juts his out.

I surprise myself when, without hesitation, I link mine through.

TWENTY

A FEW DAYS AFTER THE McDonald's date, I'm eager to get my head planted back where it belongs, rather than lost in thoughts of Vanderford's lips. At the end of our night, I'd let him kiss me. And kiss me. Yeah, he's got fancy words and fancier life stories but kissing is the best thing he does with his mouth, and my god is it the most glorious distraction.

He'd had to wipe away windshield fog to drive the two blocks to my house. Once there, I leaned back into him, whispering close to his ear. "Stupefaction."

He'd shivered. "I can't believe it, but I don't know that word. Help me out."

"I'll use it in a sentence. 'You, Aaron Vanderford, are the great stupefaction of my senior year. I didn't see you coming.'"

He's been on my mind since.

Seriously, though. Having a hot, very wordy friend with benefits is fun, but I still have a lot of other things to tackle.

Three Ways to Not Get Sidetracked by a Fling
1. *Really* dig into debate prep—a *real* topic next tournament, thank fucking goodness
2. Text Liv incessantly re item 1 and her string of recent college visits
3. Get my head around the stupid Thanksgiving media special thing

Reese's media strategy for the Thanksgiving special is "wholesome." Apparently Mom comes off as aloof and "snobby" to some voters, which is hilarious given that Mom came from a background of poverty and was only able to attend college because of scholarships and Pell Grants. The public's perceptions of my mom probably have more to do with casual sexism than reality, but whatever. "We do what we must" has become a Mom-mantra, and so here we are. The goal is to let the public see us as a cohesive, loving family, doing normal family things. Which shouldn't be hard, as the Crawfords are never more Apple Pie American than we are on Thanksgiving.

But there's a big kink in the plans. Grandma and Grandpa Crawford were supposed to come for Thanksgiving—they come every year, and Reese was counting on the extended family presence for "amping the warmth factor." Also: Grandma is a linchpin in the meal plan. She always runs the prep, somehow managing to prepare almost all the food herself despite her seventy-plus years. But Grandma got sick enough this week that my grandparents need to stay home in Iowa.

Which is why it's the day before Thanksgiving and I'm lying in bed, pinning recipes that our little family can manage without looking like train wrecks on camera. I add Four-Step Pumpkin Cheesecake and Green Bean Casserole with All Canned Ingredients to the master list. Grandma's from-scratch cranberry sauce comes to mind, and I wonder if there's a recipe. Grandma makes most things from memory.

There's a soft knock at my door.

"Come in, Dad."

"How'd you know it was me?"

"Process of elimination." Issy and Lucy always barge in unannounced and Mom's gone.

He flops down next to me, propping himself up against the headboard. "What're you doing?"

"Pinning Thanksgiving recipes," I say, now saving a recipe for gravy.

"Ah. Shouldn't you let me and your mom handle that?"

I roll to face him. "I'm well aware that either of you would rather prepare an airtight stance than a pie crust."

"Guilty. Still, you don't have to take this all on yourself."

"I wasn't planning to. I'm going to pin recipes for everything, make a grocery list, then assign tasks."

He searches my face. "Are you feeling okay, Sweets?"

His old nickname for me doesn't really fit anymore, but hearing it makes me a little choked up anyway. I push that down. "Never better."

"Emmy. I saw your face when you heard Grandma couldn't come."

The thing is, we've *never* not seen Grandma and Grandpa on Thanksgiving. Ever. This year there'd be no making popcorn garlands with Grandma, no Grandpa fixing all the squeaky hinges in our brownstone with WD-40. "We'd go to Iowa if we could, but we've got that special to film . . ." Mom had said, looking helpless.

Anger came first. At my parents and their stupid work and the stupid holiday special and having to live in fucking stupid Washington, DC, instead of near my grandparents, who aren't getting any younger. There was a satisfaction with the rage blooming in my chest, because it felt so, so much better than sadness. If I'm angry I've got someone to yell at, someone to blame. Something to *do* with this stuff eating up my insides. But I couldn't hold it there, not for long. The sadness was too big and it took over, pushing up unwanted tears. I'd stared at my lap as I blinked, hard, and didn't face my family again until they were completely dry.

But I guess Dad saw me anyway.

"It's unfortunate," I say.

"It's more than that. It hurts, honey. You're allowed to hurt."

"I know." But I'm not. Not if I'm going to get anything done. And not if we're going to pull off the Thanksgiving special looking like the kind of family that voters want in the White House.

Dad sighs. "I'll miss them, too. And, not to be a jerk about it, but the turkey thing is kind of a problem."

"The turkey thing?"

"We've never made the turkey. No clue what we're doing."

I thumb back to Pinterest and we explore the ways to do a turkey. You can stuff it (though not recommended), and/or you can bake it on its own in a bag. You can even *deep-fry* it, which sounds delicious, though also dangerous. We're chatting about the best ways to talk Mom into a turkey fryer when Dad's phone rings and he has to take it, because it's Reese and we always answer Reese.

I text a little with Liv about Grandma and the change of plans.

> LIV: That's shitty news, friend. Here if you want to talk more about it.

But she doesn't push any harder than that, which I appreciate.

I flip over to Snapchat, where there are a few unreads waiting—including the group chat that Issy has set up with her, me, Aaron, and Gabe, which I've privately labeled DATING HELL, just in my own phone. A low growl hums in my throat as I catch up, because apparently some topics are inescapable.

> ISSY: I'm so sad. Our grandma is sick and isn't able to come for Thanksgiving
>
> GABE: What? Is she okay?
>
> ISSY: Yeah, she will be. Just not strong enough to fly
>
> GABE: That sucks
>
> ISSY: Yeah
>
> AARON: Flip side—good thing she got sick at home instead of while traveling?
>
> ISSY: I suppose that's a good way to look at it

I try to add something, but I literally have no words for this.

I reopen Pinterest, desperate to get back into that pseudo-happy planning space, but then out of nowhere, I start crying. We're talking Serious Cry, the kind that comes out of the very bottom of you. I'm gasping, tears gushing down my face. It's like there's buckets and buckets of sadness inside and the tipping of one led to the tipping of all of them.

You're allowed to hurt, Dad had said. But being allowed doesn't make this any easier. The tears are about Grandma, but they're also about everything. I miss my mom. In Iowa she was home most nights for dinner, came to every school event, even sometimes picked us up from school. Now I have to make an appointment if I want to spend more than ten minutes with her. I miss how simple life used to be, when I was just Emmy and I knew what people wanted from me—and it was just *me*, not debater me, not senator's-daughter me, not Crohn's-disease me, just *me*. I miss not having to think about whether or not my pill container is filled for the week and if I've taken that day's dose.

And *this* is why I never let myself get too down.

There's this scene in an old movie that my parents love where a guy literally gets his heart ripped out, and it's then held in front of him, still beating. That's what sadness is like. What kind of weak little girl can't stop crying when she needs to?

Not me. Even as I shudder with sobs, I push the sadness away. *Not me.*

I get up and make my bed. Doesn't matter I'm about to get back into it for the night. Tight corners, straight lines, smooth coverlet; these things bring me solace. The dresser beckons and I answer, opening the top drawer and pulling out five T-shirts. I unfold and refold, making a crisp top layer of them before sliding the drawer shut again. On my already tidy desk, I move objects to perfect ninety-degree angles with the edges, slide a paperweight to where the stapler was. All the while, my shoulders are loosening, falling away from my ears. I fuss about my room until I've made a full breath in and out without it catching.

Snapchat chirps again. If it's DATING HELL, I'm ignoring it— but it's not. My thumb is clicking before I even have time to think.

GABE: It's okay if you're not okay

That's hilarious, coming from the one who screwed me over when I wasn't okay—twice! Which is a thought best left in my head. It wouldn't do any good to share it.

GABE: Last year was the first Thanksgiving Mom wasn't home with me. I was a wreck. Thanksgiving was still sort of new for us but we'd adopted the holiday. Mom made it special. Instead of turkey, my favorites— quesadillas de hongas, flan for dessert. When she was gone, I tried to make the flan myself. It didn't turn out right, and I ended up punching a hole in Mari's bathroom wall, and *then* I cried

The tears are back to running, running, running, and won't stop. I've already plowed through a third of a box of Kleenex. Against my better judgment, I type a reply.

EMMY: I'm still mad at you. Like eleven out of ten
GABE: I know
EMMY: Are you going to take anything I say straight to the press?
GABE: No

EMMY: How can I be sure?

GABE: What happened with SenatorSlush was a fuck up on my part, and I'm really, really sorry. As I've been trying to explain to you, but you won't hear it. Nothing like this will ever happen again

I want to believe him. So, so desperately. And for tonight, because I am beaten down and exhausted and because he just shared really hard things about his life with me, I will.

EMMY: I'm still mad. But about what you told me about your mom and Thanksgiving, I guess it's nice to know I'm not the only one who sucks at feelings

GABE: I'm the *worst* at feelings

EMMY: Try me

I'm waiting for his response when the screen lights up with his face and phone number. What, he's *calling* me? Now? I'm *so* not in the right headspace to talk, especially not to Gabe. And I *really* shouldn't, because of Issy, and honestly he should know better. But I'm weak and there's this raw need to hear his voice, no matter the consequences.

"Hey," I say, my voice cracking.

"Hey," he says, his voice soft, concerned.

I wipe my nose, trying to tamp down the sniffle.

"I can hear you sucking at feelings from here."

I laugh-sob. "Yeah."

"Would busting out a round of nineties rap help? Seems like you're into that. I know 'Gangsta's Paradise' and some old-school Tupac, thanks to Mom."

I choke out a laugh. "You'd have to cover those yourself."

"If you insist." And he starts *rapping* until I interrupt.

"Okay, okay. I'm good."

"Let me know when you're ready for the encore. Real talk, though. If you're crying, then I know this news about your grandma is hitting hard."

"Real talk, how do you know I don't just lie around crying every night?"

Gabe scoffs, but his voice stays gentle. "C'mon, Emmy. I know you. You're one of the most self-possessed people I've ever met."

I know you. Does he?

"Not always," I manage, barely more than a whisper. And I wonder if he's remembering the closet, when I'd cried and cried, when I'd let him know too much. Why was I always letting him know too much?

"No one can keep that up all the time."

Something spiky is sneaking in, a different brand of sadness. "I should, though. When I fell apart, it scared you away."

"That's not quite true."

Not quite true. I don't know what he means, and now doesn't seem like the time to get into it. Not only did he stop talking to me completely after my sophomore year overshare, this is also the boy whose violation of my trust sent a paparazzi militia to our doorstep, just weeks ago. My insides toughen up. "Thanks for calling, but I'm pretty worn out. I'm going now."

"Okay. Thanks for hearing me out, even this littlest bit."

"It doesn't change anything."

There's a pause before he says, "Okay. Of course. I guess I'll say good night."

His words ring in my ear long after the call has ended.

The morning brings rain splattering my windows and a Snapchat.

> GABE: Hey. You need some more mood-boosting rap? I've got some classic Ja Rule in the tank, including the growl

I giggle and automatically my thumbs fly across the screen in response. But I freeze. I can't keep doing this. As I backspace across the entirety of my words, I think of how on his end, he's seeing the "Emmy is typing" message and my Bitmoji looking so thoughtful. Ugh, guilt *hurts*.

I leave the chat.

Ten minutes later, in DATING HELL:

> GABE: Hey, Crawford girls. How we doing today?
>
> ISSY: I've been better
>
> AARON: What's up, Isabella? And Emmy, if you ever upgrade from lurker status
>
> ISSY: It's actually Isabel
>
> AARON: What, you aren't named after the queen of Spain?
>
> ISSY: Nah, Mom and Dad got my name from this old movie Legends of the Fall. ☻
>
> AARON: . . .
>
> GABE: Just Emmy with the historical name then
>
> AARON: What's that
>
> ISSY: She's Emmaline, after Emmaline Pankhurst. A suffragette

AARON: That tracks

My Bitmoji head stays out of the chat but my real-life racing heart is *saying* something. Gabe dropped that he knew something fairly personal about me—my full name and its origin. And yet no one seems to have caught it?

GABE: Anyway, what's going on over there

ISSY: First world problems, but I'm gonna miss Grandma and her cooking. Mom and Dad don't know how to cook turkey

AARON: How about a catered meal?

ISSY: I think that's the road we're on

GABE: Wait, you don't have any turkey plans? At all?

ISSY: . . . no?

AARON: Don't you have that Thanksgiving special?

ISSY: Yeah

AARON: Yeah actually, I take back the catered meal idea. Doing your own turkey would be way better for the cameras

GABE: If you can find one that's already thawed, you can still pull it off. Mine's already in the brine

ISSY: Oh

ISSY: What?

ISSY: Wait, what's brine

GABE: Oh no

AARON: I guess Gabe's some kind of turkey expert?

Well, this is it. He had me at *turkey expert.*

EMMY: Tell us everything you know

175

AARON: She speaks!

EMMY: Um, yeah? I just don't have time to always be group
chatting it up

AARON: Oh, right. Big important debates to prepare. Essays
to write. Worlds to conquer

EMMY: Thanksgivings to save

EMMY: You get me

EMMY: Back to the turkey, though

GABE: I could try to coach you through turkey prep, but
you're running out of time. It'd probably be best to
think about other options

ISSY: Costco, then?

GABE: Friends don't let friends eat Costco turkey. How about
I just bring mine over?

ISSY: Wait wait wait. I have so many questions

ISSY: Don't you have a family Thanksgiving? If so, why are
you cooking the turkey? If not, why are you cooking a
turkey?

ISSY: Just why are you cooking a turkey

GABE: It's just me and my aunt for Thanksgiving. My mom's
old employer gives a turkey to every employee at
Thanksgiving time, and a ham at Christmas. He still
sends these to me every year, even though Mom
doesn't work there anymore.

ISSY: That's kind

GABE: It is. So I do the bird, Mari does the rest. But we
always have so many leftovers that we're eating turkey

stuff for a week. You'd be helping me out by giving me somewhere to go with this 22 lb monster

EMMY: 22 lbs!

GABE: Ginormous. More than enough for everyone

AARON: That's what she said

EMMY: Jesus, Aaron

GABE: ANYWAY. Can I bring my bird to you?

ISSY: YES! As long as you and your aunt join us. We have two empty seats at our table to fill anyway

EMMY: Is, don't you think we should check with Mom and Dad re the special

ISSY: Hold on

ISSY: We're on! Dad and Reese said it will boost our "relatability" scores if we host friends

The chat may go on, but I've had enough words for one morning.

I push away the dread and embrace the distraction of this inevitable catastrophe. Say what you want about Wholesome Thanksgiving with the Crawfords, but it won't be boring.

TWENTY-ONE

BEFORE I BECAME A C-LIST political celebrity, I thought documentary-ish TV spots must be pretty simple to shoot. One guy with a camera following people around.

But no. A small army assembles in our foyer at 8:30 on Thanksgiving morning. *Three* different cameras and three people to run them. Two sound people. A director, an assistant director, a woman who manages "appearances." And she is still separate from the three hair and makeup people. Then there's Reese, Reese's assistant, their intern, and a whole shitload of equipment.

I've made it as far as the bottom stair when the appearances lady snags me, lightly yanking the hem of my black shirt. "This won't work. Do you have something in blue?"

Without a word I head back to my room, in search of a shirt that will *work*. And happy Thanksgiving to one and all.

By the time I reemerge in blue, the crew has scattered. They're removing window treatments and pulling shades aside, rearranging the dining room table for "optimal lighting effects." The makeup people are taking brushes to Mom's face, and Lucy's hovering nearby, clearly hoping to also be made over. Someone pulls me and Issy into side-by-side chairs and swipes glosses and blushes and powders and gels all over us, then shoves rollers into our hair. I want to commiserate but Issy's got her earbuds in and her eyes closed—centering with music is one of her anxiety coping methods.

"How long will this take? We need to get started on the meal." My fingers flinch against the rollers because—surprise, surprise— they're hot.

"Ah ah. Don't fuss with those. Just a few more minutes and we'll cut you loose," says River, the genderfluid hair-and-makeup person in charge.

I stay put but slouch in protest.

Finally all of us—even Lucy, who was thrilled to get a fresh high ponytail and a few swipes of blush—are apparently camera-appropriate and told to "act natural." Which is the silliest thing I've ever heard, given what they just did to our hair and faces.

While I arrange groceries on the kitchen island, Lucy takes to pacing in the foyer, talking to herself in dramatic, *Downton Abbey*-esque tones—*We couldn't have asked for better holiday weather* and *Oh, I do hope everyone is in good spirits today.* A cameraperson captures this from a doorway, which I *know* Lucy's aware of. Suddenly she screeches, her old soul leaving her nine-year-old body for a hot minute. "Gabe! Are you Issy's boyfriend or Emmy's?"

My body goes full cringe.

I tune out the murmur of family greetings and introductions, as well as the dull thud of visitors' shoes hitting the foyer rug. Briefly, I entertain the thought of how the film producers will spin Gabe and Mari's presence here—*Gracious Crawford Family Embraces All Cultures* or *Everyone Is Welcome at the Crawford Table*. A grimace sinks deep into my face, despite there being no one around to see it. Please let my parents and Reese have the good sense to *not* exploit them like that.

One cameraperson enters my kitchen and starts panning. Now I'm wondering how they're going to spin *me*, but I seriously do not have time to worry about that. Focus is imperative if I'm going to get this meal prepared. I spread out the twelve recipes and review the battle plan for one blessed uninterrupted moment. And then a parade of people, more cameras, microphones, and one overwrought dog barge into my kitchen. Lucy launches herself onto the middle of the island, sending pages everywhere.

"Lucy! Goddamn it!"

"Emmaline Leigh Crawford! Language! And in front of our company!" Mom says, gesturing at the *company*: Gabe, who's wielding a giant roaster and a bemused smirk, and a petite woman with a heart-shaped face who must be Mari. She's got a pan of something and an eyebrow straight in the air.

So much for a solid first impression.

A camera wheels in closer and I look right into it. "Sorry. Bleep that."

Gabe and his aunt pull identical trying-not-to-laugh expressions and I sort of want to die.

Issy glides through the kitchen, her black midi skirt perfectly pressed. I check her for signs of distress—the media is *here* in our *sanctuary*—but all I see is grace under fire. Possibly because *I'm* the one balancing on flames. "You're not going to be able to do these all yourself, you know," she says as she swoops up the fallen recipe.

"Yes, I am. I've got a plan." I hold my hand out for my papers.

Issy's not letting go. "We're all going to help."

The whole gang's in here now, including most of the film crew. Dad has tied on his "Kiss the Cook" apron, and if that doesn't say "upright family man" I don't know what does.

Gabe sets the roaster on the stovetop and reaches for the oven controls, but I bat his hand away. "I need the oven for the dressing! And casseroles! And pumpkin pie!"

He cocks his head and speaks to me slowly, like I'm a child. "Well. Turkeys need fifteen minutes per pound. This is a twenty-two-pound turkey, so it'll be done around five, but only if we put it in now."

The director steps between us. "Good, good, *such* a fun little exchange. Now can you smile at each other for a second and hold . . . Yes, just like that." I should have Vaselined my teeth. Holding this faux smile already hurts.

"Now, Emmy, talk to him—it's Gabe, isn't it—warmly. Like you're so excited to host him."

I'm seriously going to murder this director.

I unclench my jaw and manage, "It's so nice to see you today." Where's my Oscar?

"And you. I'm sure we can work out an oven-sharing plan that works for all the food."

"Absolutely. It was so generous of you to provide the turkey. What temperature?"

"I've got it." Gabe sets the controls and shoves the turkey into the oven, his whole body practically waltzing through the motions. "The turkey is no problem. It's an honor to be here," he says, turning to Mom and Dad.

In the background the director nods rabidly.

Mari lays her pan gently on the counter. "Flan. At least I hope it is. My sister's recipe, but mine never turns out like hers," she says, her smile a little sheepish. Gabe's eyes meet mine and I know we're both remembering the text confession of his failed dessert and how it brought him to his knees, missing his mom. A cold blade of sympathy lodges in my sternum and sticks.

Issy beams. "I'm sure it'll be delicious."

"I agree," says Mom, glancing from Issy, to Gabe, to me, and back. Oh no. The last thing I need is *Mom* in the middle of my drama. *And on national television.*

I make a grab for the recipes, but Issy holds tight. "Emmy, I know you're planning to do this all yourself. But you're going to have to delegate."

I've had about one too many people giving me orders today, and about three too many cameras capturing it. I think I'm done. "Fine. We'll do it your way."

When it all goes to shit, Issy can take the fall, for once in her life.

Twice in her life, whatever.

Ninety minutes later, we're in the thick of it. While Lucy

"entertains" Mari with multiple rounds of chess, Mom's doing sweet potatoes and mashed potatoes, Dad's struggling his way through dressing and gravy, Issy and Gabe are preparing drinks and setting the table. I've got the cheesecake and pie put together and have shifted my focus to the cranberry relish. It's turned out to be a bigger task than I expected—lots of things to chop up, grind, measure, and mix. Issy sends Gabe to help me.

His voice, his words, the space he gave me to just *be*—all such comforts when he called me a few nights ago. Despite my still being angry and wary, he'd been everything I didn't know I needed. Today my body clocks his automatically, like he's got a tracking chip inside him that my heart is looking for. Still, I tense as he sidles up to the island. I shouldn't have shared so much. Not again. I keep making this same mistake over and over, and at some point it's got to stop. I'm stronger than this. Issy needs me to be a better sister. Frankly I deserve better, too, than to keep leaning on someone who has hurt me repeatedly.

"Don't look so thrilled," Gabe says under his breath. I follow his sidelong glance to the camera still working the kitchen.

"Don't tell me what to do with my face. I've had about enough of that for one day." I shove a bag of Jonagold apples into his stomach.

"What do you want me to do with these?"

"Peel." I nod my sweaty head toward the utensil drawer. "You should find what you'll need in there."

I'm grinding cranberries with the only tool we have for the task: an old meat grinder Dad's had for a billion years. It looks like an instrument of torture—huge, heavy metal, clamped to the edge of the counter with a little vise grip. Its gears and mechanisms spin against each other, chewing up berries and spitting them out a mouth in the front. And it's all powered by a hand crank and my elbow grease. I make a mental note to get the family a food processor for Christmas.

Gabe rakes a vegetable peeler along the red-gold apple with deftness. His hands are lean, fingers insanely long. I'm surprised I'd never noticed before.

"Did you ever play basketball?" I ask.

"That was random," he replies, glancing up at me over discarded chunks of peel.

"I . . . I was just noticing your hands. They're big."

"All the better to peel apples with," he says, grinning. "As for basketball, not really. Just pickup games with guys in my neighborhood, never on a team or anything. You?"

"In middle school I played. It was part of PE at my old school."

"Any good?"

"Five out of ten," I say, cranking away, satisfying rushes of crushed berries pouring into a glass bowl.

"Ah, so there are two things Emmy Crawford isn't great at."

My crank squeals to a halt. "Two things?"

"Basketball and forgiveness."

I scoff as I resume the berry massacre. "Another way to look at that? I never get burned by the same flame twice." The fact that I actually burn myself repeatedly, and often, is not something Gabe needs to know.

He shrugs. "You do you. But staying mad at someone and expecting yourself to feel better is like drinking poison and expecting the other person to die."

I'm cranking the meat grinder so hard and fast that berry juice is spurting out at weird angles. A stream of it pelts me in the eye.

"Who said that? Gandhi? Mother Teresa?"

"Buddha. Wise dude," Gabe says, handing me a damp paper towel, which I hold to my now-watering eye. I try to ignore the fact that the other eye is burning a little, and maybe not from the juice attack.

"Wise, stupid, two sides of the same coin," I say, blinking clumsily.

"What's so stupid about forgiveness?"

"The very idea of forgiveness means opening yourself up. And that means risk."

He takes my used paper towel and hands me another. "And?"

"I'm not a fan."

"Isn't debate inherently risky? You could lose on any given day."

"Other people lose. Not me. Almost never, anyway."

Gabe looks up from his task, squinting into the other room toward Crawford 3's cackles. I hear the clap of wood on wood as the game pieces are rearranged. Poor Mari. "So you calculate. You'll gamble if the odds are in your favor," he says.

My head bobs. "I suppose that's true."

Gabe swaps a peeled apple for an unpeeled one. "Aaron told me he's trying to get you to do fun things. Stuff that's out of your comfort zone."

"Hmph. Well, good luck to him."

"But you're smiling."

"I guess I don't totally hate the idea."

"Help me understand why you'll take risks for Aaron . . . but you wouldn't for me?"

Gabe's pretty in a way that's dangerous, like when you look right at the sun during a solar eclipse and the image is burned onto your retinas forever. Which is why I generally don't look right at him anymore. I can't afford to have his image be the one that sticks.

"I *did* go out on a limb for you. Twice. And you betrayed me. Twice. Aaron hasn't. And that's the difference."

Gabe takes big breath and I ready myself for a tirade, because this is how he looks when he's got more than a few words for me.

A camera pans closer, zooming in on our red-stained workspace. "Love this, you two. So *visceral*," says the camerawoman.

She has no idea.

"Okay, can you do that again? Pick up that apple, hand it to her," the camerawoman directs Gabe. "And smile."

Gabe's face pinches and I can't imagine mine looks much better. But we smile and pass the apple back and forth, and again, and again until she has the shot she wants. Behind the fakeness, Gabe burns. His heat radiates across the Formica.

Finally the camerawoman thanks us and moves on.

"Looks like you have something to say," I offer.

Gabe's shoulders slump and he angles away, resumes his peeling. "Not anymore."

I can't stand to be in the room with him any longer, but I'm elbow deep in cranberry flesh. "Go help Issy. I'll finish the apples."

"Okay," Gabe says, and goes. Without a fight. Which I didn't expect.

The apple requires more force to grind than the berries, but I welcome the challenge. I crank and crank, biceps flexing with every turn. The seeds of my confusion and hurt and anger spit out with the apple mash, and soon they're so diluted, it's like they were never there at all.

My bare foot catches on an uneven corner of our dining room floor and I pitch forward, nearly dropping the green bean casserole I'm toting.

"You okay?" asks Gabe, catching my elbow.

"Fine," I say, yanking myself away.

Messy, unfinished business never seems to do anyone any good, including in the world of hardwood. I can't believe Mom and Dad actually brought guests into the room—as in, *the whole fucking world*—with it looking like this. The carpet's now completely gone, exposing the entirety of the dull, uneven, scratched-up wood floor. But whatever, it's their disaster.

We eat, which is only sort of awkward with microphones intermittently dropping in front of our faces. Gabe's turkey is ten-out-of-ten excellent, a fact I can add to my longer-than-three-point list of Things to Like About Someone I Shouldn't Like.

I'd planned to claim victory for organizing and pulling off a holiday miracle, but since so many people helped, I really can't. Ugh, teamwork. All I've got to show for this day are bloodred palms and a rogue tracking chip. It blinks and lights up when Gabe licks whipped cream remnants from his lips, and when he helps my mom clear the table after dinner. It follows him to the couch, where he sits with Issy playing hangman or tic-tac-toe or something equally nauseating.

I wish I could rip this tracker right out of my body.

Two hours and one traditional family viewing of *The Wizard of Oz* later, the holiday winds down. Dad carries a passed-out Lucy up to bed, which is the last thing the film crew captures before heading out. Reese and co stay behind to talk shop with my parents. Issy and Mari are still in the den, knee-deep in a discussion of their favorite musical theater shows.

Which leaves just Gabe. And me.

"Sorry," he says, lowering himself into a dining room chair.

"What'd you do this time?"

He grimaces, then slumps. "I'd leave if my ride was ready. I know you don't want me around."

My throat swells so hard and fast, it's painful. "Sometimes life isn't about what we want."

"Tell me about it."

My heart would if it could. It wants to; it's about to break a rib with its ferocity. But I won't let it. Instead, a diversion. "Whatever. Since we're stuck together, let's play." I plunk Lucy's chessboard on the table between us, giving myself the white pieces so I can go first. I move the queen's pawn two spaces ahead.

Gabe mirrors, making the same move on his side of the board. I follow with sliding my queenside bishop pawn two spaces forward.

188

"Queen's Gambit, huh," he says.

"Control of the center."

"Only if I accept."

I feign my best nonchalance, but still I lean over the board.

He accepts.

The rush in my veins is heady and sweet. This is one of the few chess scenarios I've mastered enough to be competitive. Gabe and I are quick on the board, each move bringing me closer to the inevitable victory. Triumph sings so loud that it almost drowns out the hum of *want* that's always with me whenever Gabe is near.

And then Gabe moves a pawn and I realize I'm vulnerable. I mean, my bishop at c4 is. Somewhere in the sequence I've botched my strategy. The corners of his mouth curve dangerously upward.

The rest of the match is a mess. With Gabe gaining control of the board I'm now on the defense, scrambling for safety and abandoning conventional play completely. Good thing Lucy's asleep.

But then I see it.

"Checkmate," I say, moving my remaining castle into a space that traps his king.

At first he goes still, examining the arrangement of our black-and-white warriors like he can't quite believe it's over. But then he lays his king down on the board. Gently. Sadly. "Once again, you win, Emmy."

And yet somehow, I don't feel like I did.

TWENTY-TWO

THE DAY AFTER THANKSGIVING FINDS me *not* in my bed recovering from the food and the feels and the cameras. Instead I'm out on the town with Issy, who assaults me with a gauzy red blouse, pushing hard enough to leave a rug burn on my collarbone.

"Ugh. Remind me why you're here?" I toss the red abomination over her head.

"You need me for this. Obviously." Her hair is now a staticky nightmare, but I figure that about makes up for the torture she's inflicting on me.

Three Black Friday Activities I Would Rather Be Doing
1. Debate prep
2. Reading
3. Watching football with my parents (If they were home,

which they aren't. The big health care bill waits for
no one.)

Instead I'm in the worst possible place: a store.

But today isn't about taking advantage of sales. Today is about
a *perceived* deficit in my wardrobe. We have super official Senator
Christmas Card pictures and a tree lighting ceremony tomorrow,
and I guess we need coordinated outfits for this. Last night after
Gabe and Mari left, Mom insisted on pawing through my closet.
And I let her! Without even a peep of complaint! But being uncharacteristically chill wasn't enough. Mom took issue with my
"all black" wardrobe, insisting that I needed something either red
or green for this photo shoot. When I dug out my red "Debate Is
LIFE" T-shirt as an option, she'd stuffed a handful of cash into the
front pocket of my messenger bag and said, "Do better." Which is
why I'm now at a store Issy calls "the cutest boutique in Georgetown."

Issy is unbothered. No—she's in her element. She pulls an
emerald-green sweater off a pile and holds it up. She looks at me,
then back at the sweater, then shakes her head. We've already been
at this for ten whole minutes, and I'm pretty sure I'm going to die
of boredom.

I finger a red polka-dotted dress. "What about this?"

"That'd be great, if you want to look like Minnie Mouse."

"Wait, don't you actually have a red polka-dotted dress?"

"Yeah, but not like *that*," she says, like I should know the difference.

191

"Maybe you're taking this too seriously. The Christmas card is *only* getting sent to roughly two thousand people, and I'd bet half of them would be *way* into Disney cosplay. You could be Donald Duck, and Lucy can be Pluto."

Issy sighs heavily. Clearly, I am a difficult burden to bear.

We go in separate directions for a few minutes and meet up again over a rack in the middle of the store. At the same time, we pull at a red sweater dress. I *think* it meets Mom's guideline, which was: "If you wouldn't feel proud to wear it in front of Grandma Crawford, don't bring it home." It's not too short and it has no sparkles (Grandma thinks any form of glitter, sequin, or animal print is "tacky").

"Try it on," Issy demands.

I salute and wander over to the fitting room. Two minutes later I step out, pleased with myself. The dress is great. Not too clingy, but not frumpy.

"It's perfect," says Issy. "You can wear my black boots with it."

"Sold," I say, stepping back toward the fitting room.

"You'll have to wear a different bra, though."

I turn to the mirror, surveying my chest. "What's wrong with this one?"

Issy is aghast. "Um, it's a sports bra? I can see the outline of the racerback."

"So?" I wear sports bras almost every day. Boobs are boobs no matter what you put over them, right?

"You need to wear a normal bra, like a T-shirt bra, or it'll look gross." She eyes me narrowly. "When's the last time you bought a real bra?"

"Ummm . . ." I think Mom and I bought some at Target back in Iowa right before we moved to DC. Nearly four years ago. "It's been a minute."

"Do you even have any regular bras?"

"Yeah."

"How many?"

"Jeez, Issy. What's your deal today?" She's been weirdly focused all morning, forcing me to make paper snowflakes in front of the TV while we watched a selection of movies she'd "curated"— *White Christmas*, *The Notebook*. Morning faded into afternoon as we started *Ten Things I Hate About You*, and it was about then I suggested we take a break. "You need these," she said, but ultimately paused the movie and agreed to go shopping with me instead.

I know Issy better than anyone else on earth but sometimes I do *not* get her. Including right now—who knew she was so obsessed with undergarments?

"How. Many. Bras?" She crosses her arms.

"One that's still functional."

She pinches the bridge of her nose. "Are you sure we're related?"

"I mean, I always thought maybe you were delivered via stork."

She socks my arm and drags me off to another corner of the store. "Intimate Wear," a glittery, hand-scripted sign reads. Grandma Crawford would not approve of this sign, and I do not approve of this section. Being in the presence of this much satin and lace gives me the creeps. "Can't I just borrow one of your bras?"

"It's not like tomorrow's the only time you're going to need decent underthings. Make an effort, Em."

I scowl. Making an effort is my *thing*. I grab at a plain white bra with an underwire. "How's this?"

"That's fine. Maybe get the nude one, though. It shows up less under clothes than white."

I swap white with latte. "Okay. Are we good now?"

"Only you, in store full of *cute*, would pick *the* most basic, boring bra. Why don't you try one that's got a little . . . more?"

A nearby rack displays a variety of lacy, see-through options. I hold one up to myself, throwing my hair over my shoulder in a move meant to be faux-seductive. "Oh, like zees won," I say, butchering a French accent.

Issy grabs a pink bra with pink fur trim and garter straps—one of the most god-awful things I've ever seen—and presses it against her chest. "Or vot aboot zees wun? Très chic."

We throw back our heads and howl with laughter, loud enough that a saleslady darts over to "make sure we're finding what we need."

Fifteen minutes later we're back on the Georgetown brick, headed home after a quick stop for a coffee. In our boutique bag is the sweater dress, two bras (including a pink-and-black "fun" one, at Issy's behest), and a new pair of earrings for Issy. My phone dings. Issy's too. Like choreographed dancers, we fish them out of our pockets, unlock, and read.

LIV: SOS. Check SenatorSlush ASAP.

My breath stalls in my throat. Issy looks like she's going to gag.

The top post reads, "Cute Crawford sisters get sexy? Presidential hopeful Catalina Crawford's daughters spend Black Friday shopping for skimpy lingerie in Georgetown. I wonder who their lucky dates are? #pickme #hot #idhitthat #sexedgoneright."

And the picture is a full body shot—Issy in just the fur-trimmed bra and matching panties, which she'd tried on to make me laugh, and which some creeper *somehow* snapped in the flash of time between the opening and the shutting of the fitting room door.

The post has already got hundreds of likes and more than a few gross comments.

The world is full of sick people, and nothing makes you more aware of this than being in the spotlight.

Issy drops her phone altogether, where it lands face down on stone. *Smack.* She flinches at the sound but doesn't stoop to pick it up. She's frozen in place, staring into nothing.

An incoming call buzzes in my hand. "Get home. Now," Mom says, and hangs up.

TWENTY-THREE

BLACK FRIDAY TURNS GREEN. EVERYTHING'S in motion, like squealing tires after a stoplight turns.

The family dining room has become a Situation Room. Mom and Dad sit across from each other with dueling laptops, fingers flying across keyboards at breakneck speed.

Mom has just picked up her buzzing phone when she spies us. "Don't plan on going anywhere for the rest of the day," she says over her shoulder, then turns back to the computer. She doesn't look mad, just preoccupied.

Dad flashes an apologetic glance before returning to feverish typing.

Issy and I didn't speak on the run-walk home. Once I got her unstuck—which I achieved through a quick jostle of her shoulders and a "Hey, we'll figure this out"—I couldn't find the right words, and my jaw was too tight to talk even if I'd wanted to. This wasn't just any old paparazzi crash, this was major. Issy's body, on display for the world to see. I can't think of many things more violating than this.

I wonder if this is what Issy's contemplating as she takes in our parents, already running damage control. She freezes again, teeth sunk heavily into her bottom lip. Eyes open but a million miles away.

"Is?" I venture a hand on her arm.

She bolts, retreating to her room. Her feels are predictable because we've been here many times before. Anxiety fueled by guilt, with sadness as the cherry on top. The stress of this situation will mutate into an ugly, ugly thing in Issy's head, crushing her.

Unless I intervene.

"Is!" I bang on her door.

"Leave me alone, okay? Just for a while," she says. Her voice is tear soaked and I literally want to tear whoever did this limb from limb.

My hand's on the doorknob to let myself in anyway, but as I replay her words, I stop. This is different. When Issy crumbles, she wants to be caught and put back together, which is where I come in. She never asks to be left alone. At least, she never asks that of *me*.

But today she did.

"Okay," I say, marching straight to the bathroom because suddenly I'm in my own emergency situation. Though I haven't told anyone and can hardly acknowledge it myself, something about Thanksgiving didn't agree with me—my bet's on either the mountain of pumpkin pie or watching Issy and Gabe giggle on the couch. I'd spent a good chunk of last night making runs to and from the bathroom, and apparently *this* situation is enough to send me right back.

Someday I'll be stronger.

An hour later, I'm under cool sheets, index cards of debate stances held above my reclining head, one at a time. My body's tired but I'm alert enough, and debate prep was how I'd wanted to spend my day, anyway.

I startle as Issy lets herself in, tall (for her) and clear-eyed. Something about the way she holds her head says *tough*, and that's enough to make me sit straight up. "You look . . . okay?"

"I wasn't. And I'm still not *great*. But I'm okay."

"Really?"

"Yep."

Her face is still two shades too pale, a little blotchy and tearstained, but she's out of her room. She's breathing mostly full breaths. Her voice shakes, but she *is* talking—Issy used to not be able to speak when anxiety took over.

"But . . . how?"

Issy pulls something up on her phone. "My therapist and I have been working on this thing, for a *long* time. We call it the Issy Manifesto."

On her phone screen, I spy a bulleted list—a trick right out of the Emmy playbook. I wish I could send Issy's therapist a thank-you note, because wouldn't the world be better if everyone kept their thoughts more organized? Yet as I read, I realize Issy's bullets aren't a to-do list. "Are these . . . affirmations?"

"Not exactly. I've realized that when I'm not anxious, I feel pretty good about myself. But when I'm anxious, all the positive thoughts and confidence fly out the window. When I'm like that I can't *hear* anything positive that others say to me, no matter how hard they try."

I consider this. I wonder if she's saying, *You never put me back together at all.*

I'm too scared to ask.

Issy continues. "What I need is my own voice giving me validation and reminding me of who I am. So I work on this list when I'm not anxious, and then it's ready to pull out when I *am*. Like today. My therapist and I identified that paparazzi situations are the absolute worst for my anxiety, for obvious reasons. Today I was ready."

I read her list again.

- *I'm strong.*
- *I'm capable.*
- *I can handle hard things. I've done it many times before.*
- *Anxiety and anxious thoughts are temporary.*
- *Thoughts are not reality.*
- *I am in a uniquely difficult position.*
- *This situation may not be my fault, but it's my job to cope with it.*
- *I have skills and talents.*
- *Struggle does not make me weak.*

I falter on the last of these. Struggle *is* the definition of weakness, as far as I'm concerned. But if this list helps Issy, who am I to poke holes? "This is great. Really great. What happened today was like . . . Is it too much to say it's your worst nightmare?"

"No, that's pretty accurate. Today was a *major* violation and I feel gross about it. And I had my moment. I threw up—did you hear me?"

I shake my head—if I would've heard, I would've been right there, holding her hair back.

"Well, I did. Then I panicked in my room. I cried. I thought my anxious thoughts and felt like the world was crumbling around me. But here's where I've learned a different tactic—I know I'm not *failing* for having anxiety. I don't judge it, or me for having it. I let it be there and then it starts to calm, and when I did that today I was able to see the situation with my logic lenses, too. Another thing I've been working hard on with my therapist."

"Wow. And what did the logic lenses see?"

"What I was wearing wasn't any more revealing than last year's bikini. The difference is that I *consent* to being seen in my swimsuit, you know?" She exhales strongly through her nose. "The bottom line, though, is this—paparazzi bullshit has already cost me so much. Too much. So, no more. I'm always going to be rattled by the paps, but I'm not going to live my life in fear of them."

I'd love to respond with something equally valuable, but I'm too hollowed out to find the words. All I can manage is "I'm proud of you, Is."

"Therapy is super helpful. You should try it sometime."

Me, sitting across the room from some kind-looking gray-haired lady in flowy pants and a big white sweater? Me, answering questions politely, saying all the right things, while keeping my true feelings shoved deep, deep down where they belong? Me, admitting to anyone or even myself that sometimes I struggle? "Yeah, I don't think it's for me."

"You do you." But now her eyes are canny in the way of Mom, laser beams on my skin. "No offense, but you don't look so hot. Are *you* okay?"

I put my face in my hands, which hides my dark undereye circles and gives me a chance to rearrange my face. "I'm fine. Probably leftover makeup got smeared around. I took a nap."

"*You* took a nap?"

Granted, this *is* an odd event. Emmy Crawford is not a good relaxer, and everyone in the house knows it. "It just sort of happened."

The look Issy gives me is very, very much too old and wise and I don't like it at all. But then she turns on her heel, leaving the door open behind her. "Let's go. I'm hungry."

After turkey-and-cranberry sandwiches that my body unfortunately expels almost immediately, Issy and I sit at the dining room table. Mom and Dad are in their home office with Reese, who's here for "triage." Lucy's on a playdate, which means no forced chess matches. Instead Issy digs out the cribbage board.

"How do you think they're doing? Mom and Dad?" says Issy, playing a five on top of my ten and moving ahead for fifteen-two.

I lay down a six, taking the count to twenty-one, and internally groan in realizing I've set Issy up for another move. "They seem fine."

"I wonder what they think they'll accomplish through all of this. What's done is done." Issy plays a queen, just as I knew she would, now forcefully pegging forward two for thirty-one and a bonus point for last move. She presses too hard and the peg comes popping out, skittering across the table. Next thing I know the whole table is shaking with the force of Issy's fist, rattling the pegs, the cards, my expectations of her. I'm used to watching Issy throw punches at her internal self, but not this.

"Hey. We didn't *do* anything, okay?"

"Yeah, well, it won't stop the media from making it look like we *did* do something." She fidgets with the rogue peg, bouncing it in and out of the holes. "Sometimes I'm really sick of the whole politician's daughter thing, you know?"

"Same." And I know it's even worse for the Crawford sister who prefers peace to progress.

"This reminds me of the *last* viral paparazzi incident. You know, the one that was 'my fault'?" She makes air quotes, and I flinch. "I don't know if I want Mom in the White House. She'd do amazing things, but being a first daughter sounds less and less awesome all the time. I know you're the one who said the thing but honestly, I *feel* the thing. It was hardly even a lie, when I took the blame for it." Issy bites down on her lip, so hard I can see white at the edges of her mouth.

No amount of bright-side, silver-lining thinking can change

the fact that our lives will never be the same if Mom becomes president. We'll be signing on for years of special treatment, constant oversight, Secret Service escorts. A life of unwanted publicity, like what happened today times a hundred. Every day. Every hour. I've hardly let myself think of it.

I lean over and shove Issy's shoulder with enough force that she rocks to one side. When she doesn't look at me, I do it again. I'm not sure that picking up the pieces is what she wants from me anymore, but I'll do it anyway. "Hey. If she gets elected, it definitely won't be a perfect life for us. But it'll be ours. And you're strong. You're capable. You've done so many hard things already. Remember? Manifesto?"

Her smile is so sweet that I almost forget we're under fire at all.

By early evening, the original Instagram post featuring Issy is taken down. This is what happens when your parents are connected to a sprawling network of attorneys. Not that screenshots of the pic aren't still making the rounds, but it's a start. "Family strategy meeting," declares Mom, just after 7:00 p.m. "We need to talk about what happened today and how to move forward."

In the living room, we settle around Reese like kindergartners at storytime: Issy and I squeezed together on the loveseat, Mom, Dad, and Lucy on the couch. Reese—who's in boyfriend jeans, an oversize gray T-shirt, and a ponytail but somehow still looks great—has just gotten settled into an ottoman in the middle of the room when I speak up. "Before you all say anything, Issy and I are sorry and we'll be more careful in the future." We decided to apologize preemptively.

Mom's jaw hardens and I brace for the inevitable *You have to be on your best behavior at all times, you're a public figure now, you never know who's watching* lecture. I guess I wasn't compelling enough.

"Girls. Today, someone tried to strip you of your right to privacy. You were treated as objects, not people. Your father and I are not going to shame you or guilt you for what happened."

I gulp back tears that I didn't know had been camping out behind my face. Issy squeezes my hand.

"We're going to do what we can, as a team, to make this right for you." Dad nods at Reese, who sits up a little straighter.

"Your parents and I have been in contact with a nonprofit organization that works specifically for the rights of young women. One part of their mission statement has to do with sex—that is, that young women have a right to their sexuality, if they *choose* to exercise that part of themselves, but that being sexualized without consent is a form of oppression. Senator Crawford is about to hold a short press conference to announce a fundraising campaign in support of the organization. She will discuss how what happened to you girls today is an example of the kind of forced objectification that we, as a society, need to combat."

"That's smart, Reese," I say, recognizing a savvy political move when I see one. I like that Mom might actually be able to gain some positive press out of some predator's sleazy Instagram post. Especially because her stance on this matter is genuine, not just a power play. *It can be both*, I remember Mom saying.

Reese clears her throat. "As soon as we track down the person who snapped the picture—and my sources tell me we're close—he or she will be prosecuted for child pornography. Additionally, we've gotten the post removed from SenatorSlush. However, screenshots go a long way, and the content is already all over Facebook, Reddit, and Tumblr, as well as being discussed on the major news networks. There's no way to contain the content any more at this point. Our strategy, as a team, is to express our disgust at those who would seek to sexualize, without your consent, what is merely a picture of teen sisters shopping for clothing. We also hold that this clothing is something you have every right to own if you choose to, and that sex is yours to have if you choose, but the *point* is that you didn't *choose* this exposure. We will not apologize for *any* of what happened, Emmy and Issy, because you've done nothing wrong. Do you understand the stance? *Do not* apologize, here or publicly." Reese's face is intense, eyes boring into me and Issy like the sun. She's youngish—probably somewhere in her late twenties—but per Dad, "a gifted strategist" and has already run several successful campaigns. She's got this commanding presence that you can't help but take seriously.

Issy and I nod.

"Good. I'll see you all at family pictures and the tree lighting tomorrow." Reese walks herself out, already yakking into her phone as the door slams behind her.

"You girls hear her? You didn't do anything wrong." Dad's face oozes kindness, but I can tell he's as tired as I feel. Probably more. He runs a hand over his five o'clock shadow, making a friction sound.

Issy perks up beside me. "You're darned right we did nothing wrong. Emmy's one crappy, overworked bra was crying for help, and someone had to answer that call."

I smack her arm, but laughter rolls out of me in waves, such a welcome release after a long Black-and-Green Friday.

TWENTY-FOUR

THE FIRST DAY BACK AT school after the Black Friday from hell, Issy and I stride into school shoulder to shoulder, in step once again.

A guy I don't know steps out from a cluster of kids and says, "You wearing some new chonies, ladies?"

Issy breaks rank and gets up in the guy's face.

Let me say that again, for clarity. *The sweet-as-pie probably-a-reincarnated-princess Issy Crawford got up in a guy's face.*

She juts her index finger at his nose. "You shut your mouth, or I swear I will break you." The halls have gone silent, everyone turning to stare at Issy. As they should.

He flinches and blinks twice. "Okay, okay. Sorry. Jeez."

Issy puts her finger away and steps back to join me. I try to get us going at a quick pace, but Issy doesn't seem to be in any particular hurry.

"What the hell was that?" I mutter.

"Em, we can't control our status—but we *can* use it to our advantage, when we need to."

"Touché."

No one at school utters so much as a peep about the Insta post for the remainder of the day.

With that, Issy moves the second media-pocalypse firmly in the rearview mirror for the both of us at school. Mom and Dad and their posse of political strategists have done the same for us with the rest of the world. They managed to track down the OG photographer from the Georgetown boutique, who has not only been torn apart by the media (on *both* sides of the aisle), but also now faces criminal charges.

Clutching this minor victory, I channel my focus back into the place where major victory happens—debate. The DC regional tournament is just around the corner, my bid to nationals real enough to taste. Will I have to destroy Gabe and Aaron to get there? Yes, probably. But they know I won't hold back. I'll be bringing *all* my words to regionals. Maybe I'll even bring some of Aaron's.

AARON: Ready to lose next Saturday?

He has made a habit of Snapping this line alongside a ridiculous Bitmoji—the two of us eating a giant croissant, or side-by-side downhill skiing, or both of our faces sticking out of a hot-air balloon basket.

EMMY: In your dreams

AARON: Mmm, that's not what you're doing in my dreams, Crawford 1

EMMY: Please only think of me in jeans and a hoodie

AARON: Mmm. Hoodies

Because Aaron is incorrigible and also we belong in a teen rom-com.

I've got nothing but relief when the last class period ends. Debate practice, finally! I bound down the hall to Toomey's room, anxious to get cracking. The topic for the regional meet was just released, but Toomey wouldn't share it with us until practice. I am pumped to find out. *Psyched.* This is gift-under-the-Christmas-tree-level excitement.

The two Starbucks Doubleshots that I drank to get through today *might* be another reason for my popping energy.

Liv's already in the classroom, bent over her laptop. She missed school due to a college visit, so I haven't seen her yet today. "Ugh, what's wrong with you?" she says.

"What?"

"You look . . . happy. More than happy. Kinda bonkers."

I do a little jig-hop, for once not caring about looking silly. "Just excited for regionals. You ready to kick some preppy ass?"

"It's not going to be an easy road. The St. Jeremiah's dream team? Remember?"

I try to shrug but I've got so much adrenaline coursing that it comes off more like a shiver or maybe another weird dance move. "We'll take them down, easy peasy. But enough of that for now—how was Colgate?"

Liv goes for the subject change, hook, line, and trust fund. She gives me a full four-minute description of the campus, with special emphasis on the library, the on-campus community garden, and the hot Cuban sophomore who'd been her family's tour guide. "I'm ninety-nine percent sure she was into me," Liv says, handing me her phone.

"Who am I looking at?"

"Lucia. The tour guide."

"Are you social media stalking?"

"No! I mean, a little. We added each other on Instagram before I left campus, so her selfies are all fair game, right?"

Lucia is gorgeous and Marilyn Monroe–level glam. "Isn't she kind of girly for you?" Liv generally dates earthy, no-makeup, jersey-shorts-every-day type girls. Usually they're soccer players.

"She plays tennis," says Liv. Like this explains everything.

John strolls into the room, messenger bag over his shoulder, teeth sunk into a pear.

"Hi!" I say, punching him lightly on the shoulder.

"Um, hi. You're . . . chipper."

"Isn't a girl allowed to be excited about debate?"

Taylor walks in as I'm speaking. She takes one look at my hopeful face and holds up a hand. "Yeah, I can't handle that level of *anything* right now."

Which just makes me grin harder.

Five and a half minutes after the hour, Toomey comes rushing in, wispy hairs floofing out around his collar. He grabs a stack of paper from his desk. "Take one and pass it around."

John squints at the sheets. "Um, Mr. Toomey? This is a copy of a Robert Frost poem."

"What? Damn, this *is* Frost. Where would I have put the regionals topic sheet?"

"Here, Mr. Toomey." Preston has materialized out of thin air, correct papers in tow. I know the kid wants to debate, but I'm wondering if I should suggest a backup extracurricular of cat burglary.

The topic paper makes its way around to me last.

First, I smile. Hugely. Because now there's nothing that's going to get in the way of my total domination. Winning debaters don't stand on a gold, silver, bronze medal podium like Olympic athletes, but for a moment I imagine we do and there I am, on the top step, radiant and joyous and most importantly, *the best.*

And *then* I remember. A sick feeling creeps in, starting at my sweaty feet and working its way up to my gut, which was bubbling with excitement just seconds ago. Now, it boils with dread. I need to be able to argue *both* sides of this debate, but people I care about stand solidly on *one* side. This topic is personal.

Three Atrocities I Will Witness at Regionals
1. Gabe, arguing against his mother's needs
2. Myself, arguing against Gabe's mother's well-being—and my own
3. Mom and Dad, watching me deconstruct everything they believe in

And a fourth thing, vague but still all too real, given recent events. The media spin. If they remove the context, they can turn my debate words into something else entirely.

Toomey reads it out loud, unwittingly twisting the knife in my ribs. "Resolved: The United States should incorporate a universal health care system."

Shit shit shit.

I spend the next several days in a headspace I am wholly unfamiliar with. It's like some great puppet master in the sky is addling my brains, yanking out my common sense and replacing it with B-roll from a horror flick. Maybe Issy's rubbing off on me.

I've attempted to logic myself through this.

Do Liv and I have a high chance of going head-to-head with the St. Jeremiah's Dynamic Duo? Absolutely, yes. It's almost an inevitability with their record and ours, how we'll be seeded, and how both teams are likely to perform at the meet. I need to accept and prepare for this.

Do I know my subject matter well enough? Another absolute yes. Health care reform has been at the center of our family dinner table talks for years now, and now more than ever with the bill my mom is proposing. It's inconceivable that anybody my age knows the nuts and bolts of this subject as well as I do—with exactly one exception.

And it's that exception, and his human dictionary counterpart, who could be devastating to our bid for nationals.

Still, using just rational thoughts, Liv and I have excellent chances of winning it all. Every piece of logic points that way. I should be a little nervous, mostly excited, motivated to work hard and polish my stances until they shine, i.e., the way I usually feel before a debate meet.

Instead, I'm terrified.

Gabe's too close. His mother's health care isn't a tangential detail, it changed the entire trajectory of her life—and his. Worse yet, he knows that I know that, which I imagine might throw him off his usual smooth-talking game. If he comes into the debate rattled, Liv and I will decimate him. I will stick my finger down deep into Gabe's wounds and he will crumple.

Another me in another dimension would feel happy about that possibility. But when I think about Gabe's coffee shop face, his I-lost-my-mom-a-long-time-ago face, something heavy and unwanted drops into the pit of my stomach. An atom bomb of dread, mushrooming right in the middle of me.

And how will my parents feel, if they have to watch me (convincingly) argue against their life's work? The dread explosion redoubles within me, this one even more rattling than the first.

Life was easier when I was all-debate-all-the-time Emmy—and she's who I need to be more than ever. So, in the week leading up to regionals, I decide to pretend to be her until she makes her true appearance.

First order of business: I skip my scheduled appointment with Dr. Dalke. It was too easy, now that I'm eighteen and officially in charge of my own medical files and decisions. Dad was busy with health care bill meetings the day of the appointment, so I told him I'd take the bus. Then, I logged on to the portal and clicked "cancel" in the scheduling function. And voilà! That was it! And since

I'm a legal adult, no one can call my parents to tell them. So far, adulthood kicks ass.

It's now two days before regionals and I'm in heavy prep mode, as close to Debate Emmy as I've felt so far this week. I've turned the dining room into a command center for me and Liv, and we review debate stance index cards, craft outlines on a whiteboard, rehearse lines until I want to throw them up.

We've been at this for hours when Liv stands and stretches. "Okay, friend. I don't think I've got another round of practice in me. We're ready."

That's what I'd said to myself last year, days before the bid to nationals I failed to win for us. I'd thought I was ready, that no one could touch us. What I learned is that when I'm at exhaustion point, that's *exactly* when to dig deep, find that secret energy store, and push. But that will be something I tackle myself, on my own time. "I feel you. Talk tomorrow?"

"Duh."

After Liv takes off and I make my fifth trip to the bathroom since noon, I go back to the index cards, whispering points and paragraphs over and over and over. But with my bestie gone, the anxiety rockets. Debate Emmy slips away, despite my begging that she stay.

I switch gears. I turn on soothing music, play seventeen rounds of solitaire, draw mustaches on printed pictures of the latest Republican leaders slamming Mom in the media. But *nothing* works. The impending, inevitable doom lies heavy on my shoulders.

I stomp at the dining room's stripped wood planks. They're still not done, and today I find this even more annoying than usual.

Issy saunters into the room, hand in a bag of SunChips. "What's up with you?"

"What do you mean, what's up with me? What's up with *you*?"

"Whoa whoa whoa. I'm just trying to ask how you are. Slow your roll, sister."

I force a full-belly breath because she's right. I'm teetering on the brink of either a fistfight or tears, and neither of those is Issy's fault. "I'm sorry. I'm just . . . off."

She nods toward the empty bottle of 5-hour Energy on the table. "Isn't it a little late in the evening for one of those?"

Downing multiple energy drinks has been the only way to keep my brain and body going, for many days now. My legs are blocks of lead, my stomach is in a constant cramp—usually made worse by coffee, which is why I've been dabbling in alternative forms of caffeine. Discovering energy drinks was a relief, and they don't make me as twitchy as prednisone.

At least, I didn't think they did.

Probably after regionals, I should tell Dad that things aren't great with my body. I can't tell him now, it's way too risky. If he takes me to my doctor, they'll make me do medical things that will get in the way of my debate prep. Worse yet, what if they forced me into a colonoscopy or some other test WHEN I'M SUPPOSED TO BE AT REGIONALS? No thanks. Nope, nope, triple nope. Thus I can't tell Issy, because as we've established, Issy has zero guile, and Dad will find out within the hour. "They don't really affect me that much anymore."

"Doesn't look that way to me."

"I've got a lot to do, Is."

Her eyes rove the chorus of mustached GOPs spread out on the table. "Clearly."

"That was self-care."

"Maybe you could try something else. When's the last time you left the house after school?"

I consider. It's been a while. "Well, it's too cold to run."

"Could you maybe hang out with someone?"

"You wanna go . . . somewhere?"

Her faces scrunches. "No, I'm right in the middle of songwriting stuff."

I nod at the hand still shoveling chips into her mouth. "Oh yeah?"

"This is called *taking a break*. You should try it."

"Fine," I say, grabbing for my phone. My thumb hovers over Gabe's Snapchat Bitmoji. With as present as he's been in my head, he's the one I want to see and also the *last* person I should see. But he's not a viable option in any way.

Instead, I thumb to my greatest stupefaction.

EMMY: U up?

AARON: 8:30 is a little early for a booty call

EMMY: Shut it. Would I booty call you? Or anyone?

AARON: Re question 1—probably not, but you're invited to. Re question 2, how would I know, Emmaline? You could have a whole collection of lovers

EMMY: Well, I'm not booty calling you or anyone else, fwiw

216

AARON: Fwiw, "U up?" has a pretty specific connotation

EMMY: Fair. Anyway. What're you doing?

AARON: Nothing, actually

EMMY: Wanna hang? I need out of this house

AARON: I'll be there in ten

TWENTY-FIVE

AARON DRIVES US TO THE parking lot of a long-abandoned discount store, Bumblebee still humming. December has come with a loss of sunshine, and the weather's gone frosty. I'm nestled in my favorite long wool coat and knit hat but I'm still shivering, so I crank the heat dial to full blast.

"You trying to roast us alive?" Aaron turns the heat almost entirely off.

I notch the dial back up to somewhere in the middle. "It's freezing in here."

"You sure it's not just you?"

I *am* always cold these days, but I won't give him the pleasure of being right. "By the way, if you need to pick up a few things, I think you're in the wrong place." I nod toward the dark store, so defunct that its windows are boarded up.

"You don't really seem in the headspace for a Target run. Thought we'd do privacy instead."

"Ten out of ten on privacy, two on safety. Zero for climate control." I tuck my arms more tightly around me, absorbing a pang of something between loss and guilt. Ranking jokes is me and Gabe's thing, not me and Aaron's.

"Always so impudent."

"Impudent. That's one I've never been called before."

"I find that hard to believe."

Because I can only manage ten minutes of old-school jock jams at a time, I grab his phone and mess with his iTunes. "What's a sesquipedalian?" I say, in reference to his Apple handle. With most people I hate to admit not knowing things, but I've given up on trying to match Aaron's vocab. Aaron's more of a learning experience.

"Adjective. Means characterized by long words."

I snort.

Adele croons through the speakers, and Aaron leans back in his seat, like he's settling in for the long haul. "You all right tonight?"

"I'm freezing and we're parked in a creepy-as-fuck parking lot, but other than that, yeah, I'm great."

"Hey, you were the one who wanted to hang."

"Yes, but this," I say, flailing a hand at our shady surroundings, "wasn't what I had in mind."

"What *did* you have in mind?"

I sink farther down into the passenger seat. "I don't know."

His smile is the kind you throw someone you feel sorry for, which I'm not a fan of.

"Did you bring me out here to kill me? You've got motive," I say.

"Someone's been watching too many *Criminal Minds* reruns. Besides, I'd craft a *much* more elaborate plan if I wanted to remove my competition. You know I'm way above strangling you in a parking lot, right?"

I can't help but laugh. "Only you would take it there."

"Probably. Anyway, I was serious before. You're quiet. Pre-occupied?"

"I'm okay."

"See, I don't think you are. On the drive, it was almost like you weren't even here. I said your name three times to try to get your attention. Then I told you I was planning to get your name tattooed on my upper thigh. Still nothing."

"At least get it someplace visible. As for not hearing you, I'm sorry. Guess I'm pretty in my head about regionals."

"Oh, that's what's on your mind?"

"Yeah."

He reaches for my hand, and his thumb traces circles on my knuckles. "Were you thinking about how you and I probably have to debate each other?"

"Mm-hmm." Close enough.

"I don't want you to go easy on me just because we've been hanging out."

"You sure? Because we're gonna own you."

This earns me a full grin. "Honestly, one of the best things about winning will be seeing you mad again. You're sexy when you're ticked off."

I lightly smack his cheek, but he's quick, grabbing my hand and pulling me into a peppermint kiss. It's just a quick one, but for some reason I think of how different it is from the butter-orange of kissing Gabe—such an unfair comparison, but my brain is *not* playing fair these days. I'm convinced it's out to get me, with the way it keeps handing me all the good memories of someone I can't be with, even when I'm in the presence of someone I very much *could* be with. If I wanted that with Aaron, anyway.

My anguish shifts back to the here and now when Aaron springs up and out of the car. "Hey! What are you doing?" I case our surroundings. I'm not one to be overly paranoid about being robbed or mugged or whatever, but also, I don't usually go hanging out in abandoned parking lots at night. He knocks on my window and I roll it down.

He rests his elbows in the open space. "You promised you'd do a driving lesson. So we're doing a driving lesson."

I attempt to melt all the way into the leather seat. So much for a little easy fun and distraction on the one night I actually leave the house.

"Are you scared, Crawford 1?"

I spear him with my eyes. "No."

"Then let's see."

The leather in the driver's seat is still warm from Aaron's body, which is oddly comforting. And some of the controls in front of me *are* familiar. The headlights. The wiper dial, which I wouldn't need. I search for the gear shift on the wheel and come up short, so I look down to the console. And then I groan and lay my head on the wheel. "This is a stick shift."

Now in the passenger seat, Aaron chuckles. "You didn't notice the other times you were in here?"

I cringe, as this only further gives away my car ignorance. "Nope."

"Surprising, but okay."

"I barely know how to drive an automatic. I've never tried a stick."

"That's what she said."

"This is no time for crappy humor! I'm sort of freaking out!"

There. I said it out loud. Because I know he's not going to let me out of this and I'm not going to let me out of this either and that scares me. Breathing my real feelings out between us is weird but feels surprisingly *good*. My chest is still tight but deflates a little with my confession.

His hand is comfortingly heavy on my knee. "I'll coach you through it."

Even with Aaron's thorough instructions, Bumblebee pitches and jolts under my hands and feet. The engine dies and the car goes nowhere, even after multiple attempts. God, I hate failure. Especially in front of people. Out of the corner of my eye I see a light sheen of sweat break out on Aaron's forehead, but his face is open. Stoic. The engine grinds again, and this time, I show Bumblebee (and Aaron) some mercy and switch off the ignition. "That's enough."

The relief on Aaron's face is palpable, but still, he says, "It was a commendable first try."

"Whatever you say."

"I think it's cool that you did it at all, honestly. Like karaoke. You're hot when you take risks."

My body flushes with pleasure. I haven't thought about regionals or Gabe or the state of my body or how this debate intersects in the best but also grossest way with my parents' health care bill for the past half hour–ish, and I'm not sure I'm ready to leave this state of mind behind yet. "Aaron?"

"Yeah?"

"Can we just sit here a little while? I don't want to go home."

He pecks my cheek and there we stay, our hands linked over the console.

It's the night before regionals, and I'm losing my shit. I spent the day practicing my points in the shower and texting Liv incessantly about word tweaks. It's been all health care, all the time. That, and copious amounts of coffee and energy drinks, and also more than a few trips to the bathroom because my gut is *angry*. But I take my cue from the lives of Phil and Cat Crawford and push through my fatigue for the greater good. I hope they're proud of me.

It's getting close to ten and I should probably be getting into bed right now, but instead I'm pacing. It feels like there's motors attached to my feet, but my body itself is *tired*. Basically, I'm an animated corpse. It's fine. This is how we do.

My phone dings and my heart flies into my throat when I turn it over. Snapchat from Gabe. Tonight? Of all nights?

But I can't not look.

> GABE: Hi
>
> EMMY: . . . hi?
>
> GABE: How you holding up?
>
> EMMY: You want the standard issue answer or the honest
>> one
>
> GABE: C'mon
>
> EMMY: I'm scared

There I go again with the honesty. Who even am I? Admitting to not one but *both* of my *actual biggest threats to nationals* that I'm not okay?

> GABE: Me too
>
> EMMY: Yeah?
>
> GABE: Yeah
>
> EMMY: I guess that's kind of a relief
>
> GABE: That we're both fucking freaked out?
>
> EMMY: That I'm not alone
>
> GABE: I'd never let you feel alone, Emmy
>
> EMMY: That's incorrect
>
> GABE: You're right. I'm sorry. I did that. But I guess what I'm
>> saying is that I'm here now

How dare he. I mean, seriously, how *dare* he? Is this a strategy? Throw your biggest opponent off with raw emotion and declarations of *being here*? And what about Issy? Is he *here* for her?

> EMMY: Maybe the night before regionals isn't the best time
>> for this conversation

GABE: Maybe not. Is there a good time, though?

EMMY: Maybe not

GABE: Okay. Well, see you tomorrow, then?

EMMY: Yep

I throw my phone onto the bed and flop on my stomach beside it, burying my head face-first into my comforter. *I will not cry. I will not cry. No tears no tears no tears.*

"Em."

Issy let herself in so quietly that I didn't hear her. "Yeah?" I say, words muffled by cloth.

"I brought you something." She's holding a steaming mug—the one that says, "I EAT PIECES OF SHIT LIKE YOU FOR BREAKFAST," i.e., my mug. A hilarious birthday gift from Dad, who said it's a movie quote, because of course it is.

I sniff the air. "Chamomile?"

"Yeah."

"How'd you know I was still up?"

"These floors creak. You know that."

Of course she'd heard me pacing. Probably the whole house did. I sigh and reach for the mug.

"It's okay to be nervous," she says.

"I'm not nervous."

But Issy's not buying it, I can tell from the tuck of her lips. And as to why I'm lying to her when I've decided to be full-force honest with both Gabe and Aaron, I have no clue. I am a fucking conundrum. Despite the slow, hot slide of tea down my throat, my teeth start chattering.

"Emmy. I'm worried about you." There's something like pity on Issy's face and I do not approve.

The breath I draw through me is long, intentional, and cleansing. I can center myself. I *must* center myself. There is no choice but to be okay. I summon the calmest, most Cat Crawford–like smile, forcing it across my face like it belongs. For me, for Issy.

"I love you for worrying. But I'll be fine."

TWENTY-SIX

THE MORNING OF REGIONALS COMES in like a roar. For the event, my team and I converge on the Georgetown University campus. My debate career could end in the same place my college career will begin. This *may* be irony? According to my AP Lit teacher, I don't quite grasp the concept, which is humiliating for someone who loves to be *right*. If I can stomach it, maybe I'll ask Aaron for help with this word.

Aaron. Who I may be debating today. Along with his partner, whose face I wish I could scrub from my mind.

"You're quiet," says Liv, nudging my shoulder with hers as we walk to our first match. The click of my heels is annoyingly loud on the tile floor of the student conference center, but I can't stop. Each step is vital. My skin tingles, like the white-hot energy that flows right under it is about to burst through.

"I'm determined." I've also got a headache and I'm a little dizzy, but that's just stress.

Each team's win/loss ratio is listed in the program we were given at the beginning of the day, yet I don't need it to know exactly how lackluster our first opponent's record is. The girl's as pale as her white notebook paper, the guy's hands shake as he straightens his tie.

My conscience breathes a greedy sigh of relief when we draw the affirmative stance, which means we will be arguing in favor of universal health care. Taking the stance I'm personally on board with fuels me, gives me that extra spark when I'm at the podium.

I'm settling into my usual pre-debate routine—deep breathing, intense focus on notes—when my brain goes rogue and hands me the question I've been pushing away for two weeks. *What stance would you rather draw when you're up against Gabe?* Either I'm tearing down his very personal self-interest, or Gabe is doing it to himself while I watch and my insides rip themselves apart.

I've been at debate long enough to *know* it's an intellectual enterprise, something I should be able to detach my feelings from. But have I ever debated a topic that has drawn and quartered my opponent's heart and life? The answer changes the equation for me. It changes everything.

My breath rattles and stutters. I can do this. I have to do this. I've worked too hard to blow it now. Preston has our table set up, which increases our rock star appearance and reminds me of what I am. He hands me two of the black gel ink pens that I insist on having for every match. "You ready for this?" he asks.

"Born ready." I perch upright in my chair with the good, confident posture that one trial lawyer and one senator taught me.

Preston grins. "Atta girl. How 'bout you, Liv? Need anything else before the bloodbath ensues?"

Liv checks out her stuff: notepad, her preferred mechanical pencils, bottle of water. "I'm good," she says as she fusses with her necklace.

"Here, let me," I say, tucking back the clasp that had drifted forward.

Her eyes are sharp enough to leave tracks on my cheeks. "So. Are you going to tell me what's going on?"

"What do you mean?"

"You look like shit."

"Thanks?"

"Seriously, Emmy. Are you sick?"

"Absolutely not. I'm just nervous. Really, really nervous."

"So you are human after all."

I half smile. "Wish I was above all that."

"I'm glad you're not. I'm nervous, too. Level with me, though: Is this about getting to nationals or about debating Jeremiah's?"

I let that one ride a few seconds before answering. I want to lie, but Liv sees through me almost as well as Mom. "Yes," I say, finally.

"We talked about this. We *prepped* for this," Liv replies, but her face is sympathetic.

"I know. It won't be a problem. I promise."

Liv squeezes my hand.

"Well, isn't this a cute little lovefest?" John has appeared out of thin air.

"Don't you have a match?" says Liv, squinting at him.

Taylor joins us. "The judge is running late. Can you believe this shit? *Late*, for *this* meet? Anyway, they're pushing that room's matches back by a half hour. So we get to watch you!"

"Is Issy coming today?" John's nonchalance convinces no one.

I point to the faces who've come to watch us and there she is, smiling brightly from the center of three rows of chairs. John goes the way of an excited puppy as they exchange waves, and I wonder why I didn't just set them up in the first place and avoid this whole love-square situation I've gotten myself into.

The moderator takes her place at the podium, and something clicks. I switch into full-on debate mode and all my weeks of practice show up for me.

Liv and I slaughter them.

And so it's on to round two. We draw the negating side. Debate Emmy gets a little twitchy saying things that would make my parents' (and Mom's voting base, ugh) skin crawl, but I do what must be done. And I do it well enough, because it ends in another victory.

This is how it goes for the four preliminary rounds. We win them all.

At lunch, Liv and I meet back up with John and Taylor in the canteen area.

"Well?" I ask, as Liv and I trade halves of our sandwiches. She brings ham and Swiss on white, I bring roast beef and cheddar on cracked wheat, but we like the variety of eating both kinds. It's a ritual.

"Three and one," says Taylor, biting savagely into a banana.

"Good Lord, you're scary even when you eat."

"Grow up, John," she replies, through a mouthful of white-yellow mush.

John opens his mouth to deliver the obvious comeback, but Liv's rapidly shaking head silences him. Instead, he offers, "We, um . . . were close to winning the last one."

"I forgot one key point! One! And if I would have remembered it, we would've had them." Taylor pounds her knee with a fist. "I really wanted to beat those Jeremiah's clowns, too."

I of course play it super cool. "Huh. You had Jeremiah's?"

"Oh, don't try to act like you're not interested in knowing how your boyfriends stacked up. We drew the affirmative. John killed his part. Their guy with all the fancy words, the tall one, he was *good.* Then I got up and I botched my part. Then the other guy—Gabriel, right? He was at that party at Liv's a few months ago?—got up and he was all sweaty. Stumbled and stammered and seemed like he lost his train of thought once. And as I'm watching him, I'm thinking, 'That's the team that beat Emmy and Liv?' And then we manage to lose to them, too. Even sweating his balls off, the kid got the job done. Does he ever lose? I mean, seriously."

A hodgepodge of emotions clatter around behind my breastbone. What was I even hoping for? My team to lose? Gabe's team to lose?

Aaron's team. I keep having to remind myself it's Aaron's team, too.

The head honcho tournament coordinator, a tall, wiry dude with thick black-rimmed glasses, emerges. He's holding The List, and everyone in the room knows it, and I can tell from his furtive, anxious side-eyeing that he *knows* everyone knows it. He jogs to the bulletin board at the front of the room, thumbtacks the paper down, and bolts.

Predictably, there's a stampede. Dozens of anxious, overly verbose teens step on toes and elbow each other out of the way to get a peek. Curse words cut across whoops of victory. A blond girl stalks away, mascara tears running down her face. I spy Preston's red head amid the crush of competitors, now needling its way back to us. His teeth are blindingly white, even against his pasty skin. "You're all in the finals. Congrats!"

I jump up, last forgotten quarter of my sandwich falling off my lap to the floor, where it's trampled by my team's excited bouncing. We laugh and squeal like little kids. Toomey's face is gleaming and proud. "Well done, well done! Let's go check the room assignments."

I turn to make my way and knock face-first into Gabe's solid, too-hot body. Because of course he'd be *right there* and of *course* the one person I'd clumsily plow into has to be him, after many weeks of not seeing him. This is how life works.

"Congratulations," he says, looking genuinely happy, but his face is a weird shade of brown-gray, like he's been sick. He swipes at his brow with one sleeve while offering me his other hand.

I shake, ignoring both the stab of concern and the zap of touching him. "Thanks. And . . . you?"

"Yeah. We made it."

As if there was ever any doubt.

I'm snatched up into a bear hug, which pulls my hand out of Gabe's. Peppermint and crisp linen fill my nose.

"You did it!" Aaron squeezes me hard enough to lift me off my feet, which pushes a strangled laugh out of my middle.

"Put me down, you Neanderthal!"

So many eyes are devouring the scene we're making. On our right side is my team, looking *pissed*. Even Toomey looks slightly affronted, eyes bulgy, hands wringing. And on our left, Gabe and Issy stand close. Gabe's face is neutral, stony. And Issy wears a tiny, knowing smirk. Like she knows anything.

For some reason *this* is the thing that cracks me. Issy, and her too-sweet, too-trusting face. This is *not* the time or the place for tears but they're pushing their way up anyway, and I wish, I *wish* I better understood why. Suddenly everything feels like too much.

But then Issy's right there. She gathers me up, natural, easy, like everything's fine. My body melts as I let my nose sink into the familiar patchouli-and-rose of my sister's neck.

"Seriously. Are you okay?" She whispers this close to my ear, so quietly that no one else would be able to hear.

"I don't know," I whisper back, as close to honest as I'm able to get right now.

She tucks a stray wisp of my hair behind my ear. "I'm proud of you no matter what happens. Mom and Dad will be, too."

I hold on to her longer than what is probably normal and far longer than I deserve. If only she knew how I really felt about the boy she's seeing, she would hate me.

But it doesn't matter how I feel. My feelings will never get in the way of me protecting Issy. Also, I can't let my team see me like this. Not now. Not today.

Not ever.

I force myself to push everything away, focusing only on Issy's words, even if I haven't earned them. *I'm proud of you no matter what.*

I'm grateful for that. I am.

The problem is, I'm less and less sure all the time of how to make *me* proud of me.

TWENTY-SEVEN

JOHN AND TAYLOR LOSE THEIR first round of finals. John handles it as John handles things, graciously congratulating the winners. Taylor skulks in a far corner of the auditorium, ripping into a King Size Hershey's bar. She'll come around.

Aaron and Gabe win all their finals matches, and so do Liv and I.

And so, here we all are. Or at least, here my team is—the opponents haven't arrived yet. Liv and I sit side by side in unforgiving plastic chairs as we wait for 4:00 p.m., which is when the championship match begins. My knee's bouncing at an unprecedented pace. Probably shouldn't have picked up that last cup of vending-machine coffee a half hour ago. Liv is sitting on top of her hands, which I've never seen her do.

"Hey. What're you doing?" I say, nodding at her handless wrists.

"They're cold."

"Ah. So you're cold, and I feel like I'm about to jump out of my skin." Which is true, though weirdly also I feel like my legs are made of overcooked noodles. My cell phone clock says 3:40, meaning we've still got time to kill. "Quick walk?"

"Hell yes." Liv leaps out of her seat and is three steps ahead before I've even gotten up.

We pace the central corridor of Georgetown's Healy Hall, the famous, castle-like one that's in all the brochures and pictures of campus. Its inside is a little less impressive, but still, you can feel the history in its walls. I close my eyes and imagine the knowledge shared here soaking in through my skin, imbuing me with intergenerational wisdom. I'm going to need all I can get if we're going to beat Aaron and Gabe. This whole day would have been so much easier if they'd just lost. Or if we had. And I can't believe I'm even entertaining that thought.

I sigh, the echo of it bouncing off the wood floors.

"What's up?" Liv asks.

"I knew this was bound to happen, but I so wish we were debating any other team right now."

"Yeah. It's not ideal."

"It's going to be hard. Jeremiah's is *good*. And my personal feelings toward Aaron have nothing to do with what I'm saying."

"Oh, it's not your feelings toward *Aaron* I'm worried about."

My heels cease their clicking. "Liv."

"Look, your feels aren't always as buttoned up as you think."

There's no use even trying to verbally tap-dance my way out

of this, not with Liv. "Does Issy know?" I'm not sure I can tolerate any more stress today but I'm also unable to stop myself from asking.

"I'm not sure. She hasn't said anything."

I release a slow breath, hoping it rights the dizziness that's come and gone all day. My body wants to lean to the left, which means I'm putting a weird amount of concentration into walking straight. Good thing debates are more of a still proposition.

We do what we must, I say to myself, echoes of Mom-wisdom. I have no choice but to stay upright.

"I'll fix this. I *am* fixing this," I say.

Liv's face is half-amused, half-sad. "I didn't know feelings were something that could be fixed."

"They are when your sister needs you. Not to mention your debate partner."

Though there's so much still left unsaid, for the next several minutes Liv and I pace in silence. Debate Emmy thinks we should be using this time to re-review wording or give each other last-minute feedback. But another Emmy is awake inside, and she's demanding quiet. Time to center, time to breathe.

Finally, I speak. Some words can wait, but not all of them. "It's 3:49. Shall we?"

"We shall."

The medium-size lecture hall yawns out beyond its doors, cavernous compared to the rooms we usually debate in. It smells like furniture varnish and stale coffee. The tables are set up at the front of the room, which is slightly raised, like a stage but not quite.

Liv surveys the space. "This is it. Let's give 'em hell, Emmy Crawford."

I manage a grimace-smile in return. Yeah, this *will* be hell, but I'm not sure if I'll be the one giving it.

Liv and I have drawn the affirmative stance, which makes my insides shrivel—but then again, drawing the negating stance would have done the same thing. This round is one giant cringe, either way. The space inside my head expands, contracts, and then my notepad is covered in sparkling white starbursts that only I can see. I push both palms into the table, an attempt to get myself and the world to hold a little steadier. Maybe after this match I need to go on a short debate-cation. Much as I love my craft, this body reaction *can't* be normal.

Liv slides me her extra bottle of water. "Em. You're not okay."

"I'm fine," I insist, gulping from the bottle. The water hits my gut with a cold thud and unfurls, releasing nausea that's been lying in wait. Great. I push the water bottle to the far end of the table.

"You're pale."

"Seriously, no big deal. Just nerves." And then I turn my head and surreptitiously wipe away the thin layer of sweat from my forehead and upper lip.

"Well, here you are on the big stage again," says one of my favorite voices. She's wearing her Mom face, not her senator one, and this is possibly the biggest accidental gift she could have handed me. I jump up to greet her, but I do it too fast. My surroundings go all wavy and dreamlike, and I totter to one side a little. Two steps later, the edges of everything regain their sharpness. Mom's compact body in my arms anchors me. "You came!" I said, squeezing her tightly.

"Of course I came. Issy texted us and told us you made the finals—because you forgot to, silly girl."

"Whoops. I'll thank her later."

"Thank me now." Issy lands a kiss on my forehead. "Good luck, team!"

"Dad's coming," says Mom. "He got stuck in traffic picking Lucy up from school, but he'll be here."

"Did you see who we're up against?"

Mom raises one savvy eyebrow. "I saw. I know this puts you in a weird situation. But go with your gut, kiddo. And your big brain. Neither one has ever led you astray."

That's what she thinks.

I sneak a look across the platform to the now-occupied enemy table. Aaron's leaned back in his metal folding chair, bobbing his head to the steady drumbeat pounding from his mini-speaker, cooler than his peppermint gum. Gabe, on the other hand, looks as bad as I feel. My tiny sweat mustache has got nothing on him—he's full-on raining. Even his underarms are stained dark from perspiration. His brows are drawn together, face buried in a notepad that holds anti-universal-health-care notes. Anti-everything-he-believes-in notes, anti-happiness notes.

Heart so swollen it might burst, I force myself to turn back to my own notepad. I review my main points, then try to repeat them to myself. I get through point one, then point two, and then I hit a wall of brain fog. What's point three? Seriously, I've done this position three times already today . . . *C'mon brain, don't fail me now.* Point three comes rushing forth in my memory and I welcome it like a long-lost friend.

The moderator enters. She's the same one from the evening of the exhibition debate, a.k.a. the Sex Ed Debate That Wasn't. As she shakes my hand she leans in, speaking into my ear. "I expect you'll pay a bit more attention to the debate rules this time around, Miss Crawford?"

"Yes, ma'am."

She acknowledges Liv, then greets Aaron and Gabe. For the first time, it dawns on me that they're sitting in the wrong seats—Aaron's in the A1 seat, which is usually Gabe's. He was apparently so affected by this topic that he'd ceded his point position to Aaron. As our team's very proud A1, I am appalled, and only now realizing that this whole debacle is going to be so much worse than I'd even imagined.

As if he heard my horror, Gabe looks right at me. His half smile is dull, weary. He doesn't have to say it for me to know—he doesn't want to be here, not like this. It's one thing to be immersed in a gut-wrenching topic for an hour or two. It's another thing to be in it for seven straight hours, no matter how hard you've worked to build armor around your vulnerable heart. And that doesn't take into consideration the weeks of prep he must have put in. How many times did he think of his mom as he researched health care policy, wrote arguments, practiced in front of the mirror? Did he wonder if he'd do her proud by being a part of this activity or disappoint her by agreeing to be a part of a system in which the equity of human lives is still a point of debate?

And I thought *I* had it bad with my parent situation. I know my dad loves all of us no matter what—truly, I do. But he *also* loves to see us winning. I see it in the lightness in his step when Lucy brings home another chess medal, and I see it in his scowl when Issy refuses to participate in something she's good at. And it's there in his starry, glistening eyes when Mom manages to come away from an election with the most ballots cast in her favor. What he always says is just "to be the best you can be"—which is loving, by-the-book parent-talk. But I know full well that my performance here, and any future performances in debate or speech or Model UN or really anything else, reflect upon him and especially Mom. Because I'm not just Emmy, I'm the daughter of Senator Catalina Crawford, who may well be our nation's next commander in chief. Living up to Mom's legacy factors into every sentence I write, every position I take, and every energy drink I crush along the way.

And honestly? I'm tired. There, I said it. I am *tired*. But I don't have time for that. My jaw is clenched tight enough to shoot pain across my mouth and throat. And there's no choice but to keep clamping down, unless I want to dissolve into a puddle of tears right here on this platform in front of everyone.

The moderator takes her place behind the central table, facing us. "Debaters, are you ready to begin?"

I swallow hard and nod, now wishing I'd left my water within arm's reach. Nausea would be an improvement over implosion via spontaneous sobbing. I inhale hard, pulling the air down through my clogged throat and into my oxygen-deprived lungs, then breathe it out hot and slow. It's a technique pulled way back from my middle school choir days.

"Good luck, all of you." She nods to me. "Miss Crawford, you may begin."

I rise slowly and walk to the podium, that swirling dreamlike feeling from earlier threatening to wash me away. I pinch my left hand with my right, and the faces in the crowd go from slightly swirly to fully formed. Dad has arrived, and he winks. I manage a tiny smile back. John thumbs-up me from the front row, with Taylor, Toomey, and Preston all around him, fierce like a pride of lions.

Adjusting the microphone to my height, I clear my throat.

"'We hold these truths to be self-evident, that all men are created equal.' This is the opening of our Declaration of Independence. Yet, over years it would be twisted and skewed, with entire groups of people facing oppression from the very beginning of our country's history. Native Americans were pushed off their land by white colonists. Women were denied rights to vote and own property, among other gross injustices, for centuries. African people brought to the United States as part of the slave trade were subjugated to less-than-human status. Japanese Americans were held in American internment camps during World War II. This is only a sampling of the ways that the United States has never lived up to its billing as a free country, and these inequalities among people persist today.

"In a society in which women still earn only eighty-three cents on the dollar to what a man will bring home for the same work and people of color inordinately inherit legacies of poverty as a by-product of ancestral trauma and oppression, we must continuously seek ways to level the playing field. One way to work toward achieving more equity is to offer universal health care to every person living on American soil."

And this is where I'm supposed to now introduce our multipronged argument, in a list of three. My brain is ready, ready, ready. Triumph floods and I do what I always do—swivel my attention from the audience to my opponent. It's a nonverbal flex, the way that turn of my shoulders says, *You don't scare me and btw prepare to lose.*

Gabe's somber-devastated face catches me across the middle. Suddenly my heart is working on only one track. My feelings deflate me so soundly that not even ambition can pump me back up. I glance at my precise statistics and all my carefully chosen words one more time before pushing the notepad away.

"Right now I'm supposed to pitch our side in this debate with philosophy, facts, and figures. And I assure you I could. I've done it many times just today. So many times, in fact, that I've almost lost sight of what it all means.

"But not quite. I want to tell you what it's really like, living within the current system of US health care. For me, who lives in a family of privilege and who has the solid health care coverage that comes with that, it means I can get the care I need for the Crohn's disease I was diagnosed with two years ago. When I needed a specialist, we could afford one—and our insurance helps pay for it. When I needed medication, same thing. If I needed mental health care, that'd be covered, too."

Liv's mouth is gaping—at least, that's what it looks like from the corner of my eye, because I don't dare look at her straight on. She was right, so right—with this topic and this opponent I was always at risk, and now I'm threatening her win, too. My gaze tumbles out to the audience, where my sisters, my friends, and my dad look shell-shocked over my self-disclosure. But my eyes flick away from the shock and to the dark-headed, olive-skinned face of my mother. The reaction I most need to see. Her face is solemn but her eyes glimmer, with what I don't know.

"And though legally all health insurers are supposed to cover all these services, they don't cover them equally. This year at my school, my sister and others put together a GoFundMe for someone whose mother has cancer—and this mother of three and full-time worker *has* health insurance; it's just that insurance didn't come close to touching the enormous costs associated with her illness. And if this is the situation for someone who is covered, consider what the situation is like for those who can't afford health care coverage or who aren't covered in the right way."

I stop for a breath, as my stomach is boiling with . . . I think it's sadness, but it feels like anger, too. I close my eyes and choose my next words with care. "I happen to know someone whose mother is chronically ill, and their family's health insurance failed them in a way that has affected the fabric of his entire life. He has essentially lost his mother in part due to her not having access to the care she needs. This could have gone so much better. Better medications and services exist, it's just that she can't get to them, which is a situation that I personally find to be arbitrarily cruel. In sum, what I'm saying is that health care should be a right, not a privilege. When we don't provide access and properly cover essential health care for *all* people, we fail. Families go bankrupt. People die. Our country is only as strong as our weakest links. We fare better when all of us thrive."

Liv's hands clench the table. A quick glance reveals her face— sympathetic but desperate. I know she supports me but also, she wants to win. I'll need to get back to the original talking points if we're still going to have any chance at that. The ground is growing wavy, swaying under me, and I grasp the podium to right myself. I've got to stand firm. Keep going. It's the Crawford way, and the only right option.

But as to the direction I take as I plow forward, I have a choice.

I could try to win this debate and get my shot at nationals.

Or, I could *stand* for something.

I realize what I have to do, and I don't question it.

I'm sorry, Liv. This is so not fair to you and you might actually hate me for this.

I'm sorry, Aaron. So much for bringing the fight.

I'm sorry, Gabe. For the way you've suffered.

I look right at him, them. He's flashing me two open hands— two fives. "Ten out of ten." Gabe has finally given me his top debate ranking. I guess his was the one that mattered to me most of all.

I lean back into the microphone.

"High school debate has exceptional merit. In fact, if anyone cared to disagree with me on that topic—well, I'd debate them. And it is precisely because I so highly value this activity that I am about to say this. We—as a culture of scholars, as a collective of passionate students—are better than allowing ourselves to debate a subject that, in my opinion, has a foregone conclusion. In half of today's matches, I was forced to argue against human rights, and that's not something I can continue to be a part of. I'm foregoing my position in this match, as of now."

The crowd is now far louder out there than the usual golf-course-level muttering of a debate audience.

Or is it the roar in my head that's making everything else sound so loud?

As I step away from the podium, everything around me shifts into slow motion. I try to say "I'm sorry" to my ex–debate partner, but I'm not sure my mouth actually moves. Liv's face moves from stunned to deeply concerned. Across the stage a chair is thrown, metal slogging through water. I never even hear it clatter, though part of me knows I should.

There's nothing left in me. I give up. The swerve inside my head takes me and my knees buckle.

Warmth catches me on my way down. "Emmy! Oh no, please, are you okay?" And it's Gabe's voice, Gabe's hands, Gabe's face swirling, so close to mine.

It's the last thing I remember before I go out completely.

TWENTY-EIGHT

I DON'T LET THE TEARS come until I'm out of the building, off campus, and safely in the passenger seat of Dad's Jeep. It'll be one thing if the media gets wind of the collapse, but no way they get to see me cry about it. With just Dad, though, I can't hold back anymore. Salty hot liquid rolls down my cheeks, spelling "finally" on my face with grief and makeup.

I cry for all the things.

For losing my shot at nationals, yeah, but also because of feeling sick and helpless and for a mother and son who might have felt this way for years and with no way to fix it. And for being a disappointment, because surely Dad's going to have something to say about all this. I also manage to cry for being so far away from Iowa. If my collapse had happened there, Grandma and Grandpa would help. Grandma would be waiting at home with open arms and food that makes the whole house smell good. Grandpa would crack a bad joke. All of it would be comforting and *normal*. But they're. Not. Here. All I have to watch over me here is the DC public and the piranha paparazzi.

And I cry because I *collapsed*. I wasn't strong enough, not this time. I remember it in hazy chunks, Mom and Dad on either side of me, my team beyond them, a chorus of biting nails, whispers, worried glances. Gabe running his hands over and over through his sweat-damp hair and Aaron looking deeply uncomfortable; Issy with her arm around a crying Lucy.

Yes, Lucy cried. Which was the main thing that let me in on how scary the situation had been for everyone else. Guilt beckons and I cry in big, ugly sobs that threaten to rip me in half, like what happened when I found out Grandma couldn't come for Thanksgiving but multiplied by infinity. I can't remember the last time I cried like this. Had I ever?

I'm still crying when Dad pulls up in front of the Georgetown University Hospital. I shake my head vehemently. "No, no. I can't go in. Not like this."

"Like what?"

"Look at me! I'm a mess. I melted down, I'm a total disaster, if anyone sees it'll be—"

Dad's hand on my cheek quiets me. "Emmaline. You need help. And there are laws that protect your identity in a hospital. HIPAA."

"HIPAA was supposed to protect Issy at her therapist's office, too."

Dad closes his eyes and looks sad, so sad. "I know. This world hasn't been easy on either of you. In Issy we could always see it, but with you . . ." He squeezes my face, gently. "You always hide. And you do it so well—too well."

"Not well enough. Not today, anyway. Not well enough to save us from the 'I don't want my mom to be president' bit, either." I hadn't really *meant* to confess but I had nothing left in the defense tank. All I could do in this moment was *be*.

"I thought maybe that was you. It's okay. Truly, we're okay. These things happen."

"They don't happen to me. I need to be better."

"For you? Or for us? Because if all of this hiding is for me and your mom, it's just too much."

My chin trembling starts back up, making the next words hard to get out. "I'm . . . I'm really tired, Dad. Are you sure we can't go home? I think I just need my bed."

"You *do* need your bed, but you passed out, honey. We need to make sure there's nothing serious going on."

I'm a force, but I've got nothing on my dad.

Inside the ER there's paperwork. And lots of waiting, which gives me plenty of time to stop crying and let more comfortable feelings ease forward. Frustration and contempt, my familiar friends, especially when it comes to forced doctor visits. They balloon more and more with every minute that ticks away on the analog waiting-room clock. Funny, I've just thrown away my entire debate career over health care, and here I am, angry to have the privilege of it. (Is this irony? Do I finally understand?)

After forever, a nurse fetches us, takes my vitals, and hustles out again. A little while later, a new voice debuts. "Knock knock." A slight, redheaded man—my doctor, apparently—smiles as he raps his knuckles silently against our curtain divider. Probably the same joke he makes with every single patient. He can't be that much older than I am, if his face is any indicator—so smooth, I doubt it's ever seen a razor. "What seems to be the trouble?"

"Nothing. I'm fine."

"She fainted during a debate tournament," interjects Dad. "Which is *not* like her. It's never happened before."

Dr. Peach Fuzz surveys me, his face both blank *and* curious. A little like Mom's typical look. "Have you been feeling ill today?"

"No. I mean, I was kind of dizzy this morning, and nauseous on and off, but I'm sure that was just nerves. This was a big tournament." I choke on the last words, feeling the sadness well up in my throat again. I push it down, away. None of that has anything to do with whatever's going on with my body.

"Mm-hmm, okay. Anything else? Any dietary changes? Other stressors?" He picks up my wrist, apparently checking my pulse. Again. The nurse has already done that. And the lecture hall volunteer doctor who determined I didn't need an ambulance but did need a doctor.

Dad's quick to add more ammo. "She has Crohn's disease. I think maybe it's been acting up and she hasn't said anything. She's been working nonstop, getting ready for this tournament. She's not especially good at taking care of herself."

I scowl. "Look who's talking."

Dad crosses his arms. "Today isn't about my problems, Emmy."

"I take care of myself. How else could I have perfect grades and

250

an almost-perfect debate record? So what if I've been putting in a few extra hours lately? It's nothing I shouldn't be able to handle."

Dr. Peach Fuzz frowns to match me. "Mr. Crawford, could I have a minute alone with Emmy?"

"Sure thing," Dad says. "I'll be waiting right outside."

Dr. Peach Fuzz pulls his chair up so close that I smell the coffee on his breath, and he looks altogether too *solicitous*. This whole calamity is about to become an after-school special.

"All right, I need you to be straight with me. Are you on anything?" he asks.

"What do you mean, on anything? Like, drugs?"

"Yeah, like drugs. Specifically, meth, cocaine, or any kind of ADHD medication you might have bought off a friend?"

I know people who pop Adderall to help them study for big tests and whatnot. It's not for me, though. I want to know my accomplishments are my own, no chemical aid.

"No. What makes you ask that?"

"Hmm, let's see. You're a highly driven teenager living in a world of pressure. *And* you're a senator's daughter, *plus* the oldest, which sounds like a recipe for intense standards."

I shrug even as my stupid eyes burn. Apparently today is *only* for disappointment and crying.

He continues. "I've lived in DC a long time. I've seen what this place can do to senators' kids."

There are lines around his eyes and a few stray white hairs at his temples. Dr. Barnes—which is what his name tag says—isn't so young after all.

"Well. Yes." I clear my throat. "But this senator's kid is okay."

"Do you see anyone?"

"Like dating?"

"Like a therapist."

"That's more my sister's thing."

His smile is gentle. "Maybe you could make it *your* thing, too. But until then, let's return to the question. Are you on anything?"

"No."

"You sure? I ordered a tox screen that'll show any drugs in your system, so either you can tell me now or I'll find out in a few minutes anyway."

"It'll come back clean, I swear."

"How about caffeine?"

I scoff. "Well, yeah, I've had that. That doesn't even count."

"How much?"

"I had a Starbucks Doubleshot this morning, and a 5-hour Energy with my lunch, and then a cup of coffee at about three p.m."

His eyebrows almost fly off his face. "Have you been using this much caffeine every day?"

"Approximately."

"And how are you sleeping?"

"Poorly, and very little."

"Okay, then. I'm guessing you fainted due to palpitations, which is a symptom of caffeine overdose. You're overworking your heart, and you need to cut that out."

My overworked heart. Ha. If he only knew. "Okay, doc, no more caffeine."

"May I?" he asks, holding my hand up like a specimen.

I'm not sure what I'm agreeing to, but still I say, "Sure."

He pinches the skin just over my blue-green veins.

"Ouch! I said I'd stop; what more do you want from me?"

"See how your skin there stayed standing, rather than popping back into place? That means you're dehydrated. It can be a side effect of too much caffeine, as it's a diuretic. But also, let's talk about your Crohn's disease for a minute."

"Do we have to? I'm sort of tired of talking about that."

"Well, you can either ignore it and let it get out of control or talk about it and maybe there's something that can be done."

"It's incurable. So honestly I prefer the *ignore* method."

"And how's that working out for you?"

I want to punch his smug face, but instead I throw my head back into my pillow with more force than necessary. "Fine, until today I guess."

"I'd say not so fine, because it takes at least a few days of significant fluid loss to look like you do."

He makes me talk about my gut (nausea and some pain) and my joints (they hurt) and my bowel movements (too many). At least I tell the truth this time. I'm too tired to even concoct half-truths anymore.

"I'm going to bring your dad back in so we can talk about what comes next. I assume you're okay with him knowing about the caffeine use?"

"It's not a secret," I say, rolling my eyes.

Dr. Barnes pokes his head out and Dad comes back into the

room, a nurse with him. He gives dad the rundown on his diagnosis, finishing with, "Also, she's reporting symptoms consistent with active Crohn's disease, very likely also contributing to dehydration. She needs to see her GI as soon as possible."

Dad's forehead scrunches. "Didn't you see Dr. Dalke a few days ago?"

I'm totally screwed. "I, um, might have missed that appointment."

Dr. Barnes pecks at his tablet. "How about that Prednisone taper? I can see from your universal chart that your GI prescribed one in October. Did that help?"

"Well. I didn't take those. Prednisone makes me completely unstable."

Dad pinches the bridge of his nose.

"I'm going to give Emmy a couple boluses of fluid, which should get her feeling significantly better in the short term. She needs to cut way back on caffeine use from here on out, though."

Dad's still squeezing his face cartilage for dear life, like stanch-a-nosebleed-level hard. "How much coffee have you been drinking?"

I squirm, the exam table suddenly uncomfortably hard. "Um, two or three cups a day."

"And?" Dr. Barnes prods.

I brace myself, which leads me to realize that I'm *confessing* and thus have probably done something *wrong*. "I've also discovered Monster, Red Bull, and Starbucks Doubleshot. The last of which is really tasty, I might add."

"And 5-hour Energy. I'd recommend not drinking that at all," offers Dr. Peach Fuzz. So helpful.

"Emmaline Leigh! You know better than to put that garbage into your body!" The hospital vending machine coffee Dad *literally* holds in his hand right now undermines his message just a smidge, but I'm not about to go there right now. Caffeine *is* a chemical aid, though I'd never thought of it in the same way I'd thought of Adderall or other drugs. It sucks to realize I'm a hypocrite after all.

Dr. Barnes rocks back and forth on his heels. "I'm guessing she's been very tired. And needing more and more help—caffeine—to do the things she wants to do. Is that right, Emmy?"

"Things I *need* to do, but yeah. I guess so."

He lays his hand on my shoulder. "It's okay to go slower. Or not be the best at something. No one would fault you."

Dad says nothing, but his eyes plead. *Can you stay out of the path of the sun just this once, Emmy?*

Twenty minutes later, I've got an IV in my arm and an exhausted dad across the room. I'm cold. *Really* cold, like my body is full of ice water. Glancing down at the needle jabbed into the crook of my elbow and the half-empty bag of clear fluid rhythmically pumping into it, I remember that I basically *am* an icy-cold water balloon now.

In every conceivable way.

Dad's typing away on his phone. Drafting policy? Texting Mom? I open my mouth to ask him but it's all gummy, stuck together.

He's by my side in a blink, holding out a girthy, hospital-issued plastic water bottle. "Here, Sweets." Still taking care of me, even after I blew off doctor's appointments and medications and treated my body like a hazardous waste container.

I sip from the giant bendy straw. The water is too cold but delicious, like something I've waited my whole life to taste, a magical, life-enhancing elixir. "Thanks, Dad," I say, but it comes out sounding like "Croak, croak." I shiver.

He tucks the rough blue hospital blanket under my shoulders. "Are you still cold?"

I want to say no but I can't stop shaking. I nod, and Dad leaves our curtained-off area, returning a few seconds later with another blanket. It's warm like it's just been pulled out of the dryer, and a grateful sigh eases out of me.

He smooths stray hairs back from my clammy forehead. "Rest. We'll be home soon."

I close my eyes and force deep breaths, but it's all an act, because the inside of me is anything but calm.

I've done this to myself. All of it.

And it's up to me to figure my way out.

TWENTY-NINE

DAD AND I DRIVE HOME from the hospital in silence. A soft patter of rain and the swish of windshield wipers is our only music. I let my head loll on the passenger-side window, which is chilly against my still-too-cold body, but I'm too tired to care.

The Jeep has only just come to a stop in our driveway when my door pops open, startling me. Mom pulls me gently out of the vehicle and into her arms, and for some reason I'm crying all over again. "I'm sorry," I say into her shoulder, strangled words too high-pitched, too weak to be mine.

"For what?"

"For letting you down. I'm not going to nationals." *I didn't win. I'm not the best this time.*

She holds me out by my shoulders. My eyes shy away but she tips my chin up toward her. "I'm proud of you. *So* proud. The way you stood up for what you thought was right, even though it meant giving up your dream? That's braver than anything I've ever done."

"But now they all know. The media. About the Crohn's disease. Is this going to be like what happened to Issy?"

"Oh, honey." Mom looks like she's in pain, and I hate that I did that to her. "I'm so, so sorry that I haven't been able to keep you and your sisters safer. No one deserves to have their private lives flaunted like yours have been. But I promise I will do everything in my power to control the narrative on this. And you call the shots. If you want to talk about it or take interviews, you can. If you never want to talk about it again, that's also fine."

"But what about what's best for—"

"*No*, Emmy. It's your body. It's your decision. It doesn't matter what's 'best' for me or my campaign or politics or *any* of that. You hear me? *You* are my priority."

And then she disappears behind my tears and I let her hold me as I sob. Not a senator and her protégée, just a mom and her daughter.

Light streams through the cracks of my curtains. The clock says it's 10:30 a.m.

Whoa. The last time I remember was 10:00 p.m. After the hospital and a few minutes of much-needed Mom time, I'd gone up to my room, shucked off my clothes, and hopped into bed in just my sports bra and undies. It's been a long, long while since I've had this many hours of sleep in a row. I should be a whole new girl today, ready to take on the world. Yet I feel more like a corpse than a conqueror. My thoughts are fuzzy and slow, my face is gross from not washing it, and my mouth tastes like something died in it. Worse yet, the memory of yesterday's living nightmare eats at my bones, a slow decay. No nationals. Dreams shot to hell. My friendship with Liv, ruined. And the news outlets are probably having a heyday with my demise. Two headlines: "Oldest Crawford Daughter Cracks under Pressure, Forfeits Debate Match." "Senator Crawford's Daughter Rumored to Be Hospitalized for Overdose." All of which is technically true, but the spin matters. The spin could kill us.

I should be putting my finger right on the pulse of the situation, so I can do my best to get ahead of it. But my cadaver arms are too heavy to check for signs of paparazzi life. I can't pick up my phone. Not yet.

All I really feel capable of is smacking my sticky tongue against the roof of my mouth.

"Here," says a voice, scaring me so badly that I gasp. Issy's sitting in my desk chair, holding a sweaty bottle of water.

"Good Lord. What're you doing in here?" I slowly push myself upright in bed and accept the water.

"Waiting for you to wake up." Which is all shades of weird, as I'm the early riser, Issy's the late sleeper. "You're cute when you're asleep," she adds.

"And you're creepy for watching me."

She swings her legs around and straddles the chair, leaning her chin on the headrest. "You're gonna want to take that back."

"Or else what?"

"Or else I won't give you that." She juts a thumb at the white box on the desk behind her.

"Ooooh. Is it—"

"Duh."

"Okay. You're only a tiny bit creepy."

"That's acceptable."

Issy hands me the box and I pop it open immediately. As the gorgeous smell of peanut butter hits, I realize I'm ravenous and jam the Pretty Bitchin' CakeCup unceremoniously into my mouth. "Please let there be a Baked and Wired in my next life." Chocolate crumbs spray out of my mouth, onto the bedspread.

Issy wrinkles her nose. "Cute."

"Is there any coffee?" My head aches in the *I need caffeine* way.

She looks aghast, then it clicks as to why.

"Never mind." In lieu of what I'm convinced would be a glorious cup of coffee, I wash my cake down with water and two Tylenol.

"I've got another surprise for you!" Issy says, now brandishing her laptop.

"Ugh, please no more rom-coms. If I have to sit through 'OMG you are the worst but I loved you allllll along' one more time—"

"No, no. Not that." Issy squeezes into bed beside me and lays the computer across our laps. She clicks play and the first image is a big wooden front door. *Our* front door. The camera pans through the entrance and follows Lucy, flitting around our foyer in her Thanksgiving dress.

"Oh! It's done?"

"Dropped first thing this morning. But I wanted to watch it with you, so I waited."

Our "A Holiday with the Crawfords" video starts with talking head scenes of Mom, then Dad. Issy and I in the kitchen—they've framed it like we're chatting, though the truth is we're arguing over recipes. When Gabe and Mari arrive we really do look like a holiday ad, a shiny-happy family overjoyed to greet their friends. Cooking shots, food shots, Gabe and I so nicely handling oven sharing. All of us laughing around the dining room table as Mom's voice intones over the top. It ends with a shot of Mom and Dad holding hands at the helm of the dining room, the rest of us still eating behind them, blurred.

It's a good video. For campaign purposes, anyway. We look cohesive yet fun, and somehow the shabby dining room floor lends authenticity. *We're not perfect*, whisper the scratched, worn-out planks. And oddly, it works. I *like* how the floor makes our home look *real*.

Two beeps and another screen flashes, this one labeled "Outtake Reel." Here, we've got some footage of Dad corralling Lucy, me arguing with Lucy, Lucy smoking Mari at chess. It's pretty much the Crawford 3 show until a scene takes us back to the kitchen. Gabe and I over cranberries. I grind and he peels with an intensity that pops off the screen. He's sneaking peeks at me while I work. Looking just like he does before he digs into a scone.

And then there's me. Me, who prides herself on being *such* an actress, wears everything on her face in this footage. When my eyes well up (from the cranberry juice spray, ha), my hurt over-flows with them. As I take this damning evidence in, I breathe and remember, *Okay, he's about to leave the room now.* But before that, a pause that I don't remember being quite this long or even close to this loaded. In that moment, he and I are mirrors. And I'd like to say it's only desire splashed across our flushed cheeks and hunched shoulders, but it's so obviously *more*.

We fade to black, and Issy's reflection flickers off the dark computer screen. One look at her and I know—what I saw in those outtakes wasn't just a projection. Issy sees it the same.

She closes the laptop, a little too hard.

My fried brain tries to move fast—I need half-truths and excuses, *stat*. "I can explain."

"There's nothing to explain."

"No, seriously. That isn't what it looks like."

"Emmy, I—"

"Right away at Liv's party, I could tell you liked Gabe, and I thought I could get myself to *stop* liking him and—"

"I already know. I know you used to date him, even if you never called it dating or whatever. I've known it all along."

My blood flashes hot then cold then hot again. "All along?"

"Since the party at Liv's. I didn't know about Gabe before that. By the way, I can't believe you never told me you were seeing someone sophomore year."

"That wasn't a great year for you, Is. You were new to Frida's and freaked out—"

"What in the hell does that have to do with *you*? You don't think I'd want to hear about something good in your life, even when I'm not good?"

262

Issy's sharpness throws me off. "I . . . guess I wasn't thinking about it in that way."

"You never do, Em. Still. Anyway, when I met Gabe at the party he asked if I had a sister, we figured out that he knew you, and he told me that you used to hang out. A lot. And that he ghosted, but that he felt awful about that. He was dying to see you again but didn't know if he should, until I came along. I believe his exact words were 'It felt like the Universe aligned in my favor for once.'"

The Universe kept finding and finding us. At debate tournaments. At Safe Space. At Liv's party. And now again. Maybe Gabe had been right about it all along, that day in the closet.

"So I came up with a plan, along with Gabe, to get you two back together. I thought if we hung out in group settings you'd eventually relax and realize how great Gabe is and everything would be fine and you would be happy."

Of course Issy had gone all in on a half-cooked, uber-cheesy scheme. There's nothing more Issy than that. "And Gabe went along with that?"

"Yeah. He has a certain flair for the romantic. Honestly, though, I think he would have done anything. For you."

"But . . . you like Gabe. *You're* dating Gabe."

She shakes her head violently. "We aren't. Never were. Anytime we were talking, it was about the plan. And I tried so hard to make it be you and Gabe! I talked him up constantly. I was *always* pushing for him and you to be the duo when we were with others."

I put on these new lenses and look back. On our group date night, Issy made sure Gabe and I sat together in Bumblebee, and in the karaoke bar. She'd assigned Gabe to work with me in the kitchen on Thanksgiving, and then conversed forever with Mari after dinner so he and I would be left alone. Every time she Snapped with Gabe or went on and on about him, I thought it was part of her crush . . . but she was talking him up for my benefit? And plotting?

Issy shakes her head. "We didn't count on the Aaron factor."

"What do you mean, the Aaron factor?"

"When we all started hanging out, I thought you'd naturally drift toward Gabe. But then you seemed to genuinely *like* Aaron. I mean, we both saw you kissing him on the stoop after karaoke! So then over time, Gabe and I started to think that maybe . . . that was the way. If you were going to fall for Aaron, then so be it. You seemed happy. At least, happy-ish. Gabe was always adamant that he just wanted you to be happy. Like I do."

I put my head in my hands as new terrible questions crash through my skull. "Wait. Was Aaron in on this whole thing?"

"No. But here's one for you: If you were into Gabe *this entire time*, did you consider Aaron's feelings?"

"Yes!" I'm burning all over, because defensiveness feels like that—a gross heat rash.

Issy gives me a look that's straight-up from the book of Cat Crawford.

"Maybe not as much as I could have. But we were just hanging out, nothing serious! No labels, no expectations. It was fun and distracting. And . . . I wanted Gabe to pay for what he did to me."

"Ugh, Emmy. I know he hurt you with the ghosting, but jeez."

"Not just the ghosting. He was behind one of the SenatorSlush incidents, the time they posted the 'Crawford daughter doesn't want her mom to be president' thing. I said something like that to Gabe, and only Gabe, and the very next day the thing was live."

She showcases her feels rapid-fire: shock, confusion, and finally, anger. "And you didn't think to tell me that? *Even* when you thought I was dating Gabe?"

"I didn't want you to know anything about us, and that would have outed me. I was rolling the dice on him not hurting you in the same way." My nails cut into still-raw-from-regionals cuticles.

She goes quiet for a few ticks. "Well, at least you're a consistent liar."

I flinch.

Issy seems not to notice and pushes on. "Also, I'm not sure I buy that Gabe leaked that info."

"He's the only one who was there to hear it! And he's apologized for the betrayal. Not that it matters."

"It just doesn't sit right, doesn't feel like something Gabe would do."

"Tell me about it," I mutter.

Issy presses on. "Anyway, though, back to my point—you've at least *sort of* been using Aaron."

"With informed consent!"

"I don't think so, sister. The way he looks at you is just like the way you were looking at Gabe in that Thanksgiving special footage."

She might be right, but I'm too angry to admit that. "Whatever about Aaron—*you've* got more shit to explain. Such as, why not just *tell* me that Gabe was interested again? He could have. You could have. Why this convoluted dating scheme?"

"You make it sound like he didn't try—he did! The coffee asks, the Snapchats."

I roll my eyes. "Weak."

"You're proving my point for me, so thanks."

"How's that?"

"Listen to yourself! You're so stubborn. So I *knew* you wouldn't just *see him* again. And I felt bad for him. The other thing was that I wanted freedom to start seeing people, but you're . . . well, you're kind of controlling, Emmy."

My limbs flash hotter. "Are you kidding me right now?"

"Look, I know it comes from a good place. You've always been my protector. But I've grown a lot in the past year and it's like you can't even see it."

"And *this* is how you choose to show me. By meddling in my personal business."

"How is that so different than how you've treated me, for *years*?"

How dare she possibly be ungrateful for everything I've done. Everything I've given up, to keep her happy and healthy. "Wow."

"I'm sorry if it's hurtful, but it's true. No matter what I do, you still can't trust me to take care of myself. So I thought . . ." She stops, closes her eyes, pushes the next words out in a rush. ". . . that if you got a life of your own, you wouldn't be so focused on mine."

That more than stings. It *burns*; *everything* burns. My eyes sear, my chest is on fire.

And I'm out of things to say. Instead I sit on my absolute mountain of feelings—betrayal, rage, embarrassment—and will myself not to cry. Not again. I don't even have enough fluid left in me for that.

I wad the bakery box up into a ball, the sound of it deafening after so much silent tension.

"I think you should go," I finally say.

"If that's what you want," Issy says. I nod, she leaves, and I crumple.

When I throw myself back into bed, one arm finds an unexpected lump in the blankets. I reach in and yank out a heavy, cellophane-wrapped pastry.

The vaguely triangular gift bears a Post-it note. *Someone dropped this off. He said you'd know who. —Mom*

Because Gabe finds a way to wend himself into every part of my life. My head, my heart, my relationship with my sister. And now my bed, and not the way I *thought* he might make his debut there, once upon a time.

A part of me wants to hurl this scone across the room, and all thoughts of Gabe with it. I'm still reeling with information. He's not dating Issy. He never was. Issy's not into him, and her involvement with him was *all* for me. So many games, so much subterfuge was enacted on my behalf. And for what? A tiny, rational voice whispers, *Issy was trying to help*, but goddamn it, sometimes good intentions fail and sometimes they hurt others. And I'm deeply humiliated that Issy and Gabe thought they could manipulate me back into his arms.

And yet the sticky cellophane remains between my hands. The part of me that isn't hurt wants it right here, and of course that's the part of me that wins. I'm much too full to eat but I lie back and set the pastry on my chest, close enough that I can smell butter and citrus and my past.

Try as I might, I can never seem to stop wanting Gabe close.

THIRTY

I SLEEP TWO MORE HOURS with the scone on my chest. One of the weirder things I've ever done, but you can't accuse me of being boring. When I wake I'm hungry again and dig in, managing to both demolish and savor the pastry. Much like I'd always done with the gift giver's words.

Ugh, all this sappy, pointless reminiscing. Get a life. The thought comes automatically, but then, what else is there to do? Dad has already announced that I will not be leaving the house today and that my "only job is to rest." Which I get is probably a good idea after an ER visit, but that doesn't mean it's easy for me.

Since my body's forced into inertia, I might as well let my head go where it wants. Back to Gabe. How he must have gotten up early and gone to Safe Space to pick up the pastry (unless he keeps a stash in his house, which I wouldn't put past him), and then made a special trip across town early this morning to drop it off. Did he leave it with Mom and go? Stay and hang out in the house while I slept? It shouldn't matter, but still, my brain wants to know every detail. I could ask Issy . . . but no. I'm not ready to talk to her.

I could ask Gabe.

But I'm not ready to talk to him, either.

My phone remains plugged in on my bedside table, untouched for the longest time since I've owned it. It awaits me like a gift. Or a grenade.

I don't know if I'm ready to deal with the aftermath of yesterday. I don't know if I'll ever be ready.

My door flies open and Lucy trots in, carrying a picnic basket. "Lunch!" she announces, spreading a red-and-white checked gingham blanket on my floor, the one our family takes with us when we go eat at the park. From my perch on the bed I watch her unload sandwiches, baby carrots, a container of her much-beloved hummus. A plastic container of sliced cheddar and salami. Apples and bananas and bottles of water.

"Wow, Luce. Did you put this together?"

"Yep."

"For me?" And *because my eyes are now just tiny sieves*, they get wet again. Which is proof enough that I am not yet back to normal.

But Lucy doesn't seem to notice. She pats the ground beside her. "Yep. Let's eat."

"Okay. This looks great!" And it does. I may have just finished a scone, but the lure of salty cheese and meat is real. I'm weaker than I expect as I lever myself slowly upright and then down to the floor, but no white dizzy-stars behind my eyes so far today. Baby steps.

Lucy and I chomp on our PB&Js and the rest of the picnic spread as she fills me in on some third-grade drama—which she usually doesn't share with me, but then again, when do I take the time to sit and listen to her? Today, I guess. And maybe more often after this, because she's pretty entertaining when she's not being a shit.

"Are you sick?" she says, after a bit.

"Sort of."

"Well, you look better than you did yesterday, but still kinda bad."

Usually I'd take offense to that. But today, her cocked little head is all genuine curiosity. Maybe a tiny bit of worry, too.

"I just got worn out. I'll catch up on sleep and be back to normal soon," I say.

"Mom says that too much coffee and not enough self-care is a bad combination. Is that what happened to you?"

"Close enough."

Lucy picks at the last bite of a round of salami. "That's what Dad does, too. You've seen him—he drinks like a whole pot of coffee every day! And no toast or anything with it. And then he and Mom work all the time, just like you. Are they going to be okay?"

The truth hits me like a tidal wave. I *am* so like my parents, and that means both the commendable and the less-than-great things.

When I think of *work, my* work, I have positive feelings—pride and passion and a sense of duty. Yet when I think of my parents' work, I can't help but think of the undereye circles, and how they're always gone, and how it took us away from our grandparents.

Lucy sees the nasty underbelly of my workaholism in a way I keep hidden from myself. She must, because she sees me and my parents as the same. It's kind of unfair that at nine she's not only a chess wizard but also socially observant.

"Mom and Dad will be okay. They do work hard, but they do it because their work is really important. And they know how to take care of themselves."

"Do you?" Lucy's too-old eyes are flanked by clip-on earrings.

"Well, I'm going to need to learn how to do better, right?"

"Yes! I was thinking that tomorrow we could go to Target—that's fun, not work. And Dad says you are supposed to drink all those waters." She points into the picnic basket, which still holds three unopened bottles.

"Aye-aye, captain."

The cheese and the water and maybe even the time with my weird little sister wind up being surprisingly restorative. After Lucy packs up the basket and goes, I contemplate my phone. No time like the present to tackle the things I've been putting off. Yet also, I think of my tired parents, and the rush of ice-cold IV fluids. I probably *do* need to rest.

I decide to try "rest multitasking"—is that a thing? I get back in bed and snuggle under my blankets, but bring my phone with me.

I will, as always, do the hardest things first.

Task One: damage control. I Google my name to see what new news has been posted. Pictures from yesterday? An outside shot of Georgetown Hospital, with a dramatic headline? I click and I scan, check all my Google alerts . . . and there's nothing. No word, no mention of the debate spectacle or my trip to the hospital. A cursory scroll through SenatorSlush is also clean. I say a quick yet very earnest "thank you" to whatever gods (or attorneys) are in charge right now.

Task Two: making amends. I am so buried in text notifications that my entire text app screen is all bold and black, the previews full of OMG R U OKAY and <3 <3 <3 Get Well Soon and Thinking Of You.

I bypass them all until I find Liv's unread message, sent last night.

> LIV: I . . . am not sure what to say. What happened was a lot. Please know that I'm super worried about you and want you to be okay, though. Text me when you get this. XOXO

I start typing, stop, erase. Then I do it again. Everything coming out of me sounds defensive, and that's not what my debate partner and best friend, who trusted me implicitly, needs from me right now. I steel myself and type the easiest hardest thing.

> EMMY: I am so, so sorry
> LIV: It's . . . well. I want to say it's okay? It is and it isn't
> EMMY: I know
> LIV: I wish you would have just talked to me. About everything. If I knew you were struggling with the

Crohn's stuff, we could have like . . . gone slower, taken more rests

EMMY: Honestly, I was hiding how sick I've been even from myself. I didn't want to look at it. It's how I usually cope with the disease. Turns out that's not working very well

LIV: Yeah, turns out. But what about the part where you bowed out? I *know* how much you wanted nationals and to do that instead? It's like . . . I've got mad respect for that. But did you think I wouldn't want to come with you? Take that same stand? I would have liked the chance to *really* be on your team, like we always are

For a moment I lay my phone down, because *this* hits. Hard. Granted, I didn't know I was going to forfeit the debate until I was literally doing it, but still. I could have taken some time between arguments to talk with Liv about what I thought was right, or even let her know ahead of time that I was having serious issues with the subject matter—and the idea of debating across the podium from Gabe, especially. And I didn't, even when she gave me multiple openings to come clean. I didn't treat her like my true teammate, my true equal, and instead just took the ball and ran with it all on my own.

Have I been doing the same with Issy? Ice cubes lodge behind my sternum.

EMMY: You are so right, and I am sorry. I should have said more about what was going on with me. I should have trusted that you would see my stance on forfeiting, and

274

given you the option to join me or not, instead of taking us both down without your consent. It was impulsive and inconsiderate. I really fucked up. And I'm so sorry I took away your shot at nationals.

LIV: I appreciate that apology a lot. I'm still having some feelings about everything but I think they're gonna blow over. Because I love you and we're all messed up in our own way, you know?

Is this forgiveness? I don't deserve it, but still her words hit my icy chest like summer sunshine.

LIV: Besides, nationals is still a thing for me

EMMY: Wut

My phone rings and for once I'm grateful, because typing with shaking hands was getting hard. I skip the pleasantries and go with, "What do you mean, nationals is still a thing?"

"You haven't talked to *anyone*?" Liv sounds incredulous.

"This is the first time I've been on my phone since I hit the floor, and I texted you first."

"Aww. Well, that helps me to feel even a little bit better."

"I'm so glad, but spill. What's going on?"

"Emmy, we won. Taylor and I."

"You're kidding."

"Would I kid about this? We did it. For real. We're going to nationals."

The jealousy comes for me like a knife in the back. *Ouch*. This is why I don't do feelings. Yet then my heart hands me images of Liv's face, up there onstage, having just earned the right to the most major of the debate stages. Pride eases in, sharing space with envy. She's my best friend and equal and every bit as talented as I am but she never once questioned that it would be *me* who went to nationals. Because she knows how badly I wanted it, how much of my identity is wrapped around debate and being the best at everything. It's not like that for her. *She's* not like that.

I could stand to be more like her.

"That's awesome. You and Taylor will be great!" The words sting but still feel true and right, working their way across my lips. They *will* be great.

"Thank you! You're . . . okay, with this?"

I take another stab at that *thing* I've been piloting lately. Honesty. "Well, it's hard, too. But I know you guys are going to slay! I'm happy for you."

Sometimes relief is audible, as it is in Liv's exhale. "More work ahead of us, though. Jeremiah's probably has nothing on who we'll see at nationals."

Oh yeah. Jeremiah's. I grip the phone a little tighter as I brace for the details. "How did the final debate go down?"

"It was a close match, but in the end, Taylor's new stuff was too much for them. Since she and John had faced them earlier in the day, she'd figured out some weak points in their arguments. And Vanderford is good, but he's just not as smooth without Gabe."

"Wait—without Gabe?"

"We chatted during your . . . incident. He was super rattled. And he bowed out of the debate like you. Same reason. Human rights shouldn't be up for debate."

My heart squeezes and soars in a confusing mishmash of emotion. It's sympathy. Or empathy. Both? I'm not sure.

Liv interrupts my ponderings. "By the way . . . is it time to get real about your feels for that boy?"

"He hurt me. Multiple times. I'll fill you in on all of it some other day. And by the way, did you know that Issy was in cahoots with him, trying to get us together?"

Liv's silence says multitudes.

"No. Not you too."

"I'm sorry, Emmy. I did my best to stay out of it, but I honestly thought what Issy was up to was good for you. I say this with love, but you need to get a life, you know?"

So I keep hearing. "Yeah, yeah. Maybe after Dad releases me from mandatory resting."

"Unfortunately I'm with your fam again on this. Get some rest. I'll be here when you're better."

"Ugh, fine. Thank you, but fine."

"That fainting shit was scary. Don't do that again. Although I think John and Taylor were more hurt than scared maybe."

"Hurt? Why?"

"They didn't know about the Crohn's. So they feel out of the loop with this big important thing in your life."

My cuticles are picked to shreds at this point. "I . . . didn't think anyone would really want to know about it. It's a gross disease. And I didn't want anybody's pity."

Liv pauses before she begins again. "Remember when my parents got divorced and I told you *everything*? Every fight, every worry, every time my mom tried to pump me for information about my dad?"

"Yeah, of course I do."

"Did you pity me?"

"No."

"That's what I'm talking about, Emmy. You were my person through all of that and your support was everything. You were there even when I was messy."

"But I hate being messy," I whisper.

"You think I like it?" Liv's response is a cross between a laugh and an accusation.

"I'm thinking not."

"Sometimes spilling our guts isn't about asking for pity. It's to let people *know* you. The real you. John and Taylor want to know *her*. We all do."

I think back to the way the dining room floor looked in the Thanksgiving special video. Pockmarked, imperfect. Real. A backdrop for our family that matched.

"This is a lot of truth to sit with, Liv. But I'll work on it."

"Good enough. By the way, I guess I wanted to say like . . . sorry, I guess, for beating Jeremiah's? I mean, not really, but I know you're close to both of them."

More pain, pelting my rib cage. Poor Gabe. Poor Aaron. "Yeah. Kind of a weird situation, but thanks. I do feel bad for them. They wanted nationals as much as we did."

"Lady, you really *have* been off your phone. You haven't heard?"

"Haven't heard what?"

"A few teams with really good records still got picked to go to nationals. Wild card picks. Jeremiah's is going. Gabe told me it'd be him and Vanderford again, as long as the topic isn't universal health care."

My grin is so sudden and so wide, my lips crack, but that doesn't stop me from smiling until we're done talking.

Then it's onto Task Three: pick up the trash. Slowly, I thumb through the rest of my avalanche of notifications, focusing on just the priority people for right now. I reply to John and congratulate Taylor and apologize to both of them for not being more forth-coming. Then I bang out a quick response to an all-debate-team email from Toomey re my collapse.

Hey all, thanks for your concern. I'm doing fine and will see you back at school on Monday!

No sooner than I've hit send and reread my own words do I realize I'm doing it again—glossy half-truths, the kind that keep trusted others at arm's length. I try again in another short reply.

About the Crohn's disease. It's not something I love talking about because I like to pretend I don't have it. But I do have it. If anyone has questions, it's okay to ask. Please know that I wasn't trying to be eva-sive, I just didn't know what to say.

—ELC

Which is a *lot* of honesty and it's hard and immediately I sort of wish I could take it back. But what's done is done; the email is already lost to cyberspace, shooting into inboxes as soon as my fin-ger left the mouse. I breathe and remind myself: I do want these people to know me. My debate friends are my closest friends.

279

And I have another friend, recently close, who I need to get real with.

> AARON: Hey, social justice warrior. Text me when you're up
>
> EMMY: I'm up
>
> AARON: Hi! You're alive!
>
> EMMY: Mostly
>
> AARON: hahaha. I assume you've heard all the news?
>
> EMMY: Yep. Congrats!
>
> AARON: And to you. I mean Liv and Taylor, anyway
>
> EMMY: I'm happy for them. Truly
>
> AARON: And not disgruntled at all?
>
> EMMY: Of course it's hard to not get the thing I always wanted. But I got something else I wanted
>
> AARON: A dramatic collapse? Being whisked into the arms of a hunky ER doctor?
>
> EMMY: LOL. To stand up for what I thought was right. To really *say* something
>
> AARON: Well technically you didn't stand
>
> EMMY: Too soon, man
>
> AARON: Anyway, you want my hot take on the whole thing?
>
> EMMY: Fire away
>
> AARON: There could have been other ways of standing on principle that did *not* involve unilateral decisions and screwing debate partners over
>
> EMMY: Ouch. But yeah. I'm working on all that. Sorry about what happened with you guys. I think
>
> AARON: It all worked out. Yay wild card draws!

EMMY: Can we hang out?

AARON: Damn girl, get right back up on that horse

EMMY: I'm a bad rester

AARON: Who would've thought

EMMY: I think I'll be off house arrest by this evening. Pick
me up at 7?

AARON: Aye aye

Issy's accusations about me and my treatment of Aaron have not
been sitting well—which, sadly, makes me think she's onto something. Which means I'll have to do more hard things, which doesn't
really seem fair given that I've already been pummeled over the last
twenty-four hours, but as Dad so loves to remind us, *life's not always
fair.*

And I still have one more hard notification left to tackle. I hold
my breath as I click, hardly knowing what to expect, *especially*
given Issy's confession.

GABE: Hi

GABE: I know how much you wanted nationals

GABE: And anyone can see your passion for debate

GABE: But now the world can see some other things about
you. Empathy. And pain

GABE: Weird as this might sound, knowing about your
sickness makes me feel closer to you. It helped me
understand some things about you, I think

GABE: My life is really not normal, but that doesn't stop me
from wanting normal life stuff too. Like winning at

281

debate. And sometimes I try to not pay attention to the hard stuff and I pretend I'm okay because it's the only way to ever even get close to the life I think I want or need

GABE: Is that why you never told me about the Crohn's disease? To feel normal? It's why I usually don't tell people about Mom

GABE: Anyway. I guess all I'm trying to say is that now . . . I see you. I thought I always did but now more than ever. You gave me the courage to forfeit at regionals, which I probably should have done all along

GABE: I'm so grateful for you

GABE: I want to say so much more but it would take too many words for a screen. Also, maybe not fair to drop *all* my feels without your consent. But if you ever want to hear them, say the word. I'll find you

With trembling hands I bring the phone almost to my nose, like being close to my screen would bring me closer to him. I read the messages three, four, five times, each time picking a different sentence to burn myself with. Tears flow freely, surprising me. I didn't think I had any left in me. I chug one of my many bottles of water, as I can't really afford any more water loss at the moment.

"*All* my feels." What do you feel, Gabe?

Much as I'd like to find out, the truth of our situation is unshakable. It doesn't matter that he was so motivated to get me back in his life, he went along with one of Issy's harebrained schemes. It also doesn't matter that I think I can forgive him for the absence that came with his mom's illness. What matters is this: he leaked my secret, shameful thoughts to SenatorSlush and I'm not over it. Maybe I can't get over it.

My thumbs hover long moments over the screen before finally choosing a response.

EMMY: I'm okay

I'm not sure I've ever told a bigger lie.

THIRTY-ONE

AARON AND BUMBLEBEE ARRIVE AT 6:50.

I'm sure gonna miss this guy's punctuality. Among other things, probably.

Lucy greets him in that weird, washed-up Hollywood starlet way that she has, Maple losing her shit underfoot. Aaron takes it all in stride, matching Lucy's old lady energy, patting Maple on the head. So chill. Almost too chill. He's got this bubble of logic and calm that he lives in and it never pops. Which probably helps him in debate—it's sure as hell easier to argue a topic if it doesn't *move* you. Yet I'm realizing his charming coolness keeps me at arm's length. Does anyone else *ever* see the real Aaron?

Pot, meet kettle.

Aaron drives us back to that abandoned parking lot. "I thought we could try another driving lesson."

"Uh, I don't know. That didn't go so well last time."

"C'mon. It's a life skill you need to have."

I'm nervous, but still I push open the passenger door. This will probably be my last shot at *this* life lesson—at least, in *this* car with *this* boy—why not give it one final go? I get situated in the driver's seat and clamp my hands at nine and three.

"Okay, now remember. Release the clutch as you depress the gas . . ."

I kill the engine. And then I kill it again. I lay my head on the wheel, between my sore-from-gripping-too-hard hands.

"You'll get it. Let's take a little break and we'll try again." He runs a finger down my cheekbone, feather-light. "C'mere. Let's use your break time wisely."

My shoulders come up around my ears and stiffen. Aaron draws his hand back like he's been burned.

I force myself to look right at him. "Okay, so, we need to talk."

"No conversation starting with that phrase has ever ended well for the other person." He slumps back in his seat.

"Look. This whole . . . whatever . . . between us has been way more fun than I ever expected."

"This *whatever*. What is *this* to you?" he asks, gesturing to the space between us.

"Um. I was thinking of it like a friends with benefits operation."

"Close enough. Though I was hoping maybe someday . . ."

I let my silence speak for me.

"Wow. Okay, then," he says, facing straight forward again. "I mean, I know I didn't exactly dazzle you with my first impression.

But then after karaoke, everything was different."

"It was, yeah. And since then I've learned that you're silly and kind. Fun. Incredibly good-looking. And you like me even when I'm saucy."

"Especially when you're saucy." I get a full-on smile, a real one, but it fades so fast it's like it never happened. "But it's not enough."

I worry my hoodie strings. "It's . . . I just don't think we're right for each other." And I swallow my cringe, as I can't believe I've said *that* again. I seriously need to prepare a better breakup script.

"Because I'll never be Gabe. That's the issue, right?"

I swallow, hard. "It is. And there's more."

"Yeah?"

"I was . . ." I stop and put my thumb cuticle in my mouth, as blood is starting to drip down my hand. "This is really hard. I'm trying to be more honest with myself and others and it honestly *sucks*."

"Just hit me with it, babe."

"Ew, don't call me that."

"Doesn't sound like I'll have any need to, after today."

"Fair. Okay. So, here's the truth. I started spending time with you to make Gabe jealous. And to be a distraction from my feelings toward him."

His face falls and this puts a stranglehold on my windpipe. I babble on, "But as we got to know each other it was more than that. I like you. I'm attracted to you. We have fun together. It's just that I'm lying to myself and to you and to everyone if I try to make this anything other than that."

286

He lays his head back against his seat, letting his eyes fall closed. "If we're working on honesty: this hurts."

I ache in knowing I'm causing him pain, but there's gratitude in me too, because he's being real. "I'm sorry."

"Much as I'm tempted to try to talk you out of this, I know you too well to try. And I'd be lying if I said I didn't know how you felt about Gabe. Any idiot could see it. I always knew, and I went along with it anyway."

"Again, I'm sorry."

He shrugs. "I can see how much it cost you to be up-front with me."

"Yeah?"

"You're literally paler than my bedsheets. And they're like eight-hundred-thread-count hotel white and get washed every week."

I catch a glimpse of myself in the rearview mirror, and he's right. My face looks sunken, hollow. "It's been a rough couple of days. I'm exhausted."

"Never thought I'd hear *you* admit defeat."

"I'm trying not to lie so much, to myself or anyone else. Which is about as fun as being mauled by a garbage truck."

"Sounds hard." His jaw's working overtime again, and he messes with the zipper on his leather jacket.

"Important, but yeah."

There's a long pause before he offers, "I guess if we're doing this, there's something I need to show you. In the spirit of veracity."

"Okay?"

He fiddles with his phone for a few seconds, then hands it over.

I'm looking at an email. It's one line of text. Teenage daughter of Senator Catalina Crawford doesn't want her mother to be president.

I scroll up. Message recipient is SenatorSlush@gmail.com.

Message sender is SmoothSesquipedalian@icloud.com.

I stare at the screen forever, because it makes no sense. Gabe's iCloud handle is SconeMaster.

And then it hits me with the force of a bucket of water upended over my head.

"You."

He hitches his chin and I see a glimmer of his old cocky disguise, but quickly, it falls. He's sheepish, eyes crinkling in guilt.

"How *could* you?" My voice is shrill, like I've been sucking helium.

"On a lot of Sunday nights we have these informal debate team 'jams,' and one night Gabe showed up *pissed*. When we asked him why, he spilled. 'I've been rejected by someone I really care about and I don't know why' were his exact words. I always remember words just as they were said."

I gulp. "Wow."

"There's more, obviously. He went on to say that he'd moved mountains to forgive this girl for something she said, but that she was in her own, privileged world. And that her biggest life problem was that she doesn't want her mom to be the fucking president."

For one thing, ouch. But beyond that, what in the hell had I said that Gabe had to "move mountains" to forgive? And whoa, what, Gabe was trying to forgive *me*?

I'd have to come back to that, though, because I wasn't done

288

filleting Aaron Vanderford. "So I'm guessing you knew who he was talking about."

"It had to be you or Issy, and you were the obvious candidate. And I sent the info to SenatorSlush intentionally vague, in case I got it wrong."

"Gosh, how considerate of you."

He grimaces. "Yeah, it wasn't. It's awful. Maybe almost as awful as using someone to get back at someone else."

I smash my mouth into a line but absorb that blow as gracefully as possible. "Okay. So we both suck."

"Yeah, a little. A lot, maybe. I want you to know, though, that this whole thing went down before I knew you, like *really* knew you. We'd only had that one interaction, after Gabe and I killed you and Liv at that debate tournament, and you were kind of a jerk to me."

"*I* was a jerk to *you*, Mr. Date Me for My Trust Fund?"

"Well, fine. It wasn't my best work."

I snort.

"In any case, sending the information to SenatorSlush was an impulsive mistake. A huge one that I've regretted since."

My pulse is making a case for anger as a form of exercise. "Is that an apology?"

"I'm getting there. I'm so sorry, Emmy. I know the information leak hurt you and your family. I feel terrible. I'd never do it, now."

"You do realize that if it hadn't been *us* you still would have been hurting some other girl, some other family?"

"Yeah, I know. Consideration of others' feelings isn't really my strong suit—or so I've been told—but I'm going to start working on it. I *am* working on it, real time."

My hands are clenched in my lap, useless. I want to move, I want to *bolt*, but I'm stuck here in this car with this guy who isn't what I thought. "You didn't post the other thing, did you? The lingerie pic of Issy?"

"No! God, no."

I sit staring at my clenched hands. What I thought was truth has shattered, and now I'm left scrambling to make the pieces fit back together, but in a new configuration.

"Why did you let Gabe take the blame for it?"

Aaron exhales a long breath, letting his cheeks puff as he blows. "When I saw you in that Expo debate, in all your disastrous glory, I realized my interest in you was going to be more than a fleeting thing. You were so articulate, so . . ." His face scrunches, as he uncharacteristically searches for the right word. "Dynamic! And it was too late by then, I'd already sent the thing, but . . ."

"You let Gabe take one for the team. So you could have a chance with me."

"Essentially, yes."

There's a part of me that wants to scream and spit nails, but the longer I sit, the more I realize my leading feeling isn't anger. It's disappointment. In Aaron. In me. In how this situation turned out.

"For what it's worth, I really am truly sorry. It was such a dick move. All of it." He looks genuinely contrite. Though I wouldn't put it past him to fake remorse, I'm not sure why he would. He chose to come clean about everything on his own volition.

My shoulders are painfully tight and my fingernails are digging deeper and deeper into my raw cuticles, and I'm *this* close to completely writing off Mr. Aaron Vanderford, the Smoothest Sesquipedalian, who it turns out I don't even know.

But I do. I do know him. It's just there are many pieces of him, and some of them he keeps locked down. Just like me.

And then I realize what I have to do and *fuuuucccckkk*.

"Okay, so. This is a lot. A lot lot. And it's going to take me some time but I want to . . ." The words feel sandy in my mouth. I swallow and try again. "Work on forgiveness."

"You serious?"

"As a heart attack. Or maybe Crohn's disease."

"Hilarious. But why?"

"Because I know what it's like to make impulsive choices that end up hurting others."

He sucks air in through his teeth. "You're talking about the debate forfeit?"

"That's one of them. But god, there've been so many. I've done a lot of lying, and hiding, and trying to control situations that weren't mine to run—and I'm now discovering the extent to which these things hurt people I care about." And apparently I hurt Gabe, too, only I don't know how. "A bunch of folks are working on forgiving me. If I deserve forgiveness, then so do you."

He nods, though his brows still come together in confusion. "Okay. Then . . . I guess I'll work on forgiving you, too?"

"I'd appreciate that. We don't have to be besties or anything. But civility would be good."

"Just so I'm clear, is this a self-growth thing or a 'he's friends with Gabe so being civil is practical' kind of thing?"

I remember my Mom's kitchen table words on forgiving Senator Livers. "Both. It can be both." We let that idea ring for a few seconds, giving it the space of semi-comfortable silence. "Anyway, you ready to take me home?" I say, making to open my door.

"In a minute. Let's see if we can end this driving lesson with a little success," he says, gesturing to the steering wheel.

"Are you sure?"

"Yeah, let's do it. Why not?"

"Because I suck at this and have already wreaked havoc on poor Bumblebee?"

"Let our pain be our parting gift. I mean, on top of the other shit."

I sigh. "I'll do my best."

I kill the engine on my first try, and on my second. But on my third I get it to go and accelerate the car around the parking lot, switching gears with Aaron's help. Holy wow.

"See? Doesn't it feel amazing to do something you didn't think you could?" Aaron's face sheds all traces of anger as he splits wide open, all lit up.

I smile just as brightly back at him. "It does, doesn't it?"

Aaron's just dropped me off when my phone buzzes.

> AARON: Sorry, got so caught up in our Camaro
>> Confessional that I forgot one important thing
> EMMY: What's that

AARON: My parents are throwing this holiday party thing
next weekend. Since you (are/were/someday?) a
friend, you're invited. Issy too. And John and Liv and
Taylor. Kinda bonded with the whole team when you,
um . . . hit the ground

EMMY: IDK, that sounds awkward. Especially after . . .
everything?

AARON: Nah, it'll be okay. We can mostly ignore each other

EMMY: Wow, you're really selling it

AARON: Lemme try again: Dresses. Ties. Caviar and also
Bugles and Chex Mix. Music, maybe dancing. It's
basically an opportunity for Mom and Dad to show off
in front of their friends. You know the drill

EMMY: What, are they renting out a place for this?

AARON: No. Our house is sort of, um, big. We've used the
dining room for social events and dances lots of
times

EMMY: Whoa

AARON: yeah

EMMY: Guess it'd be my chance to see how the other other
side lives

AARON: ☺ You could say that

EMMY: I'll think about it

AARON: I really think you should come. Some people will be
there who you probably need to see. Like, one person
particularly

EMMY: Too soon, man

AARON: I know. I also want to puke a little. Tryna be a
decent person though
EMMY: A for effort

I am definitely *not* going. I'm not sure who would define "fun" as "going to a social function at the home of your social media betrayer you are working on forgiving but haven't yet *plus* everyone who just witnessed you having a medical event *plus* Gabe effing Castillo," but it isn't me.

I don't need to tell Aaron yet, though. I've said enough hard things for one day.

THIRTY-TWO

THE AFTERNOON OF VANDERFORD'S SOIREE finds me in bed. In joggers and a T-shirt, no makeup, and absolutely no intention of changing this state of affairs.

Three Reasons I Will Not Be Attending Vanderford's Ridiculous Party
1. Gabe
2. Issy
3. Dignity

Issy and I haven't spoken since the big dating scheme reveal. Not only will I look like a clown without her fashion guidance, but hashing out our problems in front of a slew of rich strangers—*or* our friends, who also just saw me have a medical event—does not sound like a good time.

Neither does seeing Gabe. I'm not ready.

Also, it's highly likely that some kind of media outlet will be there, and I'm so not in the mood. We've just finished a string of family campaign appearances, including another family photo shoot. All of the hand-holding, hugging, and wide-fake-smiling was extra extra gross with the emotional distance between me and Issy, but *we do what we must.*

If it weren't for all of this, I'd totally go to Aaron's party. I'm more than a little curious about the Vanderford mansion, and I could use an excuse to laugh and dance and not be so serious for a night. Aaron has always been good for that, even if he'd have to be good from a distance this time.

All afternoon, I've been listening to the sounds of Issy preparing for the big event. Clomping around the hallway outside my door, I'm guessing a trial run with new heels. A shout of "Mom, can I borrow your little black purse?" and the soft footfall of our mother, no doubt walking to her closet to fetch it. A gaggle of appreciative murmurs and shouts when Issy exits her bedroom and clatters down the stairs in those shoes, which must have soles of lead. The doorbell rings. More high-pitched exchanges, the door shuts, and the house goes quiet again as Issy leaves.

A knock on my door. "Emmy? Don't you need to get ready for the party?"

I curl up into myself a little more. "I'm not going." I purposely waited until now to drop this particular news. I wasn't up for any harassment, and that's what it would have been, if they'd known— constant Mom-hounding, not to mention *Lucy.*

Mom lets herself in. "I wondered. But why?"

I go right for her soft spot. "I'm dizzy."

She crosses her arms and her face settles into Honorable Catalina Crawford. "You wouldn't now be using your recent health scare to get out of a function you should absolutely be attending . . . would you?"

"I didn't bow out of any of the campaign events all week, did I? I showed up for you. But just this once I don't want to show up." And, wonder of wonder, my lie becomes the truth, surprising even me.

Mom sits at the edge of my bed. "You do show up for us. Always. I see it every day."

I blink away tears as I stare studiously at my knees.

"But sometimes you don't show up for you."

How can that be true? I run and I study and I debate practice (*practiced*, I remind myself, with a wave of nausea). I never miss school.

"Tonight is supposed to be a fun night, Emmy. To celebrate and be with your friends. To see you parade around a campaign event with a fake smile but sit this out? I'd rather you reversed it."

"But I *have* to show up for your stuff."

"Any of that could have been rescheduled if your tank was empty. I assure you."

"Right, your campaign people would be *thrilled* about rearranging some big preplanned thing because I was tired."

"The campaign people work for us, honey. Not the other way around."

"Doesn't seem like it."

Mom lays a hand on my leg. "I know. The conundrum of you, my Emmy, is that you come across as tough and self-sufficient and limitless, and I think maybe that's how you see yourself. How you want to be seen. But you live your entire life in the service of trying to make other people happy. You see that, right?"

My tears spill over as the power of what she's saying hits home. I really don't want her to be right . . . but she is. "Yeah. But it's more like: I don't want to let anybody down."

She hugs me to her. "I know."

Of course she does. She might be a bigwig senator now, but she's still Mom and somehow knows everything. She lets me soak the shoulder of her fancy yoga sweatshirt, the second time in as many weeks my careful levees have broken and a parent has shored them up. I burrow myself tighter against her body, hoping she can feel my gratitude without me having to say it.

"You know, when you were a baby, you *never* liked to lay your head down like this. If you were awake, it was head up, eyes out and facing the world, even from the first day home from the hospital. You were a ridiculous bobblehead of a thing, because baby necks aren't meant to support baby heads that early, but you were stubborn. It's like you never wanted to miss anything."

I scoff a little, but my heart is gooey. I've never heard this story.

"But then when you got tired, you wanted to be *right here*, right where you are right now. You would only let yourself be cuddled when you were utterly exhausted. And you're still *exactly* the same. Eyes up, head out, refusing comfort until you're too tired to push it away."

"Are you actually a psychologist, Mom?"

She chuckles. "My second-choice career, if the whole law and politics thing wouldn't have worked out."

"You know, the ER doctor told me that maybe I should see someone. Like a psychologist. Or a therapist like Issy's." I'd never told Mom, or anyone, about this part of my ER visit.

"What do you think?"

I'm prepared to say what I always do, *I can handle it all on my own.* But clearly that isn't working anymore, with all this crashing and burning. "Maybe it's a good idea."

"We'll get it lined up. In the meantime, I can be your helper for the evening."

"Okay, Dr. Mom."

"That's almost as nice as Senator Mom!"

My nose rubs against her neck as I shake my head. "You're the worst."

"I am. Now, what are we going to do about tonight?"

Getting myself dressed and coiffed and plastering on a smile seems impossible, even aside from the tangled-up relationships and feelings I'd have to deal with if I went to the party.

But then . . . there's this *other* thing. A tiny spark. How long has it been since I hung out with my friends in a silly, brainless, no-pressure kind of way? I imagine us laughing on a backdrop of twinkle-light trees and menorahs and fancy finger food. And while pretty dresses and high heels usually aren't my scene, I'm not above getting dolled up once in a while. I even have a real bra now.

"I think I should go. Guess I'm still the baby with FOMO after all."

"That's my girl," Mom says, and boops my nose.

A wave of unwelcome realization plunges into my gut. "Small problem."

"What's that?"

"I don't have anything to wear. I . . . see, I sort of thought all along that I wouldn't go, and so I didn't worry about figuring that out." And without Issy and her aesthetic sensibilities, I'm lost.

Mom is unfazed. "I've got you," she says. Within minutes, she returns with a short satin dress in timeless, elegant black—my signature color! Perfect for something like this party, and it looks like it should fit. I whistle. "Holy smokes. When did you wear this?"

"Inauguration party, my first term. Which was years ago now, but Little Black Dresses never go out of style." In her other hand are a pair of black peep-toe stilettos. "I think these will do."

I eye the spiky heels with deep suspicion, but ultimately pull them onto my bare feet. Uncomfortable as fuck, but the fit is perfect. I'll likely fall on my face tonight—in more ways than one—but I suppose that's a risk I've decided is worth it.

THIRTY-THREE

I STEP UP TO VANDERFORD'S red front door at 7:46. I'm late, and it's weird, but everything's weird this month so why not? Tasteful white Christmas lights adorn the trim and columns of the ginormous house, and it's not even the biggest one on the block. Aaron's family lives in Kalorama Heights, home of some of the richest of the rich people in DC.

My hands tremble a little as I reach for the doorbell. I'm used to being around wealth, but not *this* level of wealth. Also, it's cold out here.

Also, Gabe is somewhere behind this door.

Also, *Issy* is somewhere behind this door.

But first behind the door is a fifty-something Black woman who I can only describe as regal. She wears a sleek black skirt and blouse set off by large pearls that are no doubt real, and her dark hair, streaked with gray, is drawn back into a chignon. I see traces of Aaron in her sharp cheekbones. "Welcome! Let me take your coat," she says, ushering me inside.

I try not to gape, but it's like a miniature White House in here. *Be cool, Emmy.*

I jut my hand out at the woman, you know, in the spirit of that coolness I'm channeling. "I'm Emmy Crawford. Thank you for having me."

She grasps my hand with both of hers. "Oh, Emmy! I'm Aaron's mom, Rhoda. It's so nice to finally meet you. We've heard so much about you."

"You have?"

"Oh, yes. Aaron's quite the fan of yours."

I wonder how updated she is on the situation, but that's *not* holiday party conversation.

She walks me through the foyer and into a *second foyer,* this one with a grand piano and multiple bookshelves. Next is a cavernous dining room. A huge, gleaming table has been pushed off to one side of the long room, overflowing with hors d'oeuvres, crudités— but my eyes glue themselves to a fountain of what appears to be champagne. "It's sparkling grape juice," Rhoda says near my ear, smoothly placing a flute of it in my hand.

Forty or so guests are clustered in the far end of the room, many of them my age. A goateed man in business casual attire approaches, camera slung around his neck. "Emmy, will you stand for a picture? I'm with *Washington Life* magazine." I'll never get used to complete strangers knowing my name, but at least this one asked for permission. I nod. He deftly moves forward, snaps his shutter, then thanks me and moves on. It's not so bad.

And then I'm alone, more of an observer than a participant. Aaron's across the room, right in the thick of all the people, in a neatly tailored navy blue suit. He sees me and flips a one-finger salute, and I know that's all I'm going to get. No bear hug. No big smile. Things between us needed to change, but that doesn't mean I don't have an achy heart over it.

Suddenly, my heartache amps to a whole other level. Gabe has stepped out from the clump of teens, and he looks . . . like himself, but better. Black pants and jacket over a charcoal gray shirt, black tie. Hair with some kind of product in it, glossy as his tie and even darker than usual. White Chucks, of course.

And he's looking at me like I'm an orange scone.

Issy steps out beside him. Her fidgeting hands and nervous smile do not detract from her overall appearance, which is stunning. She's in a close-fitting green dress, midi length, with little cap sleeves and tall black heels. Her hair is half-up, the part that's down cascading in perfect burnished curls over her shoulders. They would make an extremely good-looking couple, those two.

But they're not. They never were.

I'm suddenly self-conscious, standing here in my mother's dress and shoes. My hair is simple, down, and Mom and I managed to put a loose wave in it. I'm wearing the makeup I'd wear for a debate meet, but with a bolder eyeliner, punchier eyeshadow, more blush. My lipstick is straight-up *Scarlet Letter* red, because if you're going to go hang out in a room of people who've seen you totally crash, go big or go home.

Even from across the room I can see that Issy's face is contoured, her brows impeccable, everything I don't know how to do. It's hard not to feel inadequate next to her. Which is not a way I'm used to feeling. Next to her. Next to anyone.

Liv sees me and squeals, hobbling over in what must be four-inch heels. "Hey, you! Miraculous recovery from the big feels?"

"No, but I decided I wanted to come anyway," I say, relieved to find a safe harbor in my best friend. Before Mom, she was the only person I'd disclosed my misgivings about this party to, and it feels weird but good to be so open about where I'm at emotionally. I think Liv and I are going to end up closer than ever—the opposite of what I would have predicted, after everything that went down. Life's funny like that. "Is it hot in here, though?"

"Nah, that's just you in that lipstick."

The sound of tinkling glass bounces off the walls. In a matter of seconds, the crowd hushes for a tall white man with a receding hairline, who must be Mr. Vanderford, standing on a small platform at the front of the room. "Thank you so much, everybody, for being here to join us tonight! Rhoda and I are honored to host you."

He relinquishes the microphone—yes, a *microphone* is needed to be heard in the Vanderfords' ginormous dining room—to Rhoda. At the same time, music kicks up. It's this song my parents always jam to in the car, "Sweet Caroline." For the first time, I notice a man behind a small table in a back corner of the room. "For a little entertainment, we thought we'd bring karaoke to the party!" She pronounces *karaoke* in the proper Japanese way, *car-a-okay*, which somehow makes it sound classy. The twenty or so "youth" side-eye each other and the awkwardness is so thick you could slice through it with antique silver (which is featured at the cake table).

Aaron hoists himself onto the platform and grabs the microphone. "Christmas karaoke, you guys! Let's do this." He launches into a cheesy but undoubtedly sexy rendition of Elvis Presley's "Blue Christmas."

Liv has darted off and so I stand alone again, sipping my sweet bubbly beige, and wonder who else is even safe to talk to at this thing. *John and Taylor*, I remember, and I lift to tiptoes, scanning the crowd. I spy them near the food table, but *of course* they're chatting with Issy and Gabe. My feet reel backward until I'm up against a wall and there I wait, trying not to look too pathetic.

After what feels like an eternity but is actually only one "Have Yourself a Merry Little Christmas," later, John shows up at my side. "Hey, you!"

"Hey, yourself," I say, hugging him briefly.

"Man, that Gabe Castillo. I *get* the whole consorting with the enemy thing now. He's kind of awesome!"

"Do *you* wanna date him, John?"

He laughs. "I'm hoping to be otherwise indisposed, or maybe I would. But I think he's cut out better for someone like, say, you."

I bare my teeth in that smile-grimace that comes out when I don't know what else to do with my face.

"Oh. You *don't* like him."

"It's not that."

"You like him too much." John examines me over the top of his glasses.

305

"It's not that, either." I like Gabe just the right amount, it's just complicated.

"Well, whatever, just know I have a man crush on Gabe. I can take or leave that Vanderford guy, though. He's too smooth or something."

I follow John's eyes to Mr. Smooth. He's near the faux champagne, handing some to Gabe and to Issy. They all clink glasses, and the Polite Paparazzi moves in to capture it all on camera. I watch as Issy's shoulders come up around her ears and her cheeks pinch and I wonder how long it'll be till she bolts. Yet she hangs in, smiles prettily. As soon as the cameras clear out, she takes a three-second pause with her eyes closed, then continues her conversation with the boys.

Huh.

She catches me watching, but I shift my gaze. Like I don't see her. Like she's not even here. I'm an ice sculpture in the center of the room, a fixture of the celebration but not really part of it. Untouchable. And slowly melting, melting, until there's nothing left of me at all.

I can't let much more of myself evaporate if I'm going to make it through the night. I walk away, toward where I don't know, but maybe getting lost in this place will help me keep myself intact.

"Um. Hi, everyone. Merry Christmas!" says a voice that halts me. I find myself swiveling back to the stage. "This is a big, scary ask for me, but I've been working on an original song. Would you mind if I tried it out on you?" Issy's cheeks are pink, but in the happy way.

My stomach swoops in surprise, heart soaring. No matter how

angry I still am with Issy for meddling where she didn't belong—and for the words that cut me—I am *proud*. Aaron somehow materializes a guitar (who knows what they keep on hand at a place like this?) and hands it up to her. Issy throws the strap around her neck and tunes it by ear, unhurried, natural. "This one's called 'Too Strong.'"

My little sister's smile goes from sweet to megawatt. She's a star, *utterly* a star and made for this, even if she's spent years being too scared to own it. Her voice is smoked honey in the mic, which sends tingles from my toes to my neck by way of my spine. But then I listen. And listen. This time, Issy has all the words.

Go harder / Run faster
You can do it all
Be better / Push longer
Make your feelings small

Be the champion / Be the winner
Don't let 'em see you sweat
Don't crack and / Don't flinch
Your skin's too thick to need rest

But when you're too strong
Your grip becomes your weakness
Too tight to let the real in
It all falls through your hands
When you're too strong
Your life slips by untasted

You stay safe but miss the good stuff
You're perfect untouched numb
When you're too strong

You're quick / And all-knowing
You're a gorgeous shiny mess
You're powerful / And broken
But won't settle for less

You're tired / But can't say it
You don't know how to rest
You're everything / But nothing
If you're not the best

But when you're too strong
Your grip becomes your weakness
Too tight to let the real in
It all falls through your hands
When you're too strong
Your life slips by untasted
You stay safe but miss the good stuff
You're perfect untouched numb
When you're too strong

Would you ever, ever believe
That you can hurt
And bleed
Like me

You are too strong
Your grip becomes your weakness
Too tight to let the real in
It all falls through your hands
When you're too strong
Your life slips by untasted
You stay safe but miss the good stuff
You're perfect untouched numb
When you're too strong
Too strong

The last chorus she sings right to me, which confirms the tears wrecking the makeup I'd tried so hard to get right without her. No longer an ice sculpture, my sister has (once again) thawed me out.

Issy looks just as soft. Her glow as the crowd lights up for her, her gracious nod and "thank you," her molten eyes that ignore everyone else and stay riveted on me. She steps off the stage, parting the audience like the Red Sea, and then she's right here, mouth open to say something—but the words die on her lips. Instead, she reaches for my hand. A question. A plea?

I throw my arms around her, not sure if I'm more gobsmacked by her performance or by how she *sees* me.

THIRTY-FOUR

I HAUL ISSY OUT OF the room, in pursuit of somewhere quiet and away from prying eyes, not to mention eager cameras. When we come upon what appears to be a dark-paneled, bookcase-lined room, I steer us inside. Maybe the inherently safe vibe of a library will help me weather yet another difficult conversation.

Issy and I stand eyeing the carpet, physically close but miles farther than we've ever been from each other.

"Well?" she finally says.

"Well, what?"

"Well . . . everything. You haven't spoken to me in days."

"I couldn't find the words. And I wasn't ready."

"I tried really, really hard to give you space." She's chewing the hell out of her bottom lip, one of her many anxiety giveaways. My stony silence must have been awful for her, something I'm only now acknowledging.

"The fact you did that is honestly impressive. And more than I could say for myself. According to you, I suck at giving you space."

"Yeah. You sort of do."

I sigh. "Work in progress, I guess. And there's more, huh? The song?"

"What'd you think?"

"So far I've just got one word. Wow. Whoa."

"That's two words."

"When did you get like this?"

Issy's laugh is wide and real, which melts me a little more yet. I've missed this—her laugh and our easy, comfortable way. The last few days have been anything but. "I've always been like this. Anyway. You heard me? In that song?"

"Yeah. Loud and clear."

"And you're . . . not mad?"

My head chooses this moment to go wavy. An overstuffed leather chair beckons, and I sink into it. Issy takes the wing chair across from me. "Uh-oh, what's wrong?" She's leaning in but I warn her with my eyes, and she snaps back her solicitous hand.

"Nothing. I'm good."

"Emmy, you've got to stop lying. Seriously."

There's a firmness to her voice that I'm not used to. "Okay?"

"My song, did you *really* hear it? You've got to stop *all* of this. Stop trying to protect me. Stop trying to hide your real feelings from everyone. I know you think it helps but it makes such a mess. Maybe that pisses you off to hear, but it's true."

"I'm not mad. More like overwhelmed."

"Well, that's a start."

I slump back into the cushy leather. Surely this will help straighten my spinning vision.

"Breathe. In for five, hold, out for seven. Can you do that?"

I nod and Issy leaves, returning a few minutes later with a bottle of water. "Drink some, then hold it to the space right under your ear."

I do as she says, and soon the stars behind my eyes go dormant again. "There's a nerve there that connects the brain to the body. Getting it cold stimulates it and sends a relaxation signal to your organs," she informs me.

"Thanks. And sorry about this," I say, gesturing to my body.

"It's okay. I want to help."

"I don't like needing help."

"Obviously." Issy stares past me for a second, out into nothing. Or maybe to one of those movies in her mind. "You've always been my protector. For a lot of years I really needed that and clung to it. But I've grown a lot lately and it's like you can't even see it."

I think of what she did onstage tonight. And the karaoke bar, and how she took the fall for the first SenatorSlush incident, and getting in Miguel's face at school for gossiping. In confronting me about my true feelings for Gabe, in giving me loads of space even though our distance made her anxious. "I see it now."

"And it only took me getting up on a stage in front of god-knows-how-many people and performing. A *second* time. With an original song. And a guitar."

I grimace. "Fair point."

"Anyway, good job finally catching up."

Vague strains of "Deck the Halls" sneak in from under the closed door, and I absorb an unexpected pang of wanting to be back in the party. Well, back at *a* party. A simple one, without a web of complicated relationships. Just some time to be jolly and eat a bunch of cheese and dance in the untrained, uninhibited way that only Issy and I do, at home in our pajamas with Mom's old CDs in the player.

Like we *did*, anyway.

"Where do we go from here?" I ask.

She takes a beat, like she wants to get the words just right. "I want us to be *us*. EmmyAndIssy, because what we have is special. But we need to be a different us."

I nod, then stop. My head is too wavy, still. "I don't want to lose what we have . . . but I don't know how else to be, Is. To love you has always meant to have a sword ready, basically."

"Well. It's time to lay down your weapon."

"*How?*"

"Can you remember *way* back? The Iowa days, before my anxiety kicked in?"

"The tire swing days?"

"Yeah, tire swing days, T-ball days. 'Wannabe' and 'Creep' on the front porch all summer, with the never-ending supply of Mr. Freeze while we made up dances. I think that one summer we literally smashed a box a week."

"How do we not have diabetes, by the way?"

Issy laughs. "One genetic victory, I guess. Anyway, you remember. We were equals then, or almost. You were always more serious than I was, but I held my own. Remember that time Micah dropped that huge garter snake on the porch?"

I'd cowered on the porch swing while Issy shooed it away with a broom then screamed at Micah—the neighbor kid, a little older than us—for scaring me. Later, she left very realistic-looking rubber spiders on his bike seat. She'd been fearless, back then. "Yeah."

"Let's be those kids again. Like . . . grown-up, cleaner versions. Baked and Wired instead of Mr. Freeze."

I laugh. "I think we can do that."

"Me too. I'll always protect you, but I'm not going to lie or keep things from you anymore. I guess that's when protection becomes something else, you know?"

I consider. There's so much I've hidden from Issy over the years, in the spirit of keeping her safe. Or so I thought. I wonder how many times I unwittingly shorted her an opportunity to take care of something she absolutely could have on her own. And I wonder how much she's kept from me, in an attempt to free herself from what felt like constraints. "Agreed. I'm already working on being more honest. I talked to Liv and John about Crohn's disease stuff. And I 'broke up' with Aaron, if you can even call it that."

"How'd he take it?"

I give her the rundown, including his SenatorSlush info-leak confession.

"Wow. That was a dick move. Why are we at this party?" says Issy, looking like she'd sucked a lemon (again).

"I'm working on forgiveness. Since so many people are working on forgiving me."

"I can get behind that. But in case you forgot, even your health stuff has to come out in the open. You don't always have to tell me but you've gotta tell someone when you're not feeling right. What happened at regionals freaked me the hell out."

"I know. Problem is, I need to get better at telling *me* when I don't feel good. Yet another work in progress. Mom's helping me get going with a therapist, so maybe I'll learn it there."

"Therapy! That's great!"

My black heels shuffle on the richly woven oriental rug. "I don't know if I can do it, though. I'm too big of a control freak. Doesn't it bother you, having someone tell you what to do all the time?"

"Oh, therapy isn't like that. It's more just this space to go talk things out, and then you realize stuff about yourself. Sometimes my therapist teaches me a new skill that I can use if I want to, but I don't think she's ever outright told me what to do."

Huh. *Not* what I thought. "I guess it's worth a try."

"Yep."

"Great, glad we're figuring out how to get me less fucked up."

Issy crosses one ankle over another, now fully relaxed in her chair. "We're all fucked up, sister. You, me, everyone in the world in their own ways. It's what we do with our fuckery that makes the difference."

I melt fully into my own chair, my shoulders softening as Issy's words sink in. The spin in my head slows and stops; my world rights itself again.

Being seen—fully—is hard. It's raw and vulnerable and scary.

But there's something here, on the other side of vulnerability. It beckons like a long, cool drink after spending hours with a parched mouth.

To feel un-alone in my problems, and yes, in the *pain*—my very real pain—maybe that balm is worth the price of fear.

THIRTY-FIVE

THE REST OF THE NIGHT flies by in a haze of sweet bubbles and sweaty, dance-soaked teens. Liv spends much of the evening tucked away in a corner of the room in deep conversation with a girl sporting a bright red pixie cut and a killer pantsuit. Taylor commands the stage, regaling us with song after song. And John gets a Christmas miracle, as Issy has *finally* noticed he is alive. All night the two drift closer—first in the big group, then over celery sticks and cider for two, and finally, on the dance floor. He looks down at her with the reverence he usually reserves for an airtight debate argument, and her shy, eager smile is everything.

Much as I'm aware of my friends, my true north is Gabe. I could close my eyes and I'd still know right where he was at any given time. Once, twice, so many times, our eyes crash into each other but mine stumble away.

The crowd has dwindled to just a few of us when finally, he's right here. Like he never left. "Emmy."

I say nothing, but I know he hears me anyway. I step toward him.

Over Gabe's shoulder I lock eyes with Issy, who stands across the room with her hand entwined with John's. This time I'm wanting *her* approval. Her validation. Her vote of confidence. The corners of her mouth turn up and she says it all with the flick of her free hand. *Stop hiding. Go live your life.*

If she can do it, so can I.

Gabe's hand cups my elbow gently, like he's afraid I'll startle and fly away. "Can we talk?"

After a quick stop by the coat room, I follow him all the way out the front door. Our feet unexpectedly crunch beneath us. A thin layer of white glistens on the front steps and beyond, much of it still untouched.

"I didn't know it was snowing," I breathe, as I automatically stretch my hand out to catch flakes. The white clumps swirl and sparkle in the streetlight. "So beautiful."

"Very." But Gabe's not looking at the snow. He's beautiful, too, with shadows playing across his sharp cheekbones.

"Here," I say, brushing away a snowflake that's stuck in one of his lashes. He catches my hand and mashes my wool chest into his. My body tenses reflexively, but then I remember. It's okay. He's okay. And I'm . . . maybe not okay, but will be.

My head falls to his shoulder, which leads to his arms around my back. I absorb the length of him against the length of me as my body breathes *finally, finally.* We are engulfed by the muffled silence that always accompanies light snow, so quiet that I swear I can hear flakes hitting pavement. The white lays in pristine sheets that go on forever, as infinite as I feel in his arms. A Polaroid image of this moment would be heartbreakingly lovely, and I don't want to speak. I want this, just this perfection and this peace, forever.

But that's part of my problem. I want perfect in a world that's not, and expect it from people who can never be. *I* can never be.

When I finally speak, it's into his neck. "You said you had more to say. When I was ready."

He shivers. Maybe he's cold. Or maybe it's my breath against his skin. "I do."

"Please say it."

"Why *now?*"

"So many reasons. But the big one—I know the SenatorSlush leak was Aaron, not you."

His shoulders tense. "Well. You're right that I wasn't the one who sent what you said to the press. But I was the one who got angry enough with you and the situation to blurt your business to my debate team, and I really, really shouldn't have done that. I'm sorry."

"I know. And I know you tried to apologize before. And I know you took the fall for *all* of it because you wanted me happy, even if it meant I was with Aaron."

He squints one eye, something he's been known to do just before eviscerating a debate stance. "Yeah. And what about Aaron?"

"That's not a thing. Never really was."

"Seemed like a thing."

I want to return my nose to the crook of his neck, and for a second I let myself believe it's because I crave the closeness. One more second, and I understand it's really about not wanting to look at him during this discussion. *Stop hiding.* I stare boldly into his eyes, rejecting every impulse that tells me not to. "I was angry and sad. Part of me was using my time with Aaron as a distraction. And part of me was trying to make you jealous."

His lips settle into a line. "Well. I was."

"I shouldn't have done it. I'm sorry. I've apologized to Aaron, too. We're still friends, but at a distance for now."

"I appreciate that. All of it."

"Look, Issy and I have had some long, difficult talks. I know about the entire scheme."

"I guess it's my turn to apologize. Again."

I shrug, because yeah. "I'm not saying I think what you and she did was a good thing, but I understand I'm not always the easiest person to bring around on a new idea."

This coaxes a chortle out of Gabe. "That's putting it mildly."

"I maintain that my stubbornness is one of my greatest assets, even if I don't always use my powers for good."

"I maintain that while your stubbornness bit us both in the ass this time, I still find it incredibly hot. Always have."

My body surges heat, even in the midst of a night chilly enough for snowfall. "I like that you like me the way I am."

His hands clasp at the small of my back, pulling me firmly to him. "Imagine that. Emmy Crawford, making an *understatement*."

My smile cannot be tamed but neither can the pull of his lips.

They part, silently beckon, and I answer that call like I'd never stopped answering. His cinnamon mouth matches the raw, red *want* that explodes behind my closed eyes. I reach up to stroke the nape of his neck, to run my fingers through his shock of hair. With a soft groan he pulls my hips closer, closer . . . so close, and still, we don't stop kissing. I will never want to stop kissing him.

Yet I pull away first, chest heaving, breath blowing white against the cold black of 11:00 p.m. My knees quake and every limb tingles. Something that feels painfully *real* builds within me, and for once I let it.

It all feels good, so good, and I know Gabe and I are *right*. We've cleared our misunderstandings, we care about each other, and for god's sake it's *snowing*. Issy's sappy little soul will delight when I one day tell her about this moment.

So it's a mystery, why this other thing swells within me, elbowing for space with pleasure. Something like anxiety. Something that sounds like, *I need to do right by this.* Because there is still a reason I kept myself from Gabe that I have not resolved.

"I want us to be together," Gabe says, his forehead pressed up against mine.

"I want that, too." And then I say the thing driven by insights I'm only barely starting to understand. "But I'm . . . not okay."

"What do you mean, not okay?"

"I'm sick."

He holds me out, taking an exaggerated look. "You don't *look* sick."

"That's the whole thing, though. In the mirror I see a person who looks relatively healthy. My sick is on the inside, and because no one else can see it, I've learned how to hide. I even hide it from myself."

"The Crohn's disease, you mean."

"Yeah. And . . . it's like your mom, Gabe. Doctors and drugs and something that I can treat but it will never actually go away." I've never said that out loud, and my voice catches and trembles on the truth of it. "I don't know if I can do this to you."

"Do *what* to me?"

"Weigh you down with my disease, and what it will need from me." The idea that my disease might *need* something from me is new, but as soon as I say it, I feel it. My body has been asking me to come through for it, to take care of it—and I've said no, again and again. Maybe I need to start saying something more like *I hear you, I'm here to help.*

Our chests rise and fall, rise and fall, two bodies breathing one pain. Finally he detaches from me and I brace myself. *This is it. This is how he lets you go.*

But he takes my hands. "Oh, Emmy. This is what you actually meant, sophomore year. That time in the closet."

I'm hit with a wave of dizzy shock. "What's that?"

"I don't know if you remember, but it's been hard for me to forget. You said you wouldn't want to be around someone who was 'freaking out' all the time. And that people just need to work harder, if they're struggling and not getting better."

I don't remember saying the words, but I remember how I felt that day. And I don't doubt his memory. "That does sound like me. But in reference to *me*."

"I get that now. But even beyond Mom needing a lot of help at the time, those words were ultimately the reason I stayed away from you. I didn't think you'd take well to her mental illness."

I remember Aaron's words, and guilty fingers threaten my air supply. *This* was the thing Gabe had been trying to forgive me for. "Oh, god. *No.* I *get* mental illness, at least sort of. Issy, you know—well, I don't want to say more than that. It's not mine to share."

"It's okay. She more or less told me about everything right away at that party at Liv's."

A snowflake lands in the center of my gaping mouth. "She did?"

"Yeah. When I caught her last name and realized you were sisters, I asked where you were. Issy said you were probably alone with Liv, somewhere only you two would know to go. I'd made some flip comment like, 'Too good for the commoners who have complicated lives,' and she stopped me. 'Oh, no no. You've got her *all* wrong,' she said. She told me about having anxiety and how you're always there for her. I'll never forget that. And so I told her about you and me and the past, and I decided it was time to try again. With Issy's help."

Issy was *that brave* all the way back in August. Brave enough to meet a stranger, befriend him, correct his wrongs, and stick up for me. I really hadn't been seeing her right, for months upon months.

"She's so much better now, but in the past she struggled. Significantly. So yeah, I know a little of what it's like to love someone with mental health struggles. As for me—that day I fell apart in the closet, I'd just found out that I was sick. Minutes before you followed me in there. There'd never been anything I hadn't con-quered if I just worked hard enough. I guess I thought my disease would be the same."

"And now?"

I face the sky, letting snowflakes pelt my cheeks. "I know it's not just about work. There are things I can't control . . . and also things I guess I can't ignore. As for the freaking out thing, *I* didn't want to be around me, when I was like that. And I assumed no one else would, either."

"Including me."

"Yeah. I thought that's why you ghosted."

He opens his mouth to respond, but my worry bubbles and swells and explodes, beating him to it. "I have more fears. Can I just say them all before I lose my moxie?"

"Let's hear them," he says, rubbing my upper arms.

"Now that you know about the Crohn's, I'm scared you'll resent me, because I have access to the best doctors and medicine and your mom doesn't." The words come flying out in a blur, erupting from somewhere I'd smashed them way, way down deep.

He almost looks like he's in pain, like his heart is swelling through his eyes. "I could never. I'm glad you have exactly what you need, even if Mom doesn't. Health care isn't a zero-sum game, you know? I want good treatment available for everyone."

"Me too. More than ever," I breathe.

"I know you do. Any more fears in there?"

Just the one. The one huge one. "AmItoomuchforyou?"

He pushes a loose strand of hair back from my face, not allowing me to break our eye contact. "You are exactly the right amount of everything. Even when you're freaking out. Even when you're sick."

My exhale is fast and cleansing, even if it's also part sob.

"And I don't think Crohn's disease is the same as schizophrenia. You might need medicine or times you need to go slower, that sort of stuff. With Mom, I will always, always love her, and I'm so glad I still have her, but some of the things that made her *her* just aren't there anymore. I don't think they're coming back." He closes his eyes, lets his shoulders rise and fall. "But you? *You* are right here. And the *you* I've known has always had this illness, right?"

I nod.

"That's all I care about. That I get to be with *you*."

I grip his hands tightly, like I need them to keep me tethered. The tears feel oddly good on my snow-chilled face, but my ribs might crack open with the force of my emotion. It's joy and pain and gratitude and nervousness and something, something else. And it's that indefinable *thing* that leads me to say, "Can you give me some time?"

His head cocks in confusion, and I clarify. "I need to make sure I'm all the way okay before I take on a new thing. And I know we're kind of an *old* thing, too, but not like this. Not this you and this me. You know?"

His face is open and full of things more tender than liking. "I know. And good for you for asking for what you need."

"We all have limits. Apparently."

325

"Apparently," he says, but the kiss he dances across my forehead feels limitless. "Take your time. I'm not going anywhere."

As he tucks me back into his arms, I feel another thing.

I think it's trust.

THIRTY-SIX

THE WINTER SPECIAL EDITION OF *Washington Life* comes out, and the "Elegant Crawford Girls" are splashed, in color, across a feature near the middle. Me with my fresh glass of cider and my forced "media face" smile, which crinkles my eyes but doesn't light them up. Issy onstage with the guitar slung over her shoulder. Her smile is real.

Issy flips through the coverage with one hand as she shovels Cheerios into her mouth with the other. "Not a bad write-up this time, right?"

My sister has come so far.

In the spirit of her growth, over the next few weeks I try to do the same. Mom gets me set up with a therapist. Her name is Dr. Shannon but she asks me to call her Mina. She wears funky wide-legged pants and big earrings and her sunny office is decorated in rainbows and a ton of plants. I'm surprised when I like her immediately and start spilling my guts within ten minutes of sitting on her blue velvet settee.

"So," says Mina, as we near the end of our first session. "You're terrified of failure, most of your emotions scare you, and you ignore your limits. Do I have that right?"

I cross my arms and make a face, but she's so clearly on my side that I can't really be mad. Instead, I say, "Weekly appointments, then?"

Alongside my many therapy visits, I go back to Dr. Dalke. I eat crow for missing my last appointment with him and Jo and Dad and everyone. There are jabs and vials of blood taken, so much sitting on soft vinyl chairs in waiting rooms. There is standing on the scale and having my stomach palpated, there is talking at length about my bowel movements. There is also the colonoscopy, and before it, the dreaded day of broth, Jell-O, Gatorade, and the Lemon Pledge–tasting liquid that chains me to the toilet and empties my stomach completely.

But these are the things I have to do. Much as I'd rather ignore my disease, I'm learning it'll scream for my attention if I don't willingly take care of it. *We do what we must.*

Just as Dr. Dalke feared in October, the tests all show that my current medications aren't working, and I'm in a bad flare. He says I need to change to a biologic medication—an IV infusion, given to me at the doctor's office every eight weeks. I cry when I'm told, and Dad holds my hand. Issy goes with me to my first infusion and also the second one. This all happens within a span of two weeks because they need to "on board" the drug into my system quickly.

The first go is rough. Even though I've been poked and needle-jabbed so many times already in my life, I still cringe and get dizzy when the nurse inserts my IV. Issy hands me water and we wait for my vision to clear, but then we play cribbage there on my hospital tray table, as the slow drip fills my whole body with intense cold.

The second time isn't as bad.

And by the fourth week after I start the medication, I notice some things. My knees stop aching. It's weird, because I hadn't even noticed how *much* they'd hurt until that pain is gone. My bathroom breaks decrease by half, and the need isn't as urgent when it comes. I stop feeling lightheaded when I stand up. I can run longer, faster, more often. And when I get up in the morning, I don't feel like I've been mauled by a semitruck—instead, I almost always feel re-freshed.

Apparently, this is what healing feels like.

My family goes home to Iowa for the holidays. Mom and Dad take three whole weeks off. "We need the rest," Dad says, multiple times. I'm not sure if he's trying to convince himself or model something healthier for the workaholic daughter who just had a breakdown, but either way, I'm stoked to get some time with my parents. Together we watch the entire Lord of the Rings movie series, we attempt to tackle apple pie with homemade crusts, and we manage to deep-fry a turkey without burning the house down.

We stay back at our old house, which my parents still own. It's weird but so comforting to be back, sleeping under the beloved T-shirt quilt Grandma made me one Christmas. I'd intentionally left it in Iowa, so when I come home I know it's still *home*. I hold the blanket right up to my face as I sleep.

We spend hours and hours at Grandma and Grandpa's, frosting sugar cookies and listening to Mannheim Steamroller Christmas albums and trimming their tree. Christmas itself feels almost as magical as it did when I was little. There's just something about the open Iowa sky in the deep of winter, all the stars are burning and visible, that feels like Christmas *should* feel. Cold, and a little mysterious, and also like for at least one night of the year, all is calm. All is bright.

In my downtime I voraciously read the Outlander book series that I pillaged from Grandma's bookshelves. It's so *not* on my precollege reading list but *is* highly engaging. And Claire's struggle to figure out where she belongs—either where she came from *or* the place she's unwittingly been transported to? Relatable.

When we go back to DC, I bring my T-shirt quilt with me. I realize I've left enough of my heart in Iowa. I'll always feel a sense of belonging there, even if I let myself start to think of DC as home, too. Maybe some of us are meant to feel home in more than one place.

Mid-January finds me readjusted to that DC, parents-always-gone life. The dining room floor is finally done. It's still pockmarked in places and some of the planks aren't completely straight, but it *is* pretty. These days I can't help but think of the history these boards have absorbed, how strong they must be to have lasted this many years. The floor isn't perfect and it will never be. Maybe it never was. Maybe *I* never was, either. But sometimes the best things in life come from imperfection—like growth and individuality and closeness with others who share our shortcomings. At least that's what Mina keeps saying.

I contemplate getting excited about going back to school. At Mina's gentle suggestion, I ask Lucy to watch an hour of TV or YouTube with me most nights of the week. I get another IV infusion, which I'm now convinced is breathing life force back into me. The skin across my cheeks looks brighter, fuller, and my usually brittle nails are growing long and strong for the first time in forever.

The third week of February, I make a decision. It's cold but not snowy, so I pull on my Adidas rather than boots. Joggers and a hoodie, a swipe of lip gloss, a little mascara. An effort is made.

Issy pokes her head into the bathroom as I tame my hair into a side ponytail. "And where are we off to?"

I clear my throat and try to look nonchalant. "I thought I'd swing by Safe Space."

By now Issy knows this is Gabe's haunt. Her face splits open into that huge, star-worthy smile that she no longer saves only for me. She's done two open-mic nights since we got back from Iowa and she's absolutely killing it. There's even been talk of her auditioning for the spring musical this year. "Ooohhh. Is he there?"

"I don't know. I hope so? He's usually there on Sunday afternoons."

"You didn't tell him you were coming?" The hand Issy thrusts onto her jutted hip is not a pleased one.

"No. I don't know why."

"You're still scared. It's okay."

My impulse is to cock my hip right back. *What're you talking about? I'm not a coward.* But I'm getting better at being honest. "I'm a little scared, yeah." In the mirror, my eyes are bright, but there are nerves alongside the excitement.

"Understandable. But we can be scared . . ."

". . . and do the thing anyway." Which is one of Issy's new performance mantras, and now I use it, too.

Safe Space is the same as it always was. The sign on the door says "All Are Welcome." It says "Black Lives Matter" and "Refugees Matter" and "Love Is Love Is Love." Before I walk in the old-school wood-and-glass door, I whisper something between a wish and a prayer. *Let him be here.*

Inside, more familiarity. There's the bulletin board with postings for events happening all over the city. The smell of coffee-over-books is tantalizing, perfect. Conversations ramble, spoons clink against ceramic mugs. My favorite barista's behind the bar, multiple nose rings intact, and possibly with one more tattoo on his sleeve than when I was last here. He nods in my direction as the door swings shut behind me.

The shop is full, as it is on most Sundays. On tiptoes I survey the crowd, eyes itching for the back corner table nearest the window.

And there he is, bent over a spiral notebook, writing furiously. He pushes hair back from his face with his right hand while never losing pace in his writing with his left. I buy an orange scone at the counter and breathe, breathe, breathe. I want to drag my feet, but also, I want to run to him. This is what happens when you leave all the feels inside, rather than kicking some of them out. Turns out, I have room for them all.

He's got his earbuds in and they're cranked so loud, I can hear the AC/DC from feet away. He doesn't look up, not even when I'm right there at the table. What do I do? Clear my throat? Tap him on the shoulder? Throw myself into his lap?

In the end I just unzip my hoodie and throw it over the back of the empty chair across from him. My old seat. Mine again.

I might be holding *a lot* of emotions, but what Gabe shows when he finally sees me is straightforward. Pure. He's happy. Just happy.

"You came!" He says it like he'd been waiting on me all along.

"I came."

"You're here!"

"I'm here." I set the orange scone on our table before yanking him to his feet, throwing my arms around him, and burying my head in his soft T-shirt.

"Here?" he murmurs. "What about paparazzi?"

He's right, of course. The greedy cameras, their bored and desperate operators—they're everywhere.

But I've got a life to live, and Gabe is my truth. "Let 'em look, I guess." And I catch a hint of his grateful, incredulous smile before I cover it.

"Mmm. Solid nine out of ten," I say when we come up for air.

His breath tickles my ear. "I can do better."

And he does.